The Wrinkled Crown

Also by Anne Nesbet

The Cabinet of Earths
A Box of Gargoyles

The Wrinkled Crown

Anne Nesbet

HARPER

An Imprint of HarperCollinsPublishers

Library of Congress Cataloging-in-Publication Data
Nesbet, Anne.
The wrinkled crown / Anne Nesbet. — First edition.
    pages cm
    Summary: Twelve-year-old Linny embarks on an epic quest to save
her best friend and discovers that she is the link between the magical
and logical halves of her world.
    ISBN 978-0-06-210429-8 (hardcover)
[1. Fantasy. 2. Magic—Fiction.] I. Title.
PZ7.N437768Wr 2015   2014047814
[Fic]—dc23   CIP
                                                          AC

Typography by Andrea Vandergrift
15 16 17 18 19 PC/RRDH 10 9 8 7 6 5 4 3 2 1
❖
First Edition

For all those who would go down into the Plain
for a friend, and, in particular,
for Isa and Jayne.

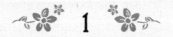

NEVER TOUCH A LOURKA

It was maybe Linny's last day of all—a pretty horrible thought—but the air in the meadow was humming with sunlight, as if nothing were the slightest bit wrong. Green and warm, the smell, with a tang to it that was all from the sheep: three parts wool, one part manure. Or maybe it was better to say the whole meadow smelled just slightly of sheep's cheese—sheep's cheese and hay. *Hey!*

Linny gave her head a shake to get rid of the webs cobbing there. This was no time to be thinking about sheep!

Tomorrow she would be twelve, no longer a child. Twelve was not any old ordinary birthday, not up in the wrinkled hills, not for a girl. It was a gate that didn't let everyone through. Even Linny—who had once sucked actual real snake venom out of a friend's arm and spat it boldly on the moss, where it sizzled like hot grease—even bold Linnet had to turn her mind away from the thought of the birthday coming for her, inching closer with every *tick rattle tick* of the village clock. *Tomorrow is not now. Tomorrow is very far away.*

And to rub it all in, the faint sweet strum of a lourka rose up from the village behind them, making Linny's heart sore.

Round bellied, four stringed, golden voiced—there was nothing anywhere quite like a lourka from Lourka.

Whether the village was named after the instrument or the instrument after the village, nobody knew for sure. What mattered was this: if a girl so much as touched a lourka during her child days—even by accident! even tripping over her own papa's instrument in the dark!—then on her twelfth birthday, the Voices would come, and off they would take her soul to Away.

"Oh, let's go!" said Linny, tugging the cord that tethered her and Sayra together, the mismatched twins. "It's late already, and there's so much to do!"

No one knew where Away was, up past the most wrinkled parts of the highest hills, but it didn't sound like a place you could sneak home from.

"You can't get there from here, nor back again neither." That was what the miller liked to say about Away. And there had been a girl taken when he was a boy, so he must know.

It made Linny mad just thinking about it, so mad she kicked the ground—and Sayra stumbled. That's the way

2

tethers are. Cause and effect, always causing trouble.

"No stomping!" said Sayra, but she laughed as she said it. "You're the one with the birthday coming! You should be happy as a duckling. *Tomorrow* you get to throw this tether *right into the creek*, if you want to. Tomorrow you'll be free."

Being Sayra, she didn't point out that she, Sayra, would also be free from that tether tomorrow. Maybe she didn't even think that thought, she was so good (but Linny thought it for her). No, Sayra just picked up a couple of spilled needles and tucked them cheerfully away:

"And so I'd *think* you'd be starting to be happy already today, knowing it's your birthday tomorrow."

"Tomorrow!" said Linny. She was grumbling, she knew it, but she couldn't help it. "*If* I'm still here. *If* the Voices don't come and—"

"Don't tell such stories!" said Sayra, and gave Linny's hand a sharp tap for good measure. You had to be careful about the things you said, this high up in the wrinkled hills, where stories had a way of coming true. "Nothing's going to happen to you. There's been the tether protecting you in the village, and the woods keeping you safe out here. And tomorrow you won't even have to worry anymore. A miracle, that's what my mother says. A mira-cle!"

It was a miracle because there hadn't been a girl born

as hummy as Linny in a hundred years. Linnet's father had even made a cage to clamp over the top of her cradle, though how could a cage do much to protect a child so hungry for music? Oh, but the whole village loved Linnet and had been willing to take desperate measures to keep her safe.

Which was why she was tethered to Sayra during most of every day.

No music fire in Sayra! Her talents were the safer ones of needle and cloth, and she had a quicksilver smile and green eyes and a face that could play tricks on you, shifting from sweetness to monster scowl in less than a blink. And back again. With eyes that sparked and laughed, sparked and laughed, the whole time.

Linny and Sayra knew each other far better than even the best of friends usually do, because Linny had been tethered to Sayra since she had learned to crawl.

"You are a good girl," the grown-ups had said to Sayra then, who was only a toddler herself at the time. "You will not let your friend Linny get near a lourka. We have all promised to keep her safe."

Sayra was a good girl, but she wasn't *that* good, thank goodness. Here's a secret: sometimes she let Linny run free in the woods, and both of them were happy, and nobody else could ever, ever know.

"Tomorrow you'll be free like a rabbit! Wait . . . stand

4

still—you've got a thread loose there."

Sayra hated loose threads.

"Free to hop around Lourka," said Linny, making a face. While Sayra tied off that thread, Linny shuffled from foot to foot and thought grumbling thoughts about hopping around Lourka.

Lourka was a very small world, as far as Linny was concerned. The village; the meadows; the woods; the hills. And everyone knew that if you walked away too far downhill—if you went past the boundary trees or around one too many bends in the creek—you would never ever find your way back.

You were born in Lourka, or you had wandered there, but it was not a place you could return to by choice, once you had left. That was the story. Once in a blue moon a breathless stranger might wander in from elsewhere, as Linny's own mother had long ago done, all footsore, hillsick, and amazed, but no one Linny had heard of had ever left, striding off past the boundary trees, and then actually returned.

"Don't grumble," said Sayra. "You'll be free to hop anywhere you want, I guess. And to make music, too, once you're officially twelve and it's safe. That should make you happy! Not to mention—now I can give you your birthday present! Which I made myself, you know, so you'd better like it."

Sayra could make anything (anything) with needle, thread, and a scrap of cloth.

"My birthday's *tomorrow*, not today," said Linny.

"I dreamed I shouldn't wait. I dreamed I should give it to you today," said Sayra, and she looked with her green eyes right at Linny, trying very hard to keep her gaze steady. But the blinking gave her away, and the wobble at the corner of her mouth. Linny felt the worry surge up in her again.

"Anyway," said Sayra. "Tomorrow they'll all be fussing over you, and I won't get a word in edgewise."

They were settled comfortably on the rocks they liked best, in a clearing nobody else ever came to, high in the Middle Woods. Sayra reached into her sewing bag and opened her hands so carefully that Linny thought the gift must be something living, a new-hatched chick or even a frog.

But no, it was a wonderfully wrinkled gift: a band of cloth, all embroidered with pictures of things they knew from their woods, and tucked into a little pocket in the middle, there was a bright bud of a flower, sewn from the prettiest scraps of satiny cloth. The best of all possible birthday sashes, with satin ribbons to keep it safely tied around Linny's waist.

"Oh!" said Linny, delighted, as she was always delighted by the things Sayra's thin, clever fingers made.

"It's got the wolf and the snake!"

They had saved each other's lives three times already. There was the sinewy blue wolf with huge teeth, way back when they were still very small, that Sayra had thrown pinecones at and somehow driven away (and the grown-ups had gone looking afterward and seen no trace of it, so Linny had been unfairly warned against telling stories, which is such a dangerous business up in the hills), and there was, of course, the snake that had casually sunk its fangs into Sayra's arm. They never told anyone about that.

And right there on that embroidered sash was also the tree Linny had fallen out of, when she had climbed up to get a sense of the hills. Sayra had retethered her, picked her up, and carried her all the way down to the village, which goes to show how much stronger Sayra was than you might think, just by looking at her. And that had been the third time.

"Shh, silly, that's not all," said Sayra, narrowing her leaf-colored eyes. "Watch now. I put some of you and some of myself right into it, because it's your birthday."

The threads that ran through that rosebud must have been spun from wrinkled silk, magic in every fiber, because the bud was already blushing a deeper pink as Sayra held it on her palm. (Sayra's mother had a glass-walled warm room where little silkworms spun their amazing cocoons.) Oh! And now it began to open up, blossoming into a red rose flower. Linny clapped her hands in wonder, but Sayra put her finger to her lips: there was more. The rose darkened and purpled and changed, until it was a butterfly of silk, fluttering its pretty wings—and the wings of the butterfly had pictures sewn on them in threads of many colors, and those pictures shifted as Linny watched. She saw herself, Linny, running under the trees, and a tiny Sayra bent over her sewing while a few blue stitches flowed by, to make a thready creek, and there was Sayra's house, and Linny's, and even Linny's young brothers, waving the tiniest of little silk hands. And then the butterfly curled up into itself and became a flower bud again, and Sayra tucked the bud into the pocket on the cloth band there, and folded that whole incredible silky present right into Linny's amazed hand.

It was like a song, inside a story, made out of silk.

There was no one like Sayra.

Sayra gave Linny's shoulders a hug.

"Want to spend the day quietly singing to me? Wouldn't that be the safest safest thing to do? No, no, all right. Look at you twitching at the thought of it. Go run wild in the woods, then, like you always do. But don't mess up!"

"Mmm," said Linny, made frankly itchy by the worry that wouldn't get out of her head.

"I'm serious: one more day! Don't even go near the village where a lourka might grab you. Don't get caught, and *don't get lost*," said Sayra.

That was an old joke of theirs, because getting lost was something Linny could pretty much not possibly do. It was one of her private wrinkles, quite separate from the music fire burning in her; Linny always knew where she was in the ups, downs, and side ways of the world. Other children get their eyes from some parent, their noses from some other parent. With her wild dark hair, Linny looked nothing at all like the rest of her family, but she had inherited humminess from her father and the gift of not getting lost from her mother. Her mother didn't even like to call it a wrinkle, because down in the Plain, where she had come from, things and places and people were not wrinkled, and all the unmagical squirrels were the same shade of rock gray (said her mother) and stayed that color always, not winking from purple to green on a whim as the squirrels did here. It was hard for Linny to imagine what that would be like, the land of squirrels as gray and unchanging as rocks.

Linny had tried describing to Sayra how the not-being-lost wrinkle felt, but it was like explaining to a blind person what it means not to be blind. Most people were so awkward and helpless, the way they stopped halfway up a hill and looked around and didn't know which way to go or even which direction they had come from anymore. Sayra herself was slightly frightened of wild places, Linny could tell. That made another thought unfurl in Linny's head, an unpleasant, icy thought:

Guess maybe you'll never—

But she bit her own tongue, because it felt like those words fished too deep in her and might drag up things she didn't really want to see. Awkward, sharp-edged thoughts, like *Maybe you'll never come back out here again with me, Sayra, once you don't have to.*

Instead she gulped, and turned the gulp into "Thank you," and skidded her palm across the top of Sayra's smooth head, which was the fastest, fondest possible way to say good-bye to someone holding needles in her hands, and sped away into those trees, moving fast so that the sharp-edged thoughts couldn't catch her. And sure enough, it worked, running off like that. Soon her head was humming with all the possible ways she could fill these last free hours—all those many familiar variants on "breaking the rules."

Because she had spent her life breaking the rules, hadn't she? Oh, yes.

If even Sayra knew . . . but she didn't know.

Linny scrambled up the familiar slopes of the Upper Woods, to a fold in the hills where the old stone sheep shed stood, keeping its secrets. Keeping her secrets.

Nobody ever came here. Nobody ever pushed through this door, as Linny was doing now, or went over to that corner there and swept the hay off the wooden chest it was hiding.

And that meant nobody knew what Linny had gone and done, all those years when the whole village had been trying its absolute utmost to keep her safe.

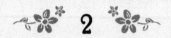

2

SOME THINGS NOBODY KNEW

It had started with a stolen ax, but it certainly hadn't ended there.

The pilfering had been going on for years, by now. That first ax, years ago, had been the same one, not coincidentally, that her father had just used to fell Elias's prentice trees: his maple and his pine. "Wood learns slow, like boys." That was what Linny's father liked to say. It was always a happy day in the village when a boy's prentice trees came down: sun and wind and time would cure the wood, and when the boy was ready to start the work on his first real lourka, three or four good years later, his wedges of maple and pine would be waiting for him, sound and well seasoned.

All of Linny's pilferings kept themselves safe and dry in a pair of old boxes. She even went to the bother of stealing some hay from the sheep to pile over the top of the boxes, as if anybody were likely to come up all this way and find her out for the wicked girl she was.

But oh, if they had. They would have seen what Linny saw now, as she knelt at her old work chest and lifted the lid. A box, filled with awls and planers and knives and sandpapers that had gone missing from her father's workshop, over all those years. And in that box, another newer box, and in it, wrapped in a swatch of stolen cloth and cradled in wood shavings and wool, the one thing a girl must never never go near, if she didn't want her doom to come hunting for her, on her twelfth birthday.

Yes, a lourka.

So that's how it was with Linny. She hadn't just "gone near" a lourka or stolen a quick touch along the polished neck of one. Nothing so innocent as that! No, she had to go and *make* one.

You grow up knowing there is ONE THING you must never ever do, and then you go and do that one thing. Why? Linny had thought about this about a hundred or a thousand times while she worked, and every answer she came up with fell apart when she poked at it. It wasn't that she wasn't afraid of what might happen. Although her mother had come up from the Plain, where they scoffed at things like curses and dooms, when Linny heard people talk about the Voices coming to carry girls off to Away, she didn't scoff—no, her heart wrung itself out in her chest like a wet rag. Sometimes she thought her ribs must be made half of fear, and only half of bone.

But still she could not help it; she *had* to make herself a lourka. She did. So maybe it was the force of the music fire in her, that so many children born in Lourka carried in them.

There had been this raw, jealous place in her heart ever since Elias started spending his days in the workshop of Linny's own father, back when they were eight or nine. She had thought then, and still thought it: *unfair.* She was the one, of all of them, who truly cared about music, about instruments, about making up songs. It should have been her, being taught how to shape a lourka, not that lummox Elias. And so on and so on and so forth, all her angry thoughts just running in tighter and tighter circles in her head.

She had begun running in circles too—or rather sneaking in circles, around and around the outside of her father's workshop (where she, of course, as a girl—*unfair unfair*—was strictly not allowed), looking for chinks in the walls and windows best suited for spying. And she found them, yes, and haunted them, and learned as much as she could from watching her father teach Elias how to choose a good wedge of wood, even grained and knot free, gleaming like silk when the blade splits it—how to season it and then shape it. She was a very good spy. If they had found her like that, untethered, all her freedom would have been taken away that very instant; she knew that well, and it made her extra sneaky. She let them think all she cared about was trees and woods and being out-doors. She kept them all fooled, even Sayra. But what she really cared about, all that time, was this: the lourka she brought out of its wrappings now and cradled with such love in her hands.

All the other instruments she had tried to make over the years had come to nothing in the end. The neck had warped because she'd calculated the tensions wrong, or a flaw in the glaze had eaten a hole in the wood, or her unpracticed hands had slipped and something had splin-tered. That's how learning is, and she had seen the same and worse happen to Elias, as she spied, like a sneaky, greedy shadow, through the workshop windows. But now, finally, just at the very tip end of her child days, guess what? She had made a lourka that looked like a lourka. So there! There was even a pretty five-petaled linny flower on the front as decoration, to be a secret reminder both of the lourka's making and its maker—linseed oil was the heart of the varnish, after all, and since linnet birds are harder than flowers to draw, Linny figured the compro-mise was fair.

The last of the fifteen coats of varnish had finally dried, so she took out the old discarded strings she had been scrounging the past few months and wound them (her fingers trembling a little) through the lourka's pegs. And it was marvelous. She could feel the tensions in the wood all balancing out just so; the lourka coming to life in her arms; her fingers plucking round, sweet notes from the strings as she tried to tune them.

Linny had even made up a special song in her head for this occasion, a birthday song for this amazing instrument she had finally managed to bring into the world. *It won't be easy,* she told herself as she took up the lourka, the proper way, tucked under her right arm so her left hand could shape the notes. But this was a golden day, and her fingers remembered the shapes they had seen her father's fingers make, as he played the songs Linny loved best, and it *was* almost easy.

She felt her way along the path the melody made for her, and it was a little like climbing up a hill through the woods: she could sense the direction that music wanted to go.

When she next looked up, it was midafternoon already, the sun low in the sky, and her stomach was growling and her head was light. She could play her song, though, more or less. She could do it.

If she had had the sense to stop for a moment and eat something, maybe her head would have cleared and she wouldn't have done the foolish thing she did do. But her mind was one gleaming fog of amazement and pride.

She was thinking, *Now someone has to hear my song, or it won't really be real.*

Of course it was impossible. How could Linny go around showing off her beautiful lourka, when everything about it was forbidden, against the rules, and wicked? But the longing to have someone hear that song was so large already, so vivid and large, and getting larger every moment. The golden haze of longing filled Linny up and left no room at all for logic or thinking.

She put the lourka back into its (stolen) soft cloth bag, her fingers tripping over themselves a little, now that the wild thought had swallowed up all the sensible parts of her brain.

I'll be very careful, she thought. *I'll just show Sayra. Just to play her the song.*

Sayra always liked Linny's songs, didn't she? Sometimes a wild thought will do that—scatter all good sense.

Linny put all her tools away and tucked the lourka into her carrying bag, next to her uneaten lunch, and set off back to the place she knew Sayra would be waiting for her, down by the creek they called the Rushing.

It was still a beautiful day, but the sun was low, and there was a hint of a chill waiting in the shadows of the trees.

Linny poked her head over the bank, and there Sayra was.

"Sayra!" she almost said. But the word died in her mouth. Sayra wasn't there alone—hunkered against the creek bank next to her was Elias, hunched over and clutching his own knees. They were in the middle of some weighty conversation, looked like. Linny's chest burned with indignation. She never liked the thought of the two of them doing anything that left no room in it for her. And the woods, the untethered woods, that was her secret, hers and Sayra's. Elias was certainly not supposed to know.

"Sayra!" she said again, this time for real. Her voice sounded kind of silly and high-pitched to her ears, and that just made her madder. "Elias! Why are you hiding here?"

Their heads whipped around to look at her: two faces, each one wearing an expression that brought Linny no particular joy. Elias looked irritated and angry. And even Sayra, though her face brightened eventually, once she was looking her way, seemed distinctly worn down.

"*Hiding?*" said Elias, almost spitting, he was so full of scorn. "*You're* the one hiding. How many hours have you been running around loose out there? On the last day, too! And Sayra—"

It made Linny want to scratch him, when Elias

sounded like that. All the same, she did notice that he seemed to think this was a one-time crime.

"Leave Sayra alone," she said quickly. "It's not her fault. I made her do it."

"Linny," said Sayra. "*Please*, Linny."

Sayra hated lying. And she hated being lied about. Her eyes were full of sparks and warning.

"What's that you're holding?" said suspicious, unwanted Elias.

"Nothing," said Linny. "I mean, something I was going to show Sayra. But now—"

But now she was beginning to come back to her senses. Frowning faces, like splashes of cold water, have a way of waking a person up. Linny turned around, confused, and her feet took half a step back to the woods. But by then Elias had jumped in front of her.

"No, really. What have you got there?"

"Just something I made," said Linny, trying to step to the side, to get away from him. Two fires were burning in her at the same time: the music fire and plain old smoldering jealousy. "Something better than you could make."

"Oh, right," said Elias, turning away in disgust. "What could you possibly make, out in the woods? A flower necklace, maybe? Acorns with cute little smiles painted on them?"

"Elias!" said Sayra. She had not moved her eyes from Linny's face, and she was probably reading disaster there, because disaster was definitely on its way. The fires burning inside Linny were jumping up and consuming everything. There was nothing of her left that wasn't on fire.

"Acorns!" she said. "Ha about *acorns*! Look at this, Elias! I happen to know you've NEVER finished anything as good as THIS!"

And she whipped her brand-new lourka out of its bag and held it up in the air in front of her: her revenge, finally, on Elias, for every day he had gone happily off to Linny's own father's workbenches, leaving Linny behind, just because she was a girl.

His head snapped back around to see, and the color drained from his face when he saw that lourka in her hands, and then flooded back with his anger, all salmony pink.

And Sayra put her hand to her mouth. She went pale and stayed pale.

"Where'd you steal that from?" said Elias. "Put it down. Are you crazy?"

"I didn't steal anything," said Linny. "I made it. It's my own. And I can play it, too."

"Oh, Linny," said Sayra.

"You went and stole a lourka!" said Elias. "You raving

idiot! On the day before your birthday!"

Some kind of madness had come over Linny by then.

"You're just jealous," she said. "Because it's a good one, and I made it myself. It took me years! It took me years, but listen!"

She played one note, and the sweetness of it hung like honey in the air. It was a very good note! But before she could get as far as note number two, Elias made a lunge at her new-made lourka, and Linny had to spin around and dodge back up to the top of the bank, out of reach. His eyes were furious and frightened under his mop of dark hair, Linny could see that clearly enough. But there was something else in them, too. He had heard that one golden note—he had seen that lourka—he knew it was good. He knew. She could read that in his eyes, and it satisfied some bitter, hungry part of her, seeing that.

Elias made another grab at her lourka, but Linny was smaller than he was—she was still pretty scrawny for someone almost no longer a child—and she danced out of his way.

"You can't have it!" she said. "You can't have it! You're just jealous, that's what!"

It was kind of exhilarating, being so angry and wild, but already Linny could feel the solid lump of bad feeling she was going to be left with, once all the anger burned off.

"But it's awful. What will your father say?" said Sayra.

"It's all my fault. He'll hate me. He'll be right to hate me. Oh, Linny. You couldn't wait one more day?"

There was a moment of silence, there, with just the creek water rustling through it and the thin whistle of some bird in the bushes on the far bank. Linny couldn't help thinking how much longer she had actually been working on lourkas than this "one more day" suggested. Then her mind shifted to thinking about her father, and the lump of bad feeling was soon getting lumpier in her belly. He could not actually hate Sayra, of course. No one could hate Sayra, who was kind and funny and could turn mere threads into a little person that actually looked like the floury baker.

But what would her father say? That was an icy sort of thought.

None of the daydreams she'd had all those years—of her father listening to a few sweet melodic lines played by his talented, talented daughter on some bright shining new-minted lourka and saying, full of pride, full of joy, "Oh, Linny!"—none of those dreams made any sense, out here in the late-afternoon light of real life. In fact, he would—

And Linny's mind refused to go that way, too. Her mind just balked and sat down, like a sheep or a goat.

"No," she said. "You can't say anything to him."

Sayra and Elias looked at her, one with sadness, the

other with—well, a kind word for Elias's expression might be *disgust*.

Linny wrapped her lourka in its cloth and put it back safely away in her bag, turning to the side a little so they wouldn't see her hands tremble.

"Honestly, Linny," said Sayra, and she wiped the back of her hand across her eyes with a shuddering sigh. "It's like you always have to do everything exactly the hardest possible way."

It was too much for Linny to stand, hearing Sayra sound so unhappy.

"And what were you even thinking we would do," Sayra went on, "if . . . if bad luck came for you? I would know, all my life, that it was my fault. Because it *would* be my fault. I was supposed to keep you safe. There's more than a cord tethering us together, by now. Whatever happens to you, it might just as well happen to me instead. That's how it feels."

Linny didn't even know what to do with her own face anymore. There was nowhere to look and no expression to make that could possibly fit. No, by this point she was just a sodden mass of ick and bad feeling. She would be actually crying in a moment—she was beginning to feel most peculiar around the eyes—and Linny never, ever cried. She was way too bad to *cry*.

Elias fortunately rescued her by snorting in scorn,

which of course made her want to smack him, and wanting to smack Elias pulled her right back from the brink of that cliff.

"Don't worry too much, Linnet, you idiot," said Elias. "We'll know whose fault it really is, if the Voices come after you: your own fault and nobody else's. So there. And I guess you'd better run home now, fast. Your mother wanted you home early today, she told me. I went looking for you earlier, but you were off in the woods."

So Linny let Sayra tether her back up and take her home. She couldn't think of anything else to say or to do.

All the gold of that day had evaporated. It was cold suddenly, too, as soon as the sun had vanished behind the brow of the hill. Linny wrapped her arms around her chest, letting the bag with the lourka in it bobble against her back, and she and Sayra made a pretty miserable home-going of it.

It should probably have been the happiest day of her life, too, because, she had done what maybe no child had ever done so well before. She had made a real, singing lourka with her own hands. In another place, surely she would have been as happy as happy!

But this was the village of Lourka, high in the wrinkled hills, and she, being a girl, was exactly the wrong sort of child.

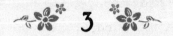

WHAT DOOM SOUNDS LIKE

Linny slouched through the door of her house to find her mother had made broth and dumplings for dinner, her old favorite, the puffy dumplings that almost sing out in the mouth as the wind picks up outside the door.

But even puffy dumplings could not make Linny smile this evening, weighed down by worry as she was. She had sneaked her bag into her own corner, and there it lay, filled with the evidence of her enormous and unforgivable wickedness. This was probably the last hour of her parents not knowing just how wicked she had been. How the shock would climb into their faces when they saw the lourka there! That was the image that kept elbowing its way into Linny's mind; it entirely ruined the taste of those dumplings.

She came back to herself about halfway through that meal, when she realized all four pairs of family eyes were leveled on her. Those eyes were full of worry, too, even the ones belonging to the twins, who (she realized now) must have scrubbed clean for this occasion.

"*What?*" she said impatiently to all of them at once.

"No need to bark, Linny," said her mother. "You can't be *that* gloomy and expect us all not to notice. What happened out there today? Did you quarrel with Sayra or something?"

The lightness in her voice was spread on thinly, like a very quick coat of paint.

"No!" said Linny. Then she realized that was a lie. "Yes," she said, and scowled.

"Ah," said her father. "And you two went home still all quarreled up, letting some little thing fester. That's varnishing flies, Linny, and you oughtn't do it."

His wife looked at him. She hadn't grown up in a place where lourka-making shaped even the words people used.

"Got to let each coat dry, Irika, when it gets to the varnishing stage," he explained. (*Fifteen coats,* thought Linny, but she kept her lips pressed together, and the thought stayed put.) "Got to pick out any dust or little critters stuck there before the next coat goes on. Otherwise you're just varnishing flies, see?"

"*Flies!* Well!" said her mother. "Normal enough for friends to bicker, I guess. These things happen. And everyone so tense these days, riled up about all that twelfth-birthday nonsense."

"All that nonsense" was Linny's mother's phrase for stories she disapproved of, or maybe (the thought was a thin, thin sliver in Linny's heart) feared.

Linny's father opened his mouth to protest, but her mother interrupted him by standing up with a clatter of plates and noisily sending the twins off to bed.

"Tomorrow we'll all feel better," said Linny's mother. "It really will be your birthday, Linny!"

"So long looked forward to," said her father. He couldn't even pretend to be anything but anxious. His hand shook when he put down his knife. "Our dear, wild, hummy Linnet, safe and grown."

The twins—named after the lourka woods, maple and pine (but known since babyhood as Maybe and Pie)—were having one of their private, silly, twinnish conversations on their way up the loft ladder: "Grown up! Maybe tomorrow she'll look, you know—"

"All completely different—"

"Tall, tall, and bumpy chested!" Giggles and whispers.

"You entirely ridiculous boys!" Linny heard her mother say, and that was comfortingly normal.

But when Linny put her own foot on the stairs, her father stopped her.

"We thought we'd sit up with you tonight," he said. "We'll just pull the chairs in front of the fire here."

"We'll have the quilts," said her mother, adding a

gloss of brightness to her thin coat of good cheer. "It'll be cozy."

Not so very cozy if you happened to be Linny, however, whose stomach felt like it was tying itself in knots. The bag she had left in the corner began again to pull on her eyes, wanting her to look over at it and give herself away.

It was not the sort of secret that could stay a secret. Elias would tell on her for sure, and maybe that strand of goodness in Sayra would win out over her inner mischief and make her feel like she had no choice but to confess. Linny frowned to herself and picked at her fingernails for a while, feeling squirmy again under the concerned eyes of her parents.

The minutes ticked away, slow as tree sap. Linny counted cracks in the wooden walls. She did that trick with her eyes to make her brown hand turn into two hands in the firelight. She waggled all those extra fingers. Still time refused to budge.

She wasn't the only one suffering. Her father shifted in his chair for the tenth or twentieth time.

"There's something I have to say to you, Linny," he said suddenly. He was too earnest—Linny found herself wanting to be somewhere far away. "I'm sorry we had to be so tough on you, all these years. It's not natural, is it, to keep children tethered together! But you know it was out of love we did it, Linny. Keeping you safely away from music and all that, for the twelve years. I know it's been hard as hard—"

"Doesn't matter now," said Linny's mother more brightly. "Another couple of hours and we'll be past all that foolishness finally, won't we? I don't so often miss the Plain, you know, but at times like these—"

"Irika," said Linny's father, almost pleading.

"No, it should be said!" said Linny's mother. "After all, for all the troubles down there, at least in the Plain stories stay stories, you know that. In the Plain there wouldn't be some doom that strikes girls just because they touch some foolish musical instrument. If you get sick in the Plain, there are medicines no one uses here. That work on the cells of the body to fix them, when they don't work as they ought. There are *doctors*."

Her father was looking appalled.

"Never mind all that now," he said. "The important thing is here we are, and in an hour I will break the wax off a bottle of last year's wine so we can be properly glad together. Our Linnet has made it through her child years without touching a lourka, despite the music fire being so fierce in her. Many said it couldn't be done, that we would see her safely through, and keep lourkas out of her hand all that time, when she was born such a very hummy baby."

"Um," said Linny, and she caught herself accidentally glancing over at the bag in the corner. Her father perhaps did not see her do that, but her mother certainly did.

"What's wrong, Linny?" she said. "Is there something we should know?" And there was worry in those questions.

"But *you* don't believe all those stories, do you, Mama? That a girl who even just by accident bumped into a lourka sometime—"

The words kind of petered out in her head, because it turned out that her mother thinking it was all nonsense had been the ground under her feet. And a tremor had just gone through that ground.

Her father took a breath that was meant to be calm but sounded rather gasping.

"Did that happen to you, Lin? You're remembering something now?"

"No!" said Linny. Well, it wasn't a lie, in the strict sense. But the fear she had been working so hard to keep at bay was beginning to trickle into her from all directions. "Anyway, in the Plain they know better, right, Mama?"

Her mother shifted in her chair.

"In the Plain they know differently," she said. "That's the thing. Here in the hills, stories make the world. You know that. Up here people see one of those owls with

30

the crystal beak and the wings that shed ice when it flies, and they say, 'Someone's been telling stories about ice owls again.' Right? That's not the way things work in the Plain, that's for sure. And yes, some part of me still thinks it's nonsense. But another part knows better than anybody how stories can come true up here. Look at me! I came up here looking for a girl just like you, and here you are! So I'll be glad when it's safely tomorrow for real, and we can move on past all this, all this—"

And this time she wouldn't even say the word. Wouldn't say "nonsense." Under Linny's feet there was only shadow, where not very long ago there had been everything solid. It was not a good feeling.

"Now, now," said her father. "I'm sure we'll all be glad. Don't let's be worrying when we don't need to. We've been so very careful, all this long time."

Linny's heart was sinking lower and lower.

"Linny," said her mother. "Think hard, sweet girl, just to be extra cautious. Did you ever, even slightly, even completely by accident, even with one elbow, even sleepwalking, even because someone bumped into you on his way somewhere—did you ever touch or take some lourka? Your father's or anybody else's? Did you?"

Hearing her sensible, Plain-spoken mother start talking this way . . . that put knobbles of fear in her stomach. Linny looked over at that bag in the corner. The fear knobbles rolled about like ice-cold marbles in her.

"Mama, Papa," she said in a whisper. "You'll hate me."

"Never," they both said.

"Tell us, then, quick," added her mother. "What have you done? What have you touched or borrowed or begged from someone?"

It was like jumping from a cliff right into an icy pool. There was no going back now. Linny couldn't even think right now, about what she should do or shouldn't do or shouldn't have done already long ago. She was at the bag in the corner before she knew what she was doing, unswaddling the lourka, turning around to face the stricken, horrified faces of her parents just as the clock in the corner ticked another minute closer to midnight.

"I didn't beg anything from anyone," she said. "I didn't have to. It's my very own lourka. Made by me. *I made it.*"

Which was the exact moment the wind rose up outside, blew the door right open, and came whistling through the room, so that the fire in the hearth threw out a fountain of sparks and then almost died away entirely, making everything terribly dim.

Something was wrong in that dim light. Linny could see her parents leaping from their chairs, could hear them crying out in alarm, but the chill had wrapped itself right around her heart, like the coldest possible boa constrictor, and for a moment she could hardly move her own lips to shout. Then the cold air rushed out of the room again, taking her breath with it; it was the strangest thing.

In that hollow space left by the wind, there were voices.

Not voices that you can hear—that would have been less terrible. But the shadow left by voices that you somehow knew had been jabbering at you a moment ago angrily, ironically, bitterly, and that now, in this moment here, were gone. Linny found herself on her feet, the lourka in her hand, but that hand, like her other one, was desperately and awkwardly trying to cover her ears, to block out all that sound that wasn't there, the awful words that no one was saying.

It was not an echo, because an echo is also a kind of sound; this was the ringing absence of something that *had been* there, in some impossible prior slice of time— the sense that a scream had filled the air just a second ago, had come ripping through the air, here and gone. This was the silence where a second ago there *had been* voices, and it was the worst thing Linny had ever heard (or not heard) in all her life.

Her heart was fluttering in jagged bursts, and her ears straining after something that could not be heard, not with ordinary human ears. The room was completely silent, but the air trembled with all that unheard sound. Sound's ghost.

The spell of those silent, absent voices held them all in

its fist. Linny was dimly aware that her parents had their hands at their ears as well, but she couldn't move an inch.

A nightmare's got us, she thought, but even as she thought that, she realized she could feel the floorboards again, solid and real under her feet. And that was already the sign the spell was fading. She turned her head (she could turn it now), and she saw the ashen faces of her parents, both turning to look for her at the very same moment, both faces already shifting from fear to relief as they found her still there.

"Linny!" said her mother (as if from very far away). "What—"

But that's when the real shouting started, far away at the end of the village. Not ghost noises anymore. Ordinary human cries. A wail of grief, outside and far away. Linny started noticing things again: how shiveringly cold she felt, how the lourka was still clenched in her hand, how her father must have dropped the bottle of wine (when?), because a puddle of dark liquid and broken glass stretched out around his feet. Outside, the wailing grew louder. Linny pulled at the quilt still draped around her shoulders with her cold, cold hands.

"Oh, no," she said, and the shaking started for real.

She knew that voice. She had known it forever. It was the sound of a mother whose heart has been torn in two by something awful, awful, awful—

"But that means, that means—*Sayra!*" said Linny, waking up, finally. The lourka fell out of her hands onto the cottage floor. And Linny flung herself across the room, through the door, and out into the chilly night, into a world where some story was coming true, apparently, in the worst possible way.

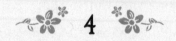

4

I WILL FIND HER

There was a thin mist winding through the village and a round, shining moon beyond the mist, so that all eaves, corners, walls, and wells looked both brighter and fuzzier than they usually would. The hard-packed earth of the road was firm and cool under Linny's bare feet. She felt a little as though she were still dreaming, running up alone through the village in the middle of the night this way, all the way up to the weatherworn cottage where Sayra lived with her mother. How many times had she come up this road? Hundreds or thousands—but never on her own.

It was strange to be running through the village without Sayra. It was like being only a fraction of yourself. To tell the truth, Linny felt right without Sayra only in two places: her own home and deep in the woods. But not among the houses here. Not running up that road at night. It actually made Linny feel a little queasy inside, to be outside and visible like this. She was used to sneaking around and hiding. But now she sped along that road like a ghost, like a rumor, like trouble, and already she could see the slight figure of Sayra's own mother, bent over in grief outside her own cottage, and hear the words in those awful keening sobs of hers.

"Sayra! My Sayra!"

The neighbors were already appearing from their houses, of course. Someone had put a sturdy arm around Sayra's mother's shoulders—that was kind Molleen, Elias's mother. She was saying something that had no words to it, that was just a kind, wordless, broken-hearted murmur. There were other neighbors on the porch and in the door. But Linny was still running very fast, and now she ran right past Sayra's grieving mother to the steps and up Sayra's most-familiar steps to the door—where someone caught up to her, grabbed her arm, and whirled her halfway around.

"You!" said Elias, as wild-haired and wild-eyed as a child with night fever (the twins had been through that not so long ago). "The Voices took Sayra. Why are *you* here?"

"Let me go," said Linny. "I've got to go in." Then she figured out what he really meant by that and could not say another word. It was true; she should not still be here if Sayra was not.

They stood there, glaring at each other miserably in the relative dark, both of them, Linny knew, probably remembering Linny's hands on the smooth neck of that lourka yesterday by the Rushing, and the stupid (but very pretty) notes she had insisted on playing. Both knowing it should have been Linny the Voices came after, if they came after anybody, not Sayra, the good one, the one they both loved.

Why? Why? That's what both those miserable, angry faces were asking as they glared at each other there.

And then, as clear and cold as a blue wolf's howl, as sharp as a snake's fangs sinking venom into her veins, Linny remembered exactly what Sayra had said: *"Whatever happens to you, it might just as well happen to me instead."*

It had been enough. It had changed the story. Something bad had come, and it hadn't happened to Linny—it had happened to Sayra instead. Horrible thought! Had Sayra maybe even *known* it might? The venom reached Linny's heart and almost stopped it still.

Surely the whole out-loud truth was about to come raining down on her then, like a ton of sharp stones, but Elias simply turned away and said to Sayra's mother, "Where is she?"

Sayra's mother looked broken—that was the word that echoed in Linny's head, *broken, broken, broken*—as she came up to the porch. Her eyes just flicked toward the door, behind which, as Linny knew well, the hall would lead a person right to Sayra's room, and her shoulders sagged, and that was enough for Elias. He went stumbling off into the shadows to see for himself, to tell whatever was left of poor Sayra how it should have been Linny taken, not her, and probably something about his undying love and so on and so on, this being Elias.

That woke the tiniest little flame in Linny, even as filled with guilt and self-loathing as she was.

"I need to see her, too," she said to the empty space where Elias had been.

"She was thinking about you," said Sayra's mother dully. "She worried about you all evening, Sayra did."

Permission enough. Linny broke away and walked down the hall, quick as quick so her feet wouldn't take fright and betray her.

She wanted to see Sayra, but of course she didn't want to, too.

What could be left of a person, once the Voices had come and taken them off to Away?

From the doorway she could see what looked like Sayra lying in her bed under the window, the lamp burning on the little table there, Elias kneeling on the floor beside her bed, his wild-haired head murmuring something to the girl sleeping (sleeping?) there, his hand holding her hand. Linny took another step through into the room, and Elias turned to look at her for a moment.

"You go away," he said. "You did this."

The little flame in Linny wavered for a moment and almost went out. But not quite.

"Let me see her," she said. "Elias, please."

"You did this," he said. "It's your fault. The men are going up into the hills to look for the edge of Away, to try to play her back. But they'll never find it. Or her."

But Sayra just looked like herself, sleeping. Didn't she?

"Doesn't look to me like she's gone anywhere," said Linny. "Let me see."

She pushed her way forward. She was not going to let Elias tell her what to do. She went right up to Sayra, her tethered twin, lying so strangely and quietly there, and she made that lummox Elias get out of the way. He always thought he loved Sayra more than anyone else could, but Linny knew better than that.

The candle was doing something strange to the light in this room. She could not focus on Sayra's hand somehow. She rubbed her eyes, and tried again.

"Thinking of you, she was," said Sayra's mother from the doorway of that room. "Worried about *you*."

The hand was definitely blurry. Light didn't respect its edges anymore. Linny took a deep breath and grabbed the hand, and it was still there, feeling just like Sayra.

Warm like Sayra. It should not be fading away the way it was.

"Sayra!" said Linny, beginning to panic, despite herself. "Please, Sayra!"

"Don't you get it?" said Elias. "She's Away. Just the shell lying there now. She'll fade to nothing here, eventually, my ma says. It may take days, it may take months, but we've lost her. We've lost Sayra. *Because of you.*"

She was braced for even worse, but Elias choked on his words, and his shoulders started to tremble. He had to turn away very fast and struggle back out of the room.

Peeking out from under Sayra's pillow, what was that? The end of a cord Linny knew very, very well. Until that second she hadn't known what she was going to do, but the tether decided things. *Whatever happens to you, it might just as well happen to me instead.* That went both ways, didn't it? You can't let your mismatched twin fade to nothing while her soul has been stolen off to Away just because of your own wild wickedness. Even wild and wicked people sometimes have to make things right again.

Linny put her head down close to Sayra's ear.

"Sayra, *listen,*" she said, quiet enough for only Sayra to hear, if Sayra could still hear at all. "I don't care where you are. Just *wait for me, wherever you are.* You have to wait. I'll come find you, even in Away. I'm going to find a

41

way to make you better and then I'm coming to Away to bring you back, Sayra. I'll fix things, I promise. You stay put, wherever you are, and wait for me. . . ."

Then she stopped. Her hand had just found the birthday sash, folded deep into her pocket. The sash that Sayra had made for her. Better than a tether. And what had she said? Her dreams had told her—*to give it to Linny . . . today . . . not to wait*—

A howl of pain surged up from Linny's heart. She couldn't speak for a moment, it was so hard to keep that howl inside.

Her fingertips had plucked the little silk rosebud out of the sash. It flickered in the dim light, warm in her hands, wanting to blossom, wanting to sing its marvelous wrinkled song all over again.

"Sayra," she whispered.

Sayra had made this astonishing thing for her. It had a bit of both of them in it. She'd said that herself, hadn't she?

Before Linny knew what she was doing, she had tucked the flower right into Sayra's fading hand.

"Don't let go," said Linny. "Sayra, hold on. I'll find you. *Don't let go.*"

And then there was nothing to do but to skim the palm of her hand across the top of Sayra's still-smooth head and stand back up in a rush.

"Sorry," she said as she pushed past everyone who had by now gathered in the room, in the hall, on the porch. She was in a hurry now. She was beginning to see what she was going to have to do, to put things right.

She ran back down the road, flying fast to hang on to that thread of certainty.

Her mother was waiting for her at the door of their house, with tears in her eyes and a quilt to wrap around Linny's cold shoulders.

Linny didn't remember dropping that quilt.

"I've got to go," she said to her mother, quickly so she wouldn't lose her courage. "You said in the Plain there would be medicines, right? Then I'm going to find them. Because it's my fault this happened. It should have been me, not Sayra."

"It shouldn't be *anybody*!" said her mother, with a fierceness Linny wasn't used to hearing.

"But it's Sayra, so that means I've got to go. I'll find that stuff that can save her, and I'll bring it back up here."

Easy-peasy when you said it that way: down to the Plain and then up to Away. If she paused even for a moment, she was afraid she would remember how impossible it all was. So she didn't pause.

She said instead, "You'll tell me where to go in the Plain, won't you, for the medicines?"

She wasn't a child anymore, right? Not being a child

means doing the brave, scary things.

Then she noticed how quiet it was in that house.

"Where's Papa?"

"He went off right away with the others," said her mother. "Taking their music up into the highest hills— looking for the edge of Away, that's where he said they'd be going. That's what they do, he says, trying to play the poor girl back."

"It never worked before, though," said Linny. They would play music as beautifully as possible, trying to draw the wandering soul back into the world. It was a nice idea, sure, but Linny couldn't remember any stories where it actually brought a lost girl home.

"Maybe they didn't find the edge," said her mother. "It's what you might call a topographical conundrum, the edge of Away."

Sometimes Linny's mother still spoke like someone fresh up from the Plain.

"Hey!" said Linny. (Her father liked to say, "Are those important words, or just long ones?")

"I just mean the hills get infinitely wrinkled, and then the edge is past that. In the Plain they'd make a graph to show you. And that's why the edge can't be found."

"*Mama*," said Linny. She almost put her hands to her ears to drown out those words. "No one can find Lourka, either, but *you did*. You came up into the wrinkled

44

country, past all the other villages that there are, down there lower in the hills, and you got sicker and sicker from the magic, but you kept coming and you kept coming, and hillsick as you were, eventually you found us."

That was the story. Linny clung to it now with a desperate hope. It had been something practically impossible that her mother had done, *but she had done it.*

"I did find you," said her mother. "Thank goodness, yes. Well, first I found your father."

And even in the midst of this awfulness, a smile danced in her eyes for a moment, only to wink out again like a snuffed candle, soon as she looked back into Linny's face.

"Oh, Linny, I don't even know anymore, what's possible or impossible in this world," she said. "And we all love Sayra."

Not as much as I do, thought Linny, and the stubbornness that was forming like a scab on top of all her fear and misery pushed her forward, forward, toward the places she knew she had to go.

"Well, what I'm doing is *possible,*" said Linny. "The Plain's a real place, right? A place a person can get to by walking? Downhill, that's all. I'm going now, and I'll get those medicines—don't look like that, Mama!"

Her mother had the strangest expression on her face, the expression of someone determined to fool the world into thinking she wasn't miserable or afraid.

"Not in rags and bare feet, surely, Linny?"

"Oh!" said Linny, looking down at her toes.

So while Linny put on layers of warm clothes and laced up her shoes, her mother hurried about the kitchen, putting together a proper traveler's bundle.

"There'll be food in here," she said to Linny. "And some things I've been waiting to give you for years and years. And even your birthday present—wrapped up in the cloth there. I made it myself, with Jenny's help. Oh, poor Jenny!"

(Jenny was Sayra's mother.)

"Well, you'll look at it later sometime. But what you need to know most of all: that lourka, sweet girl—it's not your fault."

The lourka was on the table, too, wrapped up neatly in a clean cloth sack. Linny shook her head when she saw it.

"Of course the lourka's my fault," she said, and saw Sayra again, all curled up and fading on her bed. "I was the stupid one who made it."

Her mother shook her head.

"Oh, but what you don't know, Linny, is—well, there are a lot of things you don't know. But one of them, maybe the most important fact of all, is that I came up here from the Plain looking for you. I mean, I came up here carrying the story that I would find her, the girl with a lourka. I thought the world needed her. And I had pictures in my head of what she might be like. But of course what I didn't understand then was that I was coming up to a place where stories like that have a way of coming true. And here you are! Well, never mind now. The point is, it's not all your fault. All right. Listen. You'll need help there, finding what you need. So you'll go to your aunt, my sister Mina, who lives down in the Broken City—"

Broken City?

Linny's mother caught the question in her eyes.

"They don't get along, the people on either side of the river, so they broke their own city in two."

"Like an egg?" said Linny. She meant the soft-boiled kind, that the twins enjoyed knocking the tops off with their spoons.

Her mother looked startled.

"An egg? Not so much. The river runs down from the wrinkled hills and then makes a sharp turn so it can flow right between the wrinkled and Plain halves of the city—"

"Right or left?"

This unknown place was already wanting to take shape in her mind.

"Turns left," said her mother, who understood about directions. "Standing on the hills, looking down, you'd say it turns almost as sharp as a table corner. I'd draw you a map if I had more time—a map's a sort of picture of a place. And then the river runs along through the middle of the city and then veers right again, maybe even sharper than the first time, so it can run into the Plain."

"Oh," said Linny, drinking it all in. She had known their little creeks joined up with a river eventually, of course, but she hadn't known where the river went, once it was out of the hills. "So it's the river that makes the city broken."

"The river runs through it, yes, but it takes people to break things," said her mother, and there was an edge of bitter sorrow in those words that Linny hadn't heard from her mother before. "Bend, they call the city on this side, the wrinkled side, of the river. And on the other bank, in the Plain, is the part we always called Angleside. It's been a long time since I've used those names!"

She pushed a scrap of paper (made by her own hand, that paper, and with the tiniest flowers caught in its creamy surface) toward Linny.

"So. You must go to your aunt in the Broken City. She will take care of you, and she knows about medicines. Here, I've written her address down for you—carry this close, Linny. I'm putting it in this little sack here, with some other things that will make more sense to you later, I think. Whatever you do, don't lose it."

Linny looked at the scribbled words and numbers on

that slip. Her mother had worked hard to teach her to read, but these words swam about in her eyes like little fish. And the piece of paper went into the sack too fast for Linny really to make much sense of it.

Her mother hesitated for a moment, then leaned closer and spoke almost under her breath, as if the world might pounce on her words if it caught wind of them.

"And Linny, what about when you want to come home? It's not an easy place to find, Lourka, even if I was lucky enough to find it. They say it hides itself, or the hills hide it."

"I can find my way home," said Linny, with more confidence than she really felt. "Anyway, I have to bring the medicines back for Sayra. That's the whole point. I bet I can come back. I think so, anyway."

A dog howled, rather far off. That snapped Linny's mother right out of some kind of spell.

"I don't want you to go," she said. "But if you are going, it had better be now. Linny, my dearest girl! You're good in wild places. We know that."

"And I can't get lost," said Linny.

"No," agreed her mother, arranging the bundles over Linny's shoulders. They weren't too heavy, the way her mother fixed them up. "Like me, you can't easily get lost. But if you're really like me, Linny, that won't always save you from *feeling* lost. Kiss me, sweetheart. You are brave.

Oh, you shouldn't have had to be so brave when you were still this young!"

"Twelve," said Linny pointedly. Her mother kept forgetting. Not young!

"Years younger than you should be, dear one, that's all. Well, it can't be helped. Remember you carry all my love with you, wherever you go. You are truly the girl I came looking for, when I came up into these wrinkled hills."

And Linny was out in the night again. Her mother had opened the door. No, they were already through the door and across the yard, and her mother was opening the gate with a hand that couldn't keep itself from shaking.

"Quickly, safely, quickly!" her mother was saying, and now Linny was already out the gate, and had she even said good-bye? Had she?

But she was already almost around the corner by the time that thought had risen up in her bewildered brain, and it was too late to do anything about it.

5

THAT LUMMOX ELIAS

She walked, stunned, for maybe five minutes down the road; then the dog barked again, perhaps less far away than the first time, and she decided it might be more discreet to be in the woods, where she wouldn't stick out so much like a sore thumb (the sort of sore thumb that wears traveler's bundles over its shoulders). And maybe if she hid, if she was properly sneaky, she could even steal a last look at her father, before she walked all the way down out of the wrinkled country and into the Plain. She would have liked to have been able to say good-bye to her father. That made her heart twist, thinking that. She had to walk faster, just to get those thoughts out of her mind.

She hadn't gone twenty steps into the woods, however, when something near her stubbed its toe on a tree root, stumbled forward with a loudish, but somehow familiar "Oof!" and ran (to judge from the sound) right into a tree. Linny whipped her head around, and sure enough, she had known that "Oof."

It was that lummox Elias.

She jumped back out of his path, but a sliver of moonlight had already found its way through the branches overhead and betrayed her.

"Linny?" he said. "Linny, is that you? What are you *doing* out here?"

"Strolling in the woods," said Linny. Part of her being bad was that she could never help needling Elias. "What are you doing?"

"But how'd you get up here? You shouldn't be up here."

That had Linny fairly puzzled.

"Up here?" she said. "What's that mean? We're not up anywhere. We're about twenty feet into my papa's piece of forest. That tree over there is the one he took the limb from last year for lourka pegs. You don't remember it?"

Elias sagged to the ground and put his hands to his head. Maybe he had hit that tree harder than Linny had thought.

"I've been walking for hours," he said. He was too tired even to be his usual tiresome self. Linny appreciated that. "All uphill. How can I still be way down here?"

Linny squatted down beside him, the bundles bouncing awkwardly against her back. When people get lost, it squashes their spirits somehow. Linny had seen that happen before.

"Where did you think you were going?"

Then she saw the lourka on his back and knew.

"Oh," she said.

Up to Away. Hoping to find the place that wouldn't let itself be found, up where the wrinkled hills met their limit and became some kind of edge. To try to play some song so sweetly that Sayra's captured soul would be called right back into this world (though it had never been actually done). The men had left him behind, of course. What possible use was that lummox Elias?

But she knew how it must have felt to him. He was a lummox, but even lummoxes are probably stung when everyone goes off to rescue the girl the lummox thinks he loves best of all. That made Linny feel needle-ish again, though. She couldn't believe she hadn't even thought of the most obvious thing.

"Hey, Elias!" she said. "The only one who could ever play Sayra's soul out of Away is me! I know her best, and I bet I can find her. She likes my songs. She'll come if I play. I should have thought of that right off the bat. I should have tried that first."

She expected Elias to say something rude or swat her or something, but he just looked at her in the dark, tiredness weighing him down.

"I got lost," he said. "I was trying to follow your father, but the hills got strange, and I ended up here. It's hopeless, anyway. The hills won't let people get that far. I heard the men talking, when they first set off. They said nobody really knows how to get to Away, not really. It's like living in a saucer with slippery edges. That's what they said. Nobody knows where Away even is, up at the top of the hills."

"I do," said Linny. "I could get there."

"That's a lie," said Elias.

It was, too. Elias was right enough about that. But Linny weighed that thought in her head a moment and decided maybe it was more a hopeful lie than a crazy one. She had gone pretty far up into the hills before. She knew how they tried to shrug a person off her path. But Linny was the one who never got lost.

And if she could find Sayra in Away and get her back, then she wouldn't have to leave everything behind and go down all alone into the Plain, would she? That touched some funny nerve in her throat—she had to catch her breath very fast to keep the sound she was making from becoming a sob.

And that was that. She popped back onto her feet, already running her mind's eye over the lay of the land. Thinking about the way the hills went, and the way the wrinkles thickened. Somewhere up in the wrinkliest part of the wrinkled hills was the edge of Away. All right, she could find that. She would go uphill and keep going, and then eventually somehow she'd be there.

"Hey," said Elias, that lummox. "Where do you think you're going?"

She just kept walking, measuring the slopes of things in her head and heading up.

But Elias crashed along behind her. He was never as good at walking quietly through the woods as Linny or Sayra. The deer always ran off in fright when Elias came blundering through the bushes, and Elias would just stand there looking hurt, because he liked deer. He liked all living creatures, really. Lambs came up to him to rub their furry faces against his shins. He just wasn't any good at being quiet or finding his way.

"Walk quieter," said Linny over her shoulder. "You'll mess me up."

That was another lie, actually. But Elias's crashing footsteps became a little less noisy behind her.

"Hey, Linny," he said, panting as he came along after her. "What's all that stuff on your back?"

"Stuff," said Linny. The bundles did feel heavier, now that she was lugging them uphill. But if she had left them in a heap under a tree somewhere, she would have to get back to that tree before running off to the Plain. If she couldn't find the edge of Away, that is.

These were still the familiar woods. Linny didn't really have to think yet, not down here. She just angled up the slope on a line that skirted by her old workshop, not close enough that Elias would see it, though, and start asking questions about that, too.

When she paused to change course slightly to the right, looking for the likeliest place to cross the little creek that whispered along nearest to them, she noticed that the sky was beginning to gray up already. It was no longer the deep middle of the night. That took her by surprise, somehow. Time was still padding along, then! Somehow it felt like time should have stopped, the very minute the Voices came for Sayra. Everything else had been cut short then; why should the clocks keep moving?

She shook her head roughly to get the tangles out of her brain, and pressed on up the far bank of the creek even faster than she had been going, with Elias struggling on after.

As soon as they crossed the creek, Linny could feel the ways the wrinkles of those hills began to grow thicker and deeper all around them. Elias gave a new kind of groan.

"Head hurts," he said. "Are you sure you know where you're going?"

"Shh," said Linny. "Of course I do."

The nice thing about lying is that it gets easier, the more you do it. She did not know where Away was, of course. Not ever getting lost is not the same thing as knowing where every possible place—even the ones you've never seen—might be. What Linny did know was what it felt like to follow the land's wrinkles as they became ever more complicated and deeper.

"Weren't we already here before?" said Elias. He had almost caught up with her when she paused to let the tug of the land tell her which way to go next.

"Here?" said Linny. "No."

"I don't like it. All the little valleys look the same."

Linny looked around. She was taken by surprise by Elias's words, because she hadn't really been using her eyes at all. She had been feeling her way.

The world around them was a deep, in-between gray, too light for stars but much too dark for true morning. They were standing in a very small ravine. A miniature valley. And other little canyons ran out from this one in every direction, so that the whole world seemed to be fracturing all around them. When she looked with her eyes, Linny could see how strange this place could be to a person who could, unlike Linny, get lost. She didn't usually try to imagine herself in those shoes, and for one brief moment the effort to see the world as Elias must be seeing it actually made her dizzy. She blinked to get her balance back, and Elias himself said, quietly and very nearby, "I can't see which way is up or down anymore. Can you?"

"Shh. I was fine until you distracted me. This way."

But when she moved on, Elias yelped, and she had to go back for him.

"You turned a corner," he said. His eyes were very wide. "I couldn't see where you went."

"Hang on, then," said Linny. There was no help for it, even though it slowed everything down. Elias put his hand on her shoulder, and at least he knew how to rest a hand on a person lightly, because with the bundles already weighing her down, Linny was in no mood to carry even part of a lummox.

She forged on. Elias had called it "turning a corner," and maybe his words had been powerful enough to reshape Linny's view of things, because the little canyons all around did become more like corners. You pushed past one tree, and the world turned a corner, and there were other, completely different trees, one absolutely filled with little golden birds, just beginning to chatter their welcome to the morning that was not there yet. And then you turned around another corner, and there was a creek again, taking up most of that canyon, if you could call such a tiny rift a canyon. And then a corner, and another tree, this one tall and narrow.

"Oh, help," said Elias, his hand trembling on her shoulder. "Please help. We're lost. We're so lost."

But he didn't seem to be talking to Linny exactly, so she put him back out of her mind. The world was so wrinkled all around them that she had to focus very hard to feel which way still led deeper in (and higher up).

And then finally they clambered up another set of rocks, and turned another corner, and the canyon that held them now was no larger than a closet. If you reached out a hand, you could almost feel the sides of it. But (Linny felt this in her gut) if you took another step, you'd be somewhere else. And ahead something happened to the light. Ahead there was a blur, as if they were catching a glimpse, here, of the world before it had decided how it wanted to be.

"Don't move," said Linny to Elias, and very carefully, without letting her feet shift an inch, she shrugged one bundle off her shoulder, the one with the lourka in it.

"What do you think you're doing?" said Elias in a whisper. His teeth chattered a little on the last word.

"Shh," said Linny.

She wriggled the lourka into place under her right elbow. Her left hand, the fingering hand, hesitated over the strings a little, thinking about notes she might be able to play. And then her other hand plucked a string, and the sound filled that tiny corner's worth of canyon, filled it and filled it and spilled over its edges.

"You can't do that!" said Elias into her ear. "You crazy thing! What are you *doing*?"

But Linny was squinting into the vague places in front

of them. The note had changed something in the rock just ahead. She was sure it had. She played another couple of notes, just to see what happened.

What happened was the wind kicked up around them, as if the air had perked up its ears and taken interest. And the rocks trembled a little in the wind. They shuddered. They thinned.

Elias's hand trembled on her shoulder.

Linny was still trying very hard to ignore him. She frowned down at her strings. She was trying to put those notes back together into the pattern of her song. She had known it so well, yesterday afternoon. It must be there somewhere.

A few sweet notes in a row—so it was still there! She looked up in triumph, and for a moment the rocks right in front of her eyes faded right away and became part of a different place, a hazy place, hard to see, where on the edge of something someone was sitting, someone was turning her head—

But several things happened at once just then, while her fingers stumbled on, plucking out the notes of that first song. The wind that had come back again to whip itself right around her head, chattering, fell away from one instant to the next, into that complete silence that was somehow worse than noise. The Voices were back. Or had just been back.

The someone in the different place turned and maybe held out one hand, but everything shimmered, so that it was hard to see. And it was hard to focus on anything, with the ghostly Voices still trembling in the air. They had just been jabbering everywhere all around, insisting on something. Insisting and insisting. The shadows of all those Voices made it hard to think, and harder still to see. Linny wanted very much to see clearly, because there was someone there, she was almost certain, past the shimmer.

She took a step forward, elbowing her way through the last traces of the rocks, reaching out toward that not-quite-there shape that was also reaching, reaching toward her.

"*Sayra?*" she whispered, even that much of a sound intruding rudely into the silence carved out for themselves by all those Voices.

For one instant, she felt—she was almost sure she felt—thin fingers brushing against hers, pressing something soft and cool into her hand, like a message, and she thought all in a joyful rush, *I'm doing it I've done it it's Sayra Sayra*—

And then something or someone grabbed her from behind, shouting out as he did so—it was Elias, why? What was he doing? There was a struggle of some kind going on between him and things that could not be seen nor heard, and Linny was in the middle of it like a flaxseed caught in a whirlwind. The wind was back again, and screaming.

Meanwhile Elias, that lummox, had grabbed Linny's lourka right out of her hands and was waving it around in the air. And he was shouting nonsense, too. "Go away! Go away! You can't have her! It was me! I was the one playing!"

"You were not," mumbled Linny, but it made no difference, Elias was making so much noise. And she pulled hard on something, on the beautiful lourka that was hers because she had made it, and there was a struggle, and something gave way with an awful cracking sound, and something else clonked her on the head, and the rocks at the end of the canyon became hard again and indeed scraped themselves painfully against her outstretched hands, and she would have cried from the pain of that, but the world was spinning, she was losing her balance, she was tipping over some edge while the wind screamed at her, she was gone. . . .

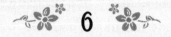

6

TWISTS IN THE PATH

Each of the first few times Linny tried to open her eyes, she caught a different glimpse of the world: a pool of trees, their pointy tops dipping into a blue sky . . . an ant climbing with enormous, heartbreaking patience up a tree trunk . . . a bruised and anxious face looking at her and saying something she couldn't hear. She knew if she were just a little more awake, she would recognize that face, and for a moment she tried to figure out why she had been asleep and where she was, but thinking made her head hurt, so she let her eyelids close again and just hid in the darkness until everything stopped spinning.

"Linny," said someone later.

It was not the voice she was expecting. It wasn't Sayra, and it wasn't her mother. She forced her eyes open again and saw that the light had changed, that it was late in the day, and that the face looking with such worry and confusion at her belonged to that lummox Elias. Only at the moment he didn't look as much like a lummox. He looked worn out and dusty. She also realized, all of a sudden, that her body felt like it had just been popped over a cliff with a river of rocks. She was pummeled all over, and her hands stung.

"Ow," she said, trying to get a look at her hands. Someone had wound strips of cloth around her left palm. And her right hand was clenched very tightly around something. Something small and soft. "Elias?"

"Is that you? Are you back?"

He sounded so incredibly relieved and exhausted. It was all very disconcerting. It was not like Elias to be worried about Linny. *I must have been nearly dead or something,* thought Linny. It was the only explanation that made sense.

"Where are we?"

She asked because she really could not tell. Which was a strange feeling all in itself. She must not have been awake when they came here.

"I don't know," said Elias. "When those awful Voices grabbed at you up there, I went kind of nuts, I think. And then there was a big shaking, and I lost my balance, and we sort of rolled around a lot of corners at once. I don't know where we ended up, but I think we're pretty far below Lourka. Someplace I never even saw before."

It was all coming back now. Linny scowled at Elias, and then had to wince, because her head was too sore for scowling.

"I almost had her," she said, remembering. The fingers of her right hand had memories of their own: they were still clenching, clenching, as if holding on now could change the past. "She was right there. I think I touched her. But then you grabbed at me and ruined it."

"You didn't have anyone, you idiot," said Elias. That was more his regular voice. "You took out that stupid lourka, and in like one minute *they* almost had *you*. I should have stopped you faster, but my head was all confused. Should have been me playing. Too late now. We messed up. And now she's really, truly gone."

He stood up with an angry, dismal jerk and walked off into the woods. Linny turned her head to watch him go, and the slightly spinny feeling she got from moving her head added to all the other bad feelings in her, until she worried she might actually be sick. But by lying very still until Elias came back, with a cookpot's worth of water sloshing around in his hands, she made it past that bad moment.

She recognized the cookpot. That made her wonder how the rest of her stuff was doing. But she wasn't really ready to look around for it yet.

So she lay there, thinking uncomfortable thoughts.

Was it true? Had she almost been trapped in Away, like Elias said? It was hard to remember the details.

Her left hand throbbed. The fingers of her right hand clenched and clenched, holding on to—whatever that was. Something almost like nothing.

"What's wrong?" said Elias, looking over at her. It was part of his being good with lambs and kittens, she figured—noticing when creatures were twitching.

"Something's in my hand," she said. "But my fingers won't move so I can see what it is."

"Hand's been cramped up all day," said Elias, poking gently at her fingers. "Fools you into thinking it's got something inside. Here, I'll try my ma's trick on it."

He sat down beside her and went to work on that hand, rubbing the life back into her fingers one by one and shaking his head at her when she yelped.

"It has to hurt some, sorry," he said, not unkindly. "That's just the blood coming back. Hey, wait—"

He bent over her fingers.

"What's this?"

Linny turned her head, trying to see what it was Elias had, but then the seasickness washed over her again.

"A handkerchief? No. A flower? Why are you—"

"Give that back!" said Linny. Because suddenly she remembered everything, and she knew what that must be: the wonderful silk rosebud Sayra had made for her from wrinkled silk. Her birthday present. "*Sayra* gave that to me."

"Sayra?" said Elias. "But what is it? Looks so strange."

Linny tried even harder to look: there were at least two silky rosebuds swimming before her eyes now. And when she made a heroic effort to bring the images together, the blossom still looked like something made of rose-colored smoke, transparent and insubstantial.

"Give it back," said Linny, closing her blurry-sick eyes. "Sayra gave it to me for my birthday, and then I gave it to her, to the shell of her, I mean, in her own room in Lourka, and then when I found her . . . *almost* found her . . . in Away, she kind of gave it to me again somehow . . . and I feel all spinny, Elias, like I'm about to fall off the world—"

"Lie quiet," said Elias. She felt him tucking the soft almost-nothing something back into her palm, and then she was dozing again.

When she opened her eyes the next time, she felt a bit better. She opened her hand and looked again, and the smoky-delicate rosebud unfolded itself for her, like a breath of magic in her palm. Sayra must have held on to that silky bud so hard that it had ended up in Away with her—but the hours it had spent in that impossible place had changed it. She tucked it safely back into the sash, itself deep in her pocket, and turned her head to see what Elias was up to.

He was scrabbling over to the left, messing with twigs and dry grass.

"What're you doing?" she asked.

"Making some supper," said Elias. "Doesn't look like you're ready to walk home just yet."

"You can do that? Make a fire? Cook?"

"'Course I can. You can't?"

Linny shook her head and winced. Elias was striking sparks off his flint, and then he knelt down and blew carefully on that little flame. She hadn't ever seen that expression on his face, that quiet concentration—it looked like her father's face, when he was polishing an especially nice piece of wood.

"Ma says you're not a full grown-up adult until you can feed yourself and at least six other people," said Elias. He even almost smiled for a moment, as he fed twigs to the flame. "Number not chosen randomly! She has all of us taking turns on meals. Seven of us, so my day's Wednesday. I'm good at it, too."

The baby fire was crackling now for real. Elias went back to rummaging around in Linny's bundles, sorting out the edibles.

"If you don't mind me asking, Linny, why are you lugging a cookpot around, if you can't cook? To whack people with?"

She would usually have flared up at that, but she couldn't get the energy together, somehow.

It was a reasonable question, too. All that stuff in her bundles—what was the point of it, really? It was useless, maybe, like Linny herself. Making wicked instruments that brought doom down on the people she loved most. Not getting lost, except that here she was now, as good as lost. And what was the point of always knowing where you were, anyway, if you couldn't find a way to find and save your best friend, really and truly lost somewhere beyond the edge of the world?

What would be left of Sayra, after spending so much time in Away?

"You all right?" said Elias.

She must have made a pathetic little noise, right out loud. That made her mad enough that she pushed herself up from the ground and heaved her body into a semi-sitting position against the nearest tree. She had to pant for a minute or so after that, just to clear her head again, but the world made a lot more sense from this perspective. She could feel the contour of the hill underneath her. To one side, through the trees, she could see a wedge of far ridgeline.

"Oh!" she said. "How'd we get down *here*?"

"The hills spat us out, remember?" said Elias. "Something like that."

"It's so far from the ridge," said Linny. "I don't remember doing that much walking."

It was way past the boundary trees. That was one thing.

"Naw. I told you. We got spat out. It was pretty weird. And I had to lug you *and* all your things."

"Oh."

That wasn't such a nice thought, having been lugged about by Elias. She tried to put it out of her head.

"You got water from a creek over there," said Linny. "Did you taste it? Is it ours?"

"Have some. You should be drinking water anyway, so you mend. That's what Ma always says."

He dug a bowl out of one of the bundles and gave Linny some water to sip. It was cold, with a sweet hint of pennyroyal and, beneath that, a whiff of buttered toast. The wrinkled creeks each favored certain flavors over others, though sometimes they experimented.

"Mostly ours," said Linny, recognizing the toast. "But some other creek's joined it, I guess. We must be pretty far below the village now. Past the boundary trees, for sure."

"You'll get us back, though, right? Bonked heads need rest, says Ma, but tomorrow you'll be walking better. Finish that water."

How had he done that? The cookpot was already

70

bubbling. Something was beginning to smell amazingly like soup. It actually made Linny's stomach forget all about how sick it had just been feeling. Fickle stomach. It rumbled.

"I'm not actually going back home right now," said Linny.

Elias curled his lip in disgust. He was definitely still a lummox, then, after all.

"Running away?" he said. "That's pretty stupid. That's what little kids do when they're mad about something."

"I'm not the stupid one," said Linny, with as much dignity as her grogginess would allow. "I have something important to do. I have to go down to the Broken City."

"You mean the place they call Bend? Down all the way to the edge of the Plain? That's a good one. Have some soup. It's pretty basic, but it's warm."

He didn't believe a word she was saying, Linny could tell. But he poured some of his miraculous soup into her bowl, and for a few minutes, anyway, she had to forgive him.

Then she said, "I'm going to the city to find medicine for Sayra. My mother says in the Plain they would cure her there with medicines. That gave me the idea."

That had Elias surprised. She could see him recalculating all sorts of things he was thinking.

"You're going to Bend *on your own*?" said Elias slowly.

"That's very far away. And you can't make fires or cook or anything, you said so yourself. It's a crazy idea."

"Sayra's my almost-twin," said Linny. "The Voices should have come for me, not her. You know that. I have to make things right. I promised her I'd save her. So now I have to."

"Hmm," said Elias.

He was letting the fire burn itself out now. The sky was getting dark around them already. How could a whole day have passed since their disastrous trip up to the edge of Away? Though it also felt like a million years ago.

"Go to sleep," said Elias. "Tomorrow you'll have changed your mind, probably. Besides—oh, never mind."

"Never mind what?"

"I promised her, too," said Elias, looking away, and the fire hissed as he dumped creek water on it. They both knew about being careful with fires, when you're out in the woods.

Linny was glad of the dark; she could roll her eyes without Elias, that lovesick lummox, having the faintest clue.

Because really. Honestly. Who did he think he was?

Everywhere all around, the trees were already dipping those points of theirs into a sea of bright stars. Elias rolled himself into a ball and fell immediately asleep, like one of the puppies that always seemed to be dozing in the corners of kind Molleen's crowded house.

Maybe she would just have to sneak off on her own the next morning. That's what she thought, all drowsy-like, and when another part of her brain remembered the boundary trees, and where they were, and how maybe Elias wouldn't be able to find his way home again, her thoughts muddled themselves up until in fact she wasn't thinking at all.

A mere moment later, however, or so it seemed, her eyes were flying open, her heart hammering like a wood-pecker. Morning had rinsed the stars away, and somebody had just given a wild, frightened shout, not very far off. Down the slope that way, it sounded like: nearer to the creek.

"What's that? What's that?" she said in alarm, turning to poke Elias awake.

But the patch of ground where Elias had been sleep-ing was now only pine needles and brown earth. Elias himself was gone.

That shout—Elias's shout?—lingered in the air.

She sprang to her feet, felt for the whittling knife in her pocket, and was halfway to the creek—slithering from tree to tree—before she even noticed that her head seemed to be feeling like itself again. Thank goodness! Sneaking through forests is hard without a clear and unspinning head.

Linny knew how to move through the woods without

making a racket, that was true. You couldn't do as much sneaking around as Linny had done all her life and not learn how to avoid breaking twigs. She was careful to stay in the fringe of the forest and on the near side of the creek, keeping her eyes and ears open and slipping from tree to tree. She hadn't gone too far when there was another bout of commotion ahead—a couple of quick shouts, and a protesting sound, and sounds that Linny could not make sense of at this distance. She scrambled through the trees as fast as she could go, her heart pounding, and as soon as she was over the next little rise of rocks, she saw a knot of people on the opposite bank. She counted them quickly: five, all in identical gray clothing without the slightest flash of color in it. Why a bunch of grown-ups would want to dress in exactly the same uninteresting, ugly clothing, Linny could not even guess.

But it wasn't the blandness of these people in gray that troubled her most. It was the way they stood in an anxious, slump-shouldered circle around something, arguing among themselves and coughing and moving angry, nervous hands in the air. Linny crawled up to the back of a conveniently placed bush and listened as hard as she could, but she still couldn't make out all the details of their speech. They were calling one another fools and idiots and other, even ruder words. Before Linny could figure out what they were saying to each other, one of them had moved off (angrily) to the side, and for the first time she got a clear look at the thing they were gathered so intently around. That thing was poor Elias. One of the gray people must have knocked him down, and he was on his knees, holding himself off the ground with one trembling hand and rubbing his head with the other.

"Told you there was a *madji* brat sneaking around," said one of the gray men, wiping sweat from his forehead. He spat out that word, "madji," as if it were some vile curse. His voice was hoarse and rough, and in between words he took desperate gasping gulps of air.

They all looked sick, Linny thought. They looked cranky and wobbly and like people at the end of their ropes. But that didn't make them less dangerous. Sick animals are worse than well ones—Linny knew that much from the woods.

"Stupid fool! What have you gotten us into?" hissed another gray man—only actually she was a woman, Linny realized once she began speaking. The woman was mad at the first man, for some reason. "Well, go ahead, bind his hands, now we're stuck with him."

"*They* take *us* prisoner when they can," said the first man sulkily. "He's got information, right? Probably knows where everything is around here, at least—don't you, *madji* boy?"

Elias mumbled something Linny couldn't hear, but

the man was unhappy with it. He raised his hand over Elias's head, but the woman yanked the hand away. She must be their boss or something.

"So tell us, boy. You got any friends out here with you?"

Elias shook his head.

"No," he said. "Just me." Linny could hear how hard he was trying to hide the shake in his voice. *Good lummox!* she thought.

"Stop and think logically for a minute," said the gray woman to the two gray men. "The hillsickness has gotten to your brains. And you call yourself Surveyors! What do we do with him now, you fools?"

"Treating him better than they treated ours. What about that officer they took years ago, hunh? Just left *her* uniform folded neatly under a rock."

"You're not making sense," said the woman, her voice like ice. "We can't let him go. Think about that."

"He'll lead us right to that lost village, I bet. He looks like he comes from way up in these logicforsaken hills. We could get a lot of land charted, if we had some help. Hey, boy! Where are you from?"

But Elias just swayed a little on his knees, and didn't say anything that Linny could hear.

"Leave him a moment," said the woman. "He's tied up, yes? The rest of you, over here. Now."

The gray people shuffled about twenty feet farther away and continued that angry discussion. They clearly didn't want poor Elias to hear whatever it was they were saying. Elias, meanwhile, was working away at the ropes on his wrists and shaking his head.

That reminded Linny of one important thing: the knife in her pocket. She sneaked forward to a slightly nearer rock. What should she do? Throwing the knife seemed more likely to damage Elias's head than to get the knife safely into his hands. All right.

She would have to sneak across the creek and do this thing herself.

7

"THANK YOU, BRAVE LINNET!"

She moved quickly up through the woods, her heart nervous in her chest, and crossed the creek at the first likely place. Then it was back through the woods on the gray people's side of the water. She was lucky with the placement of the trees—she could get pretty close to the clearing and still be hiding among the trunks and branches. But the gray people had come to the end of their discussion, apparently, and the gray woman was already walking back to Elias, who was only about twenty feet away, with the other gray people straggling behind her. Linny froze behind her tree.

"You, boy," the woman said crisply when she reached him, her voice cold as ice. She gasped for breath like the others, but Linny could tell she was fighting not to let her breathlessness show. *That one must be very tough,* thought Linny. But the woman was speaking again: "Where are the other *madji*? We are willing to be lenient if you cooperate."

"Don't know what *madji* are," said Elias under his breath. "Let me go, you people. Who are you? What village do you come from? What do you think I've done wrong?"

One of the men snorted.

"We could just drown him in the creek," he said, and Linny, who had probably thought about drowning Elias in creeks more than anyone else in the world, felt a deep and acid anger rising up in her. You really should know someone *well* before you talked about drowning him!

The woman in gray was frowning.

"Trouble and more trouble," she said, choking on her words a little. "Too much delay. Look at us—we've got to get out of here. Hillsick, every one of us. We're on our last legs."

"We could take him back with us," said the man who had wanted to drown poor Elias in the creek. "A wild *madji* paraded through the Broken City! They might like to see that, down in the Plain."

"Yes," said another man. "Take him with us. Show the fools in Bend we mean business."

The Broken City! Linny's whole mind sharpened itself, like a knife on the edging rod. These nightmarish people came from the Plain? No wonder they were all wheeze and wobble. People from the Plain got sick as anything when they first came up into the hills. Their bodies had to get used to living in wrinkled places. Linny's own mother had been so sick at first, she had almost died.

"And then how do we explain where we found him?" said the gray woman. "Well? We're not even supposed to be out here so far, you know that. Or you would know if you hadn't left some high percentage of your brains back down in the Plain."

She spat to the side in disgust, and then she held on to her stomach for a moment, as if even spitting were almost too much for her.

"If we could get the wheres of some lost village out of him, it wouldn't be a complete waste," said a third man. "Where did you appear from, boy? You must know that."

Linny could see Elias shrug. He was being very brave, she had to admit, especially considering he was only Elias.

"Oh, he'll talk eventually," said the let's-drown-him man. "I'll bring the map over so we can make proper notes."

Elias just stood there, his head hanging, looking stupid, and for once Linny approved. *Please, oh please, keep letting them think you're stupid*, she thought in his direction. *Stay stupid. But be ready to jump when I figure something out.*

She fingered her whittling knife and studied every tree within reach, looking for a good idea. But she had never had to rescue anyone from a bunch of gray people before, and the trees weren't full of helpful suggestions.

That was when she saw that one most awful man walking in the other direction, over to what Linny now saw were a few gray tents pitched on the far side of the clearing. That must be their camp, then—and that seemed like a stroke of good luck. Linny hated to leave Elias with that gray woman, but she couldn't see anything better to do. So she slipped very carefully away from the edge of the woods and then made as speedy a way through the trees as she could, following that man, all the while, of course, being as extra careful about noises as a person possibly could be. When she neared the tents, she sneaked up very close again to get a good look. There was a small metal stove with a pot on it, bubbling slightly. She had never seen a stove like that. They had set up a lightweight table between their tents, she saw. It held a big piece of paper, attached to a board. If it was meant to be a picture, it was a funny one, that was for sure—all squiggles and flowing lines and numbers. What kind of a picture was that?

But then even as she squinted squinted squinted at it, a bunch of little loose pieces clicked into place in her brain, and she almost crowed aloud in triumph (but remembered in time where she was).

That line *there*! That was the creek running down from the hills. That was the very creek she had come sneaking across, just a little while ago. She was absolutely sure of it, even though on the paper it was no more than wavy lines and numbers. She could see how the drawing of the creek bent, and she remembered the real creek bending, just in that way.

"It's the *map*," she said to herself, remembering how important and mysterious the word had sounded in her mother's mouth. A map was a picture of a place.

Meanwhile the awful man had ducked down into one of the tents. He came out a moment later with—was that a pencil? Yes. A pencil and a bunch of metal tools, though not the kind of tools you make lourkas with. Then he came over in Linny's direction to the table with the map on it, which he stopped to study for a moment, reading the secrets of those squiggles. Linny was so close she could see the veins on the backs of his hands. Way too close, that meant! She had been too eager to see what he was up to.

Her tree was only about ten feet from him. It wasn't the very best tree, either, despite the handy leafiness of the branch she was spying through now; she was pretty sure anyone who looked really closely would see her curious eyes burning through those leaves. Gazes leave little marks, like tiny insect bites, on the backs of people's necks. Sometimes a person will twitch if you stare too hard, or even scratch a gaze mark with an absent-minded hand—and then catch himself scratching, and figure out what's up, and turn. Linny knew that from experience, and that mere thought was enough to put a nervous little tickle in her throat. She willed herself as still as a tree trunk, she willed the welling-up cough away, she closed her eyes to keep them from biting, and she held her breath, which she knew she could do for longer than most people, though not forever.

It worked. Footsteps, heading away. He had left, with the map on its board in his hands. He left another roll of paper behind on the table, though. *Aha*, thought Linny. She was beginning to see the shape of a possible plan.

She was careful to wait until he rejoined the group on the far side of the clearing, because people's eyes will travel toward someone walking and might catch an accidental glimpse of someone, even a small-sized, cautious someone, sneaking about in the background. But when the awful man started talking to the group, and all the gray people's attention clumped around the sheet of paper on the board, Linny made her move.

Staying very low, she slipped over behind the table, used a quick hand to filch the roll of paper there, and faded immediately behind a tent, where she tore a strip of the paper off, twisted it a few times to made a wick, and then crept over to the stove to light it. All that was easy-peasy, for someone as practiced in wickedness as Linnet. The part she wasn't sure about was the next bit, because that depended on the material those tents were made of. Most kinds of cloth will burn, but some take longer to get going than others. She took her little flame behind the far tent and went to work on its corner, using one hand to scrabble up some dry grass and a stray twig as backup for her paper.

Burn, burn, burn, burn! she told the patch of fabric being licked by that tiny little tongue of flame. *Burn, oh, please burn!*

It darkened a little.

The wick was almost out, and the twig she was also holding to it was slow to take, too. And then the twig stopped resisting and let a bead of fire take it, and the tiny dark spot began finally to spread and to smoke, and Linny set up the twig next to another patch of tent and flung herself back into the relative safety of the woods.

Just at that moment, the voices of those gray people seemed to rise into a louder argument, and in the middle of that tangle of voices, Elias shouted out, sharply and wordlessly, like someone who has just been hurt. The woman said something angry. Others did as well. And Linny felt the icy thrill of horror dance along the bones of her back.

She had taken too long!

She was racing back through the woods as she thought this, and she was no longer quite as quiet as she had been earlier. What were they doing to him? Who *were* these horrible gray people?

Whoever they were, they were still arguing among themselves, that was for sure, arguing and coughing. Linny kept an ear on those voices as she made her way back through the trees. She was close enough now that she thought she could pick out another sound, too—Elias's breathing, the way you breathe when you've been hit. He'd better not be badly hurt, or her plan—*if you could call it a plan at all!*—went bust.

And then the voices changed tone completely, from anger to alarm.

"Hey! What's that?"

"You must have knocked the blasted stove over!"

"That's my tent!"

Linny smiled grimly to herself. They were scattering now, she could hear, back to the camp, at the lurching pace of people whose lungs are misbehaving. She peeked through the leaves—yes, there was Elias, still kneeling on the ground and left behind for the moment. He was dazed, but he had wiggled his feet out of those loops, and now he was struggling with the ropes around his wrists. Good.

"Hey, *pssst*, Elias," said Linny, coming out from behind her tree. "Quick, while they're busy."

The expression on his face—well, Linny just wished

she had the talent for making pictures that Sayra had. She would have loved a picture of Elias's face as she grabbed his arm and dragged him back into the woods, away from the burning tent and the commotion and the noise.

Thank goodness the gray people hadn't hurt his legs, whatever they had done. Thank goodness they had been a little careless with their knots. He moved along fast beside her, for once not being bossy or complaining or saying much of anything, just desperate to get away.

"Across the creek," said Linny. "Here, quick, before they figure this out."

She had to help him with the creek. It's hard jumping from stone to stone when your arms are still tied behind your back. But Linny steadied him, and they made it without too much loud splashing or inconvenient drowning.

"Good, good, good," said Linny, once they were safely back in the woods on the far side of the creek. Then it was really time to get the remaining ropes off him, as hard as it was to stand still, sawing away at ropes, when you knew gray people might be coming after you any minute.

"Quick, quick, can't you do that any faster?" said Elias—first full sentence out of his mouth. (Not "Thank you, brave Linnet," you'll notice.)

"Want to do it yourself?" she said, stepping back for a second. "They did a better job with these."

Elias made a desperate squawk-like sound, and even Linny wasn't going to waste more than a second on making Elias pay, not now. The ropes gave way, strand by strand, and soon enough she was pulling them loose and Elias rubbing his wrists and obviously trying not to cry. Under ordinary circumstances, Linny would have felt obliged to make a sarcastic remark or two, but his hands were scarily white and there were angry marks on his wrists where the ropes had been. Not to mention that flushed print of a hand on his cheek.

"Why'd they do that?" said Linny. "Gray monsters! Why'd they hit you that way?"

There was no why, though. She had never heard of people like that, who would hurt someone for what as far as she could tell was no reason at all.

"Linny, we've got to go," he said, and she knew what he meant. They needed to be farther away from people who would do something like this to a person. Plus there was Sayra, back home, fading. They couldn't let the gray people slow them down this way.

"Come on, then," she said. "I'll hide us up this slope. Can you walk?"

Elias nodded, and he shook a foot to show Linny his legs were fine.

"Okay," said Linny. "Follow me. I'll get us lost from them."

That was another thing about Linny's talent: she could find places other people would lose themselves looking for. It came in handy, if you were a person whose criminal lourka-making career called for a lot of hiding from other, possibly angry people. She sought out the crinkly places in the woods, and by the time she said, "All right—here!" and dropped to the ground in a hollow just large enough for a couple of kids about their size, Elias was looking as pale as she had probably looked the day before.

"You all right?" she said. "That was awful."

Elias shook his head, not at Linny, but like someone trying to remember how to think.

"Don't worry. They won't find us here, not right away," she said, more confidently than she really felt. "There's something wrong with them all. They couldn't run up this hill if they tried."

"C-catching my breath," he said. "Then we can go."

"I'm not going back to Lourka, you know," said Linny.

"I know," said Elias, still breathing hard. "Neither am I. Don't you see? Those gray people were looking for us—I mean, for Lourka. They kept talking about lost towns and lost villages, and it was the ones tucked up into the hills that they meant. We can't be accidentally leading them there. I'd better come along with you."

She was startled, and then, to her surprise, actually a little tiny bit glad.

"You mean, you want to come downhill with me? To the Broken City with all the different names?"

"Anyway, I should have offered to come with you right away. Ma would be furious with me for even thinking about leaving you alone."

"Why?" said Linny. "I'm fine on my own."

"It's too dangerous. Those people in gray! You're going down all alone to a whole city filled with nasty people like that? No. Not by yourself. No way."

That was Elias all over, yes? Linny had just set a whole camp on fire to rescue him from evil people in gray, and now *he* was saying *she* needed him to protect her!

"I can take care of myself," she said.

"Until you hit your head on a rock or need to eat," said Elias.

Oh, right. That.

But it was time for them to get farther away from those people in gray.

"All right, then," said Linny. "Rest for five minutes. I'll just scoot over to the campsite for our bundles. Be a shame to lose our nice cookpot. Then we'll go."

Elias looked a lot better when she came back—especially when he saw his lourka bouncing against her back next to hers. (Oh, come on! Did he really think Linny would have left a lourka behind in the woods? Lummox!)

"I've figured out how to go," said Linny. It was

showing off, a little, but she couldn't help it. "We'll angle over to the next valley, soon as the ridge lets us, and walk down to the Plain from there. That way we'll keep a little more distance between us and those awful people. The trick is to keep moving."

And so they set off together down out of the hills. It was walking away from Away, Linny knew, and that meant leaving Sayra farther behind, and that was hard. But it was going away in order to come back again, which is not the same thing as going away forever. She couldn't risk being gobbled up by Away herself before she had that medicine for Sayra safely in her hands. That made it all clear: she would get that medicine from the Plain, and she would bring it back.

Linny had promised to save Sayra, and this was the only way she knew.

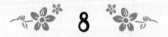

8

THE LAY OF THE LAND

Distances work differently in the most wrinkled parts of the hills than they do in the Plain, and as Linny and Elias came down out of the highest hills, they could feel the miles becoming more regular, and perhaps a bit longer, under their feet. Linny didn't mind that feeling, but Elias got a slightly stretched look as they got closer to the Plain, the expression of a person with a mild but nagging headache.

"Something's missing here, can't you tell?" he said to Linny. They had been walking already for a long time, for days and days.

But to Linny it felt like a change, not a loss, and change is often very interesting. If it hadn't been for the drone note in her brain—*Sayra is fading, Sayra is fading*—she might even have called herself happy, out here on the edges of an unknown world.

There started to be cottages from time to time. They scooted right past them, feeling shy. But in one tiny village, they passed by a piper playing by the edge of the road. Another man leaned over as he passed, and something round and metallic *clink-clinked* into the piper's hat, set out like a bowl on the ground.

Linny gave Elias a very significant look. Their food supplies were getting low.

"That could be us," she whispered. "We could play music, and people could give us things. Maybe something nice to eat."

So now and then, they took an hour away from walking to work on their music, and soon they had passable versions of several songs. Elias played the fussy technical stuff, and Linny, with perhaps excessive satisfaction and pride, plucked out the melody line, as sweetly and ringingly as she possibly could. And since Linny and Elias had grown up in Lourka, where even the flowers hummed, they didn't have much trouble cobbling together a couple of songs that sounded pleasant enough.

"All right," said Elias one afternoon, after Linny showed the trilling notes she had just figured out how to play. "I'll give you this: you learn fast, anyway."

Then he narrowed his eyes.

"Might help if you didn't look like a wild animal, though. Folks will run screaming. When did you last wash those clothes? Ma says—"

"Cobwebs to you!" said Linny. "You're the one who looks like a muddy pig."

But when she looked down at her skirt and the frayed strips of cloth dangling like ribbons from her sleeves, the rest of the insults she had all lined up in her mouth and ready to go vanished right away. She did look, pretty much, like a wild animal. Maybe worse than a wild animal, because even squirrels have too much dignity to go around wearing stinky rags. Did people offer metal coins or nice dinners to people who looked as unwashed and grubby as Linny and Elias? It might be a problem.

"All that stuff you're hauling about, and you don't have something cleanish to wear?" said Elias.

Linny did a fierce and symbolic show of digging through her bundles, even though she knew everything in there pretty much by heart.

"Wait," said Elias over her shoulder. Linny's hand was just squirming by the all-sewed-up package her mother had called her birthday present. "What's in that? Looks like cloth."

Good point. If it was cloth, she could maybe wear it as a shawl or something, and cover up some of her current ragged grime.

Linny didn't stop to think—she just untied the ribbons and picked loose a couple of threads, and to her surprise a bright flood of cloth came tumbling loose out of that package.

A dress! And not any old dress, but a very funny one, with a red patterned skirt and a blue vest and silver buttons—too fancy to wear in the woods, too bright for everyday work, an old-fashioned-looking thing, really. The last dress Linny would ever have expected her own sensible mother, a woman who had come all the way up to the wrinkled hills from the Plain, to spend time piecing together. But a huge amount of care had gone into it, Linny could see. She knew something about sewing just from having watched Sayra at work all those years. She could see her mother must have been embroidering those leaves and vines up and down the sleeves for weeks and weeks, probably.

Elias's jaw had dropped when Linny shook the dress out from the shoulders to show him its glory, silver buttons and all.

"Good grief, Linny, what's that for?" he said.

"Well, I guess you might call it 'something cleanish to wear,'" said Linny, as smug as could be.

"It's not yours!"

"Is so. My mother sewed for me. It was supposed to be my birthday present."

Elias frowned. He put out a finger to touch that fabric and frowned again.

"Odd sort of present. I mean, for a girl like you. What's in that tiny pocket bag there?"

"The address of my aunt," she said, feeling a little odd about both of those words, "address" and "aunt."

Elias was already laughing as he reached for the bag.

"What else are you carrying with you, anyway? Soft pillows? Maple candy? A few sheep? Hey! Look at this!"

Two blank cards, one smaller and thicker than the other—except that when Elias held the larger one up, it was easy enough to see that it wasn't actually blank. There was the faint trace of a picture hiding there, the picture of a girl who looked quite a bit like Linny, in a dress that looked more than a little like the dress Linny had just unfolded from her bag.

Elias turned the picture this way and that in the sunlight, trying to see it more clearly. Then they puzzled over it together. On the back side there were those few words in Linny's mother's handwriting: "I will find her." But the front of the card, where the shadow of the girl had shown up, was oddly smooth and shiny. Neither Linny nor Elias had seen any drawing quite like this before.

"That's a strange kind of picture," said Linny. She looked at it for another short minute and then put both cards back into the bag her mother had sent along with her. Just to be cautious, she hung that little bag around her neck, tucking it away so that it would remain unseen. *Things that will make more sense to you later.* That was what her mother had said about the things in that sack. And *"Whatever you do, don't lose it."*

Thinking about her mother opened a large and hollow

space in her heart. Enough! Linny jumped to her feet to clear her mind again.

"We're almost at the end of the hills," she said. "I'll put the fancy dress on now, so we can play for our supper as soon as we enter the Broken City. Aren't you *hungry*?"

The dress turned out to be more comfortable than she had expected. The sash Sayra had given her, and the half-invisible rosebud in the center of it, slipped like silk (since they *were* silk) into a nice deep pocket on the side seam. Even disguised under her ragged sweater, it was the sort of dress that made a person feel lighter on her feet.

What's more, the green hill they had just left behind was really the last of the hills, and as they moved out into the farmland below, bigger houses began to pop up here and there, and then whole little towns, and then they were walking through a town that didn't end, and that was the wrinkled half of the Broken City, the half called Bend.

There were many people, an ever-increasing stream of people, a flood of people. It was astonishing to think that each one of these people felt as much alive, and as vividly and unmistakably himself or herself, as Linny. She was so amazed as to be almost shy, faced with so much eager, busy human life. And Elias stayed very close by her side, so perhaps he was feeling some of that shyness, too.

"My head aches down here," he said at one point. That was all. But he had been more and more out of sorts the farther down from the hills they came. That was nothing very new.

Linny, on the other hand, was taking in all the clutter and clamor with great big happy gulps. Her head, unlike Elias's, didn't seem to suffer from being out of the hills. She had never been in a place with so many streets and alleys—it was different from feeling the slope of a hill, noticing which way a street went winding off and what its name was (in the few cases when a street name was splashed in paint across the wooden boards of a building), but it was as satisfying as scratching an itch or figuring out what note a song should end on.

"Let's try going this way," she kept saying to Elias. "Oh, and look at that house there—it's in three layers!"

Elias kept up with her, but his head stayed low, and his footsteps were all dogged determination. Every now and then, he leaned closer to Linny and said something quick and worried under his breath, like "Shh," or "They'll hear you," which made little sense to Linny. Everyone else in the street certainly seemed to be making as much noise as they wanted!

It was the pasty wagon that reminded her of what they really should be doing. A woman stood behind a cart, arrayed on which were a steaming pile of turnovers, stuffed (the air betrayed this piece of good news) with meat and herbs. Linny's stomach rumbled with longing.

"Hey, Elias," she said. "I'm hungry, aren't you? We need to find a free corner somewhere and start our playing!"

Whether it was coincidence or fate, who knows, but around the next corner, the road opened into a great square, absolutely filled with wagons and stands and displays of the most jewel-like vegetables and pipers and people walking on their hands before knots of lookers-on.

"Oh, wow," said Linny. She had never in all her wildest dreams imagined such a place could exist. She was hungry now, for real. She dragged Elias over to a clear stretch of wall, took off the ratty old sweater protecting the birthday dress, and then she and Elias unwrapped their lourkas and tuned up.

"Now then!" said Linny to Elias, once everything was ready. "Keep your mind on those pasties—gorgeous, gorgeous things."

Elias nodded to her, his lips thin and white. But he was born in Lourka, so no matter how his head might be feeling, the instrument he held sounded tuneful enough under his fingers.

They played one of the easier songs, and then tried the harder ones, all in a sweet, braided tangle, one after the next. It was a way to forget the strangeness of the city itself, to be standing here playing their music together.

A strange thing happened as they played.

At first, not so much. City markets have seen everything in their day, haven't they?

But then a couple of people came by, gawked, and nudged each other with their shoulders. Oh, and pointed, too!

The people's voices said things to each other:

"She looks so real," they said in whispers and behind fanned hands. And also: "Just in time for the fair!"

Linny felt strange when she first looked up and saw fingers pointing at her, but it wasn't an entirely unpleasant feeling. She figured she must be playing better than she had thought.

Then gradually the whole market square, with all its hustle-bustle, fell silent. Not right at once, mind you. Not suddenly or out of the blue. But bit by bit, like waves traveling out from where a stone plonked into the water of a pond, the music reached yet another round of people, and those people stopped what they were doing and turned their heads and became quiet.

"Psst, Elias," said Linny between songs. She was whispering, and she covered up her whisper by pretending to have dropped something close to Elias's feet. "Why are they so quiet?"

"Guess they're listening."

"Then they're listening too hard."

Not just listening. Staring, too. There was a crowd now, pressing forward, watching them. It was almost unbearable to be watched by so many eyes, whenever they stopped playing for a moment. Sometimes someone bent forward and put something on the cloth stretched in front of them, and every time that happened, Linny thought of meat pasties and became a little more encouraged again.

A woman brought a little bunch of flowers.

Linny was trying to pay attention only to the music, but the flowers worried her. What use were flowers? You couldn't eat them or trade them.

Then more flowers appeared: Long green stalks with blue blossoms at the top. Little red carnations tied together with a string. White, snowy flowers brought in the hands of a very small child, urged on by his mother.

Elias wasn't looking up. He was just soldiering through his music, thinking of food. But Linny took peeks between notes. There were tears on the cheeks of that tiny old woman over there. That seemed wrong. And the flowers were causing trouble, too. They were piling up too high, now—you could hardly see the cloth where the coin money was supposed to fall. More blossoms than coins! It was some kind of disaster, for sure. They would never get their pasties at all.

"Elias!" she said again. This time he did look up, but as soon as he did, his eyes traveled way past Linny, toward the edge of the market square, and then widened.

"Get behind me, quick!" he said, and actually pushed Linny to one side a little.

She was caught by surprise but found her balance fast and craned her neck to see what it was that had spooked Elias so. In that instant she saw them, too: the band of people in gray. The very same ones they had had their run-in with up in the hills, days before. They were standing straighter now, the hillsickness no longer doubling them over. One of them looked ahead and pointed—oh, no!—right at them, at Elias and Linny.

The crowd made a very strange sound. It was somewhere between a grumble and a growl, and Linny found it a little unnerving, to tell the truth. They did not move out of the way to let that group of people in gray easily by. But the gray people came through, all the same, the way that a heavy liquid will pour right through a lighter one and settle at the bottom of the jar, and as they came, the crowd's hissing noise of disapproval grew and grew, not that you could tell which mouths in particular were making the sound. And through that disapproving crowd, the gray people kept coming closer and closer.

Linny did not like the looks of them.

"Elias—run!" Linny whispered.

"Where to?" he said, trying to keep his shoulder between Linny and those implacable people coming toward them now.

He had a point. There was a wall behind them, and the people in gray before them, and—

"Oh, now who's *that*?" said Linny, nudging Elias.

9

A DOOR IN THE WALL

The most enormous man Linny had ever seen had just appeared out of something like nowhere. He must have been part of the general crowd, but since he was about a foot taller and a couple feet wider and several colors brighter than anyone else in that square, it was hard to imagine how he had managed not to stick out like a sore thumb. He had as many colors on him as you might see on the wildest bird, way up in the most wrinkled folds of the hills: a green belly, brown sleeves, a red sash around his waist, vast purple trousers billowing out from his legs. A black hat of an indescribable shape on his head, with papers pinned to it. Plus there was a beard large enough to serve as a nest for a dozen actual birds.

Linny was too dazzled to be afraid as he strode up close (close enough she could see the wild glint of gold in his ears), but she completely forgot to breathe. Only a foot or two away, though, he swung more gracefully around than Linny had imagined a man of that size could possibly do and put his hands on his hips—how could a single human being, even such an enormous and bright-colored one, feel so much like a boulder, a blockade, an impenetrable wall? Peeking around the side of the man, Linny could see the gathered crowd, and the people in gray pushing their way closer and closer.

The enormous man cleared his throat and spoke, and his voice was as low and rough as a growl. What he said was peculiar, too. He said, "What do you want now, you cursed grayling Surveyors, with our children?"

Linny was, of course, nervous about the people in gray who had treated Elias so badly back there in the hills, but on the other hand, she wasn't sure she wanted to be claimed by this intensely bearded man in his green and red and purple, either, whoever he might be.

She looked over at Elias, to try to see what he was thinking, and he gave her a little warning shake of the head. *No sudden moves*, that was what everything in his face was saying.

"For it does strike me," said the man with the glinting ears, and he eyed the fingernails of his mighty right hand with great thoughtfulness as he said it, "that you and yours shouldn't so much be in the markets of Bend. Should you, now? The wrinkled side of the river is no place for you lot. Time to leave, I'm thinking."

"There is some confusion, then. Because the boy indisputably belongs to us," said one of the gray men. "We've been looking for him for some days. His welfare concerns us greatly."

What did that mean, anyway? Linny was taken aback, as well as indignant. Everyone seemed to be arguing over which of them had rights to Linny and Elias. It was highly unpleasant. She certainly did not belong to any of them. Perhaps you could argue she belonged to her parents, but even there, there were limits.

"Is that so?" said the enormous man. "My boy here belongs to you?"

The gray man laughed.

"Check the rules. When we catch a *madji* boy spying, he's ours."

Linny couldn't help herself, she was so mad.

"Spying! How's he a spy?"

It just burst out of her. She would have thought better of it, a moment later, but oh well. Done is done.

The gray people all turned to look in Linny's direction. Their eyes were like icicles: sharp, pointy, and cold.

"Who's that girl there, dressed up that way?" said the woman in gray. "Little girl, who are you? Here for the fair?"

"What fair?" said Linny, and it was as if those words just hung there suspended in the dusty air.

The crowd rumbled and whispered and shifted about on its many feet. That was when Elias shouldered himself in front of Linny (making it harder for her to see what was happening, to her annoyance), and stepped out beside the enormous man.

"She's my sister," he said. "Leave her alone."

Sister! thought Linny. *Well, all right. Under the circumstances.*

The crowd sighed. Linny had the oddest sense of being on display, of performing some strange play that the people here had been awaiting for ages and ages. She knew about plays because in Lourka, the village liked to put on spectacles for itself, two times a year, midsummer and midwinter.

"Listen to the boy, you Surveyors," said the huge man in the calmest of voices. "What this all means is simple enough: you should leave this square. Do you hear me? You're on our side of the river. You'd best not stay here. No good can come of that."

"You have no right!" said the gray man, and then he turned to Elias in particular. "Are you sure you know who your sister is, *madji* boy?"

At that point, some confusing things happened. The enormous man suddenly let go of Linny's wrist, sent his hand darting into the pocket of his purple trousers to pull out—what were those things? Marbles or round stones?

106

But before Linny had even processed that thought, he sent them flying through the air in the direction of the gray people.

Did those peculiar little spheres explode? Perhaps they did. Certainly they did something bad. There was dust. Voices screaming, in shock, in surprise, in pain.

The huge hand had already clamped itself back on Linny's shoulder and was yanking her off to the side.

"Come," said the enormous man. Not that he gave her a choice. He was simply too strong for Linny to resist.

"Hey!" said Elias, right ahead of Linny. The man was steering them both off to the left now, and Elias (being Elias) had tripped. But Elias had also (despite being Elias) managed to grab Linny's travel bundles, when he scrambled back to his feet after tripping. That was good.

More shouts from the crowd in the square. What *had* the enormous man just done?

He was dragging them both right toward the wall behind them. Turning her head a moment, Linny saw, with a bitter pang, the glint of coins on the scrap of rug they had spread out. That was their coin money they were leaving! How would they ever get any food now? Beyond the rug, dust was still rising—and someone was holding his arm tight against his belly and howling. Linny could not help it; horror swamped her. Those little tiny rocks or pebbles or whatever they were had done something small but *wrong* to the world.

Linny tried to wriggle her way free from that enormous hand, but it was hopeless. They were already at the wall, and a door was opening there that had been completely, entirely invisible before.

"In we go," said the enormous man. "Quick, now."

They went into darkness and—Linny's stomach gave the most peculiar twist—came through into light: another street, but without all the crowds of the market square they had just left.

The man looked around and smiled with satisfaction.

"A good mile away. That'll do fine."

Behind them, an entirely different wall. Linny glanced up at the sun, and felt the lines and angles falling into place in her mind.

"We aren't where we were," she said. "How did you do that?"

"Wasn't me," said the man. "Wrinkled rock, that wall's made of. Brought down from the high country, back when the city was built. Or so they say. Not much of that sort of wrinkled magic left, around here."

He eyed Linny, perhaps a little too intently. She frowned right back at him.

"Were those *wrinkled* rocks you threw at the gray people?" she asked, upset enough not to be cautious. Not that she had ever heard of stones doing anything so wrong feeling as what those spheres had just done in the market square.

"That's enough," he said. No, snapped. "Quiet. It's time for us to go home. And for you, girl, to explain what made you put on such a costume, just now, and play such an instrument, when you say you've never heard of the fair. Was it the boy who told you to do this?"

"No, no," said Linny automatically. But she was more confused than confident about anything that was happening. She had never been to such a bewildering place in all her life as this city was proving to be. Even the edge of Away had been simpler than anything here; for one thing, it hadn't had all of these confusing people in it.

"Stop this!" said Elias, and he made his own feet stand still, so that the enormous man had to stop moving, too, or else just plain drag him along. "We're not pretending to be anything. But who are you? What are you doing? Where are you taking us?"

"I am taking you someplace safe," said the man. "They called you *madji*, so I'm taking you to a place hidden from Surveyors. There are parts of the city that have slipped off the grid, even as close to the Plain as we are, here by the river."

"Explain what *madji* means," said Elias. "We never heard the word before those people in gray grabbed me."

"The *madji* fight for the wrinkled country," said

the enormous man. "They fight against gridding. Soon enough, if all goes as I think it may, they will be lobbing disorder bombs into the straight lines of the Plain. They do battle against Surveyors. In Bend the right-thinking people all honor the *madji*."

"They're fighting against the gray people?" said Elias. "I'm on the side of anyone who fights the gray people."

The man laughed, a wondering laugh that ended in darkness, like a tunnel carved into the side of a hill.

"It is truly an astonishing day for me," he said, "to find two blank strangers like you in our city, who have never heard of Surveyors or the *madji*. Now come along. We are far from where we were, but I would like us even farther and more hidden, before any Surveyors can wander along this way."

Linny could see that that made sense to Elias. His whole face was beginning to relax again, around the edges. Linny was not ready to trust anyone yet, however.

"What's your name?" she said. "Who are you?"

"I am most often called Rodegar Malkin," said the man, and he paused to bow to her, which made Linny angry. Only someone being rude and mocking, she suspected, would bow like that to a person who had so very recently turned twelve. "In Bend they all know me, you will find, by one name or another. I am a businessman and a magician. Like the *madji*, many a person in this city believes he has been waiting for you, little frown-faced girl, to arrive all his life. Or for the one you are pretending to be."

"What do you mean by that?" said Elias, suspicious. "And what's a magician?"

That was Linny's secret question, too. Oh, she knew about magic—it was a word you could use for talking about the wrinkled things of this world. But she didn't see how wrinkledness could somehow become a person.

The enormous man stopped suddenly, in front of a narrow house that leaned against other narrow houses in that street. It looked a little dirty and run-down, as houses go, but in this endless, sprawling village, it was hard to judge such things. Maybe everything in a city was supposed to be dirty and run-down. There was, however, a cat in the window, Linny noted with approval.

"In through this door, young blank strangers," said Rodegar Malkin as he turned a large key in the lock, "who come from wrinkled places, but don't know what a magician is! I will explain what I mean. Or perhaps you will explain everything to me. You *should* be able to explain something to me, seems like, if you are truly the girl with the lourka."

10

IN THE HOUSE OF THE MAGICIAN

The house began with a dark hall that smelled slightly of licorice and boots. Linny had a vague impression of many thick coats hanging on pegs and piles of boxes, but her eyes were still adjusting to the dimness and could not be very helpful just yet. And then the enormous man flung open the door at the end of the hall, and Linny and Elias tumbled into the most peculiar room either of them had ever seen.

A hundred oddly shaped glass windows interrupted the room's far wall—a crazy quilt of windows, as if some enormous window had been accidentally shattered into pieces and each piece, instead of falling to the ground and being swept up, tossed onto a rubbish heap, and forgotten, had instead stubbornly insisted on becoming a window itself, in its own right. Some of the glass had a mild tint to it; some of it was rippled; some gave teasing glimpses of what looked like an actual tree out in the courtyard beyond; and through all of that motley glass, the city sunlight cascaded, dappling everything and making Linny blink.

The cat Linny had seen in the front window slithered through her legs and into a patch of particularly radiant light, right beside an ancient armchair in which someone had heaped yet another pile of ratty old coats. It was a peculiar sort of cat—sandy yellow on the left side of its body, but all smooth silver-gray fur on the other. It had a gold eye on the sandy side of its face, good for staring with, and an inscrutable silver one that seemed to be full of its own private thoughts on the other side. Perhaps it had come down from the hills, thought Linny. It was so unmistakably a wrinkled cat. It was oddness itself, padding its way through the world.

"We are off their grid here," said Rodegar Malkin when he saw Linny looking at the cat. As if that were an explanation. Then he stamped his huge foot against the floor so hard the many odd-shaped windows rattled in their frames (and Linny and Elias jumped a few inches into the air). "MA! STRANGERS!"

"Speak up when you talk to me," complained the pile of coats on the chair, and to Linny's surprise, the pile of coats unfolded itself and became a tiny, withered old person, with pale eyes and a halo of bright red hair sticking straight out from her face.

The red of her hair was not the sort of red that people are sometimes born with. It was infinitely brighter than that.

"And who are these kiddies?" said the wrinkled old person in a plaintive voice. "I can smell them, you know. In from the woods, are they? Hungry, probably? Come here and let me see your faces, you!"

"Ma can't see so well," said the magician, and he gave Linny and Elias a shove toward the ratty chair.

"Stop telling lies about me!" said the old woman, her fingers greedily reaching out for Linny's face. "I can smell them, you know. Lies!"

"Doesn't hear so good, either," said the magician.

The ancient old person's fingers were cool and quick, as they scurried across Linny's cheeks and took the measure of her eyes and nose. They were cleverer fingers, thought Linny, than the ancient, complaining person they now belonged to.

"Rodegar, this one is hungry. Isn't this one hungry?"

The old woman gave Linny's ear a little pull.

"Yes," said Linny. "We were going to buy pasties."

And medicines for Sayra—but she didn't say that aloud. Someone as good at sneaking around as Linny knew better than to tip her hand too soon. Oh, but she was still sad about the coin money left behind in the square.

"What's that?" said the old woman. "What's she

saying? She's hungry. I can smell it. And the other one's hungry, too. Kiddies is always hungry. Feed them, Rodegar. I'm napping."

And she flopped back into a heap in the armchair and began to snore.

Rodegar Malkin made Elias and Linny sit at a wooden table in that strange-windowed room and brought them bread, which surprised Linny by being not bread-colored inside, but white, and also a slab of yellow cheese. Not as tasty as Lourkan cheese, but still pretty good. There was also an apple each, the green, tangy kind, and a few pieces of some kind of dried meat that needed a lot of chewing but was pleasantly salty if you could stand it.

They were really very hungry. They ate and ate. And while they ate, the magician took their bundles, and went through them, piece by piece.

Linny squawked about that, but the enormous man gave her a look that was very nearly as impressive as his fist, and she shut up again. The price of the food they were eating was apparently letting him examine their stuff.

Not that they had much. Soon there were little heaps of things on the table. The cookpot, blacker than it had been, but still perfectly functional. He put the flint in it, and the tin cups, and their pocket-knives—everything that had brought them safely through the wild places.

Then there was a second pile of dirty clothes and the filthy blanket and unspeakably awful socks. And the lourkas, of course, which he set to the side with great care. Only the little bag of things Linny's mother had sent along missed his scrutinizing eyes, and that was because Linny was still wearing it around her neck, tucked away safely beneath her dress.

When he had examined everything to his satisfaction, he creaked back in his chair and looked at Linny.

"So, you. Who are you, strange girl? How'd you come by this instrument of yours? Who told you to wear such a dress, if you don't know about the fair?"

"She made the lourka herself," said Elias, taking Linny by surprise. "And it's good. She shouldn't have done such a wicked thing, but you can't say she hasn't got the talent for it."

"And you say what, girl? What's your name, anyway? I told you mine, and fair's fair, you'll agree."

"I'm Elias, and she's Linnet," said Elias.

"Down from the hills, you two, obviously."

"Yes."

"Come down just now, for some reason."

Elias and Linny looked at him. They weren't sure how to explain themselves and (in Linny's case, at least) weren't even sure whether this astonishing person was someone you really should be explaining yourself to.

"Coming down from the hills right in time for the fair! To lead the revolution, maybe, am I right?"

He was staring at them very intently now, as if all the earlier questions had been for practice, and now he was reaching the crux of the matter.

"What's that mean?" said Linny, squirming a little under the magician's gaze.

"Taking things over. Changing things. Getting rid of the Surveyors forever. I'm in that noble business myself, you might say. Where would the *madji* get their weapons, if it weren't for me?"

(Was that what a magician was? Someone who sold weapons?)

"Getting rid of the Surveyors sounds good to me," said Elias in an almost inaudible mumble.

"Indeed," said the magician. He stayed very calm, though. Unnervingly calm. He just stared and stared with those thoughtful eyes.

Linny popped right up out of her chair.

"Excuse me, but we're not taking anything over. That's ridiculous. That makes no sense. We are only twelve. I'm here to find medicines for someone who needs them. For my friend. There are supposed to be medicines, down in the Plain. And aren't we near the Plain here?"

"*Our* friend," said Elias. "We're here to help *our* friend, and I'm not twelve. I am thirteen."

"So old as that," said the magician. He cut himself a piece of the yellow cheese and ate it, his eyes never quite leaving Linny's face. "Sit down, young Linnet. We have only a few minutes here, before I'm off to chat with the *madji*. To tell them the good news."

"What good news?" said Linny.

"You claim to be the Girl with the Lourka, yes?" said the magician. "Their hero and their emblem, you know, and et cetera and so forth. And you look astonishingly genuine, which is a pleasant change around here. The actual, real Girl with the Lourka! I'd say that counts as news."

"I'm not claiming anything," said Linny.

"You come into Bend with a lourka in your hands and those clothes on your body? That's a claim, I think. Look! Explain that, girl from the hills."

And he pointed with his enormous hand over Elias's and Linny's heads, to something on the wall behind them.

They turned around in their chairs and stared.

There was an old painting on the wall, with ancient, gold-tasseled velvet curtains framing it.

"Hey!" said Elias. It was his turn to jump to his feet. "How'd you do that?"

Linny couldn't jump or speak, however. Anything she might say stuck like a bone in her throat.

The painting was of a girl of sixteen or seventeen or so,

standing. She had dark hair, the same color as Linny's own and wavy at the ends, and her eyes looked right at you, wherever you were in the room, the way eyes in paintings sometimes do. Her dress had a red skirt with striped patterns on it, a blue vest, and silver buttons, not to mention the leaves and vines embroidered up and down the sleeves that must have taken somebody's mother weeks to do. She had a tiny dark mole right there on her cheek, and another under her ear, and in her hand was a lourka. Not just any lourka, but the lourka Linny knew best in the world, because she herself had made it. Even the little linny flower she had worked into the wood was there, with its five pale petals.

It was a picture of a slightly older Linnet, with Linnet's own lourka.

And yet this painting had the look of something a hundred years old. Maybe even more ancient than that.

"You see the problem," said the magician, standing up and brushing the crumbs from his lap. "That, dear children, is the Girl with the Lourka. The most famous girl in all the stories told in Bend, I might add. There are plenty of fakes, oh, yes, but you have the glow of authenticity about you. And that is why our *madji* will want to meet you, though you're younger than anyone expected. So off I go, to arrange the terms of that meeting."

"I don't get it," said Elias. "How'd Linny get into that

119

picture? Looking so grown-up and all?"

The magician barked. Or laughed. It was a low and enormous sound.

"My question, and the *madji*'s question—and quite possibly the Surveyors' question, too, by the way—is how did the Girl with the Lourka start walking around outside her frame, pretending to be an ordinary flesh-and-blood person?"

He was studying their faces as he said these things. Linny tried not to look anywhere near as puzzled as she felt.

"Oh, you can be sure that won't make the Surveyors happy," he continued. "Thinking the *madji* have gotten themselves a real Girl with a Lourka. Spitting mad, I suspect they are going to be. Maybe paintings walk around on two legs all the time, where you come from, but wrinkled magic of that sort is quite rare down here. You're quite the commodity, Linnet from the hills!"

"I'm not anything but me," said Linny with dignity. She didn't understand the word the magician had just used, but it sounded (she thought) unpleasant. "And if magic is so hard to find around here, how can you be what you said you were—a magician?"

"Magic is also a commodity, in places where it is rare," the magician said. "A commodity is something with a price. And you, for instance, are definitely that, my dear.

Just the price has yet to be fully determined."

He let his enormous hand settle again, for a few heavy seconds, on Linny's head.

"You behave, and no harm will come to you or that brother of yours. Got that? This is not a game, little girl from the hills. Lives hang in the balance, not to mention a great deal of money. So from now on, whoever else you think you may be, you are first and foremost *her*—"

And he pointed at that old picture again, where the almost grown-up girl who looked so exactly like Linnet's own self stood with such confidence, the lourka in her hand.

Linny wanted to take that picture down from the wall and shake it until it explained itself to her.

Wait. What was that behind the painted girl's skirts? Linny squinted harder.

"The inspiration of the *madji*!" The magician went on. "That's you now: the Girl with the Lourka. The genuine article. The making of our fortune. And don't you forget it."

Linny gave a fierce blink to clear her eyes. Yes, there it was, painted with the most amazing precision. It was the furry tail of a cat. And as she stared, the painted tail flicked itself lazily around the girl's painted leg and changed color from tawny gold to silver gray. A wrinkled picture, then.

The magician whistled happily through his teeth as he put away the remnants of the cheese and fetched his outside jacket from the coatracks in the hall.

Not knowing exactly what the he might be up to, Elias and Linny sat as still as rabbits under a fox's eye and watched the magician force his enormous arms into the enormous sleeves of that jacket. To be sure, he was watching them at the same time (with the self-satisfied half smile of a fox on the prowl around rabbits).

And then he pounced. He clapped a huge hand, a giant's vise, onto Elias's shoulder, and steered him off toward the hall.

"This one will come with me, I think," he said. "The brother of the Girl with the Lourka! That will be my little gift to them. They'll see I mean business when they meet you, boy. You reek most convincingly of the hills."

Elias yelped and twisted, but the magician's hands were not to be squirmed out of.

"Oh, no, my boy, surely it's not such a bad fate as that!" he said, laughing his deep, resonant laugh. "That's my business, after all: selling weapons to the *madji*. Some weapons are gray and go boom; some of them have hands and feet and tales to tell. How do you feel about those Surveyors, anyway, boy from the hills?"

"I hate them," said Elias with deep conviction. "They tied me up, back in the hills. Linny had to burn down their camp."

"Good," said the magician, tightening his grip. "They'll see you; they'll hear our stories; they'll know the product I'm offering is probably genuine. Good, good, good! And then they'll take you away and train you up."

Linny squawked.

"And you'll each of you behave like a good child, won't you?" said the magician. "Not wanting harm to come to your sweet brother or sister, as the case may be. Good-bye for now, Linnet. MA!"

"Elias!" said Linny in alarm. "No. You *can't* go off with him. What are you doing?"

But really—and the glimpse of Elias's shocked face underscored the problem—there was nothing he could do. The magician was moving him out of the room as easily as a mother cat carries a kitten. He was going to take Elias away; in a moment they would be gone.

"TAKE THE GIRL UPSTAIRS, MA!"

The merest fringe of bright red hair—and one eye—peeked out from among the coats.

"It would be politer not to mumble," said the magician's ma. "Whaddayerwant anyhow?"

"GIRL! UPSTAIRS! And you, girl, stop your fussing. You don't want to make me mad. Or, I'm so very afraid to say, your brother will suffer. MA!"

The ancient old woman sat up in her chair and pointed her finger (bony! knobbly at the joints!) right in Linny's direction.

"Girl's not upstairs," said the magician's old ma, with a sly wink. "Girl's right here. I can smell her. Lost your great big eyes, Roddy?"

"Take her UPSTAIRS and keep her SAFE," said the magician, but this time he said it more with gestures than words. "This boy and I have business to attend to. Urgent, important business. And I bid you good afternoon, ladies!"

One second later the two of them—startled Elias and the enormous magician—had vanished into the front hall.

"Oh, and don't bother trying to run away, Linnet from the hills," called the magician from the far end of that hall. "You'll find I've bolted the door with tremendous care."

And then there was the great *bang* of the front door slamming shut—and Linny, whose friends kept being swallowed by dooms of her own making, found herself horribly, awfully alone.

11

LINNET ALONE

No, not entirely alone.

Already a small claw of a hand had clamped itself around Linny's arm.

"Yes yes yes yes," the dandelion-headed old woman said as she gave Linny a tug in the direction of a rickety staircase. "Up this way, kiddie. What's happened to the other one of you? My little Rodegar eat him up already? *Heh heh heh . . .*"

The stairway was narrow and dim. Linny listened to every inch of that space, as much as she measured it with her eyes. The sound of their steps had a hollow undertone to them, for instance.

There's a basement, then, thought Linny. She was putting together all the parts of this house in her mind. This was not a place where she ever intended to get lost. Quite the opposite, in fact. She would find her way out of here, as fast as fast.

Sayra was fading, way back in the hills. And now Elias being dragged off to the *madji*, wherever they were! Linny put her hands to her head in frustration, and then recognized the gesture as her mother's (when the twins were being impossible wild things) and felt a sharp stab of homesickness on top of the worry.

"In here, in here, kiddie," said the magician's ma, and she opened the door to a very small and narrow room with a simple cot set up against the wall and a wooden chair at the end of the cot nearest the door. The saving grace of that room was a slightly larger window than you might expect, tucked in under the slanting roof and letting in four dusty panes' worth of late-afternoon light.

"Young, aren't you?" said the old woman, out of the blue. She had made a quick job of covering the cot with the quilt and blanket, and now she perched a little shakily on the chair at the far end, her chin tucked on the back's top rung.

"Not particularly," said Linny, looking longingly through the panes of that window. There was a walled-in courtyard out back there, with the scrawniest apple tree she'd ever seen. No, she wasn't young. She had left her child years behind, hadn't she, when she left the hills? But she did secretly feel not quite as old as she would have wanted to be, to be caught now in the fix she was in.

"Can't hear you so clear, kiddie," said the old woman.

"We thought you'd be older, if you see what I'm saying. You're the one who is supposed to save us and lead us to victory, you know—oh, yes, I know the stories by heart. I would, wouldn't I? So many fakes, but you smell real to me. Just didn't know you'd be so puny."

The window was the kind that didn't unlatch. Linny came back toward the door and the woman watching from the chair.

"It's hot," said Linny, and she pulled the bedroom door right open.

"Hey!" said the old woman. "Go sit on that nice bed there, kiddie! I'll be minced if I lose you."

But she didn't seem to notice the opened door.

Linny listened to the subtle noises any house makes and to the silences that followed them and felt the distances of all of those walls and doors in the way the sound worked here. The old woman gave a little cough that tripped on itself and then kept tripping and rumbling until it was definitely no longer a cough but a snore. She had fallen asleep in her chair. Linny sat very quiet for a while, watching her tiny red puffball of a head loll against the back of the chair.

She was trying to be careful, waiting for a few minutes while the magician's ma snored herself deeper into her nap. Finally, when the light coming through the window at the end of the room began to dim, Linny stood up and sneaked past the end of the bed and out into the hall beyond.

She needed to know more about this house and these people. And if the redheaded granny woke up and found her wandering, well, she needed to use the privy, didn't she? That was ordinary enough.

On the other side of the hall upstairs were two other rooms, very simple and plain, looking over the street in front of the house. Probably the magician and his mother slept in those.

She was figuring all this out very fast as she sped as quietly as a breath of air down the narrow staircase to the ground floor. Her ears were stretched as wide as could be, to pick up any hint of enormous feet stomping back into the house, but she heard nothing.

She opened three doors before she found the staircase that must lead down to the basement. There was a candle in a lantern set into a nook about halfway down, and the flicker of more candlelight from farther below, so it wasn't completely dark, but it felt to Linny like there was something wrong down here, something wrong at the bottom of the stairs.

Well, but she had to know.

Linny took a deep breath and then darted down the stairs and into what she instantly recognized must be the magician's workshop. It had sturdy tables like her father's room, and storage cabinets along its sides, and shelves with tools and odd objects on them, which was also like any of the workshops she had ever caught glimpses of in her own village. But unlike the instrument-building workshops of Lourka, this basement room, lit by candle lamps, had one whole corner of it left not just undecorated, but actually blackened and barren, as if experiments there had gone terribly awry.

Worse than blackened, to be completely honest: something was deeply, deeply wrong with the world over in that corner. It was a space that Linny's mind could not make sense of, because the sense of that space had been utterly and violently undone. A part of the pattern of the world was simply missing. Melted away. Gone.

Linny found herself shaking. That annoyed her mightily, so she made a show of walking closer to that blasted corner. "Blasted" was definitely the right word. Fireworks or explosions had scarred the floor and walls and even left some drippy spots of damage in the ceiling above.

That's when she remembered the strange pebbles the magician had flung into the ranks of the gray Surveyors, and the sickening sense then that some wrong thing was being done to the world. Weapons, he had said. On the shelves were sealed cylinders that Linny thought looked purely wicked. When he had thrown those little pebbles, they had exploded, as if they had a century's worth of anger and bad feelings squeezed into them. If even a pebble could warp the world, what would these great canisters do? The back of her neck had gone all clammy.

What kind of weapons was Rodegar Malkin selling to the *madji*, she wondered? Was Elias going to be carrying one of these awful cylinders in his hands? Oh, Elias! Appalled, she scampered back up the stairs to the main floor, tested the street door in that dim front hall (and yes, it was locked), and then went outside to make her cover story true by using the privy behind the apple tree.

The walls of that courtyard were too high and too smooth to climb, even for a good climber like Linny. Elias would have to take care of himself for a little bit. And Sayra would have to keep holding on.

When she left the privy, just the last ruddy glimmers of sunset were bouncing about the yard. Time to get back upstairs before old redheaded Ma woke up from her nap and started having fits.

As she sneaked back through the many-windowed room (where the painting was now too buried in shadows to be properly seen) and up the staircase again, something warm and furry snaked up the steps, right through her legs, making her jump. It was the wrinkled cat, mysterious and self-contained, as all cats are, and on its own path.

"You're in that picture, too," whispered Linny after the cat. "Wish you could tell me why."

Cats usually skip explanations, however. By the time Linny was slipping through the bedroom door, the cat was curled up on her bed, the golden tabby side wrapped around the silver one, and its golden eye wide open and staring at Linny. The cat was not the only one staring: the magician's old ma was sitting bolt upright in her chair, running a hand through her bright red dandelion hair and frowning.

"No giddying about, kiddie!" she said crossly. "You heard my Rodegar bark about that. You're to stay up here, like a good girl."

"PRIVY," said Linny, as loud as she could manage.

Maybe the old woman heard that—hard to tell. In any case, there was a big, distracting ruckus downstairs as the enormous magician came back into the house from wherever he had gone. He bounded right up the steps and peeked his huge head in through the door of Linny's narrow room.

"Hunh! Not sleeping yet?" he said. "Well, here's something reasonable to sleep in. We'll be wanting to keep that dress of yours looking nice and bright, get the most use out of it."

He tossed a package onto the narrow bed, which made the cat open its other, silver eye, and hiss.

"COME ALONG, MA," he said. "LET THE GIRL GET SOME SLEEP. BUSY DAY TOMORROW!"

And the ancient woman pattered out the door behind him, pausing to give Linny what was probably meant to look like a wink.

"Not to worry, kiddie," she said. "I'll bring you some porridge anyway, to put some meat on your twiggy little bones."

The magician looked disgruntled.

"Well, porridge. All right. But no tricks from you now!" he said. "I have very good hearing; you need to know that. And the front door is always kept locked, don't worry about that. I'm a very cautious man. Mess up, and that brother of yours is the one who'll suffer. He's all right for now. The *madji* were glad enough to have him. But you'd better stay well in line."

So then for a while it was just Linny and the cat.

She unwrapped the package and found a plain and sturdy shift to sleep in, and another plain dress, only a little bit too big for her. And stockings without holes. How long did he mean to keep her here, then? Because Linny wasn't willing to be kept. She had her Aunt Mina to track down, and the medicines to beg, buy, or borrow, and Elias to kidnap back from those *madji*, and—oh so above all!—Sayra to find, wherever she was, and to bring home, safe and whole, from Away. She had a lot to do, when you made a list of it that way.

But for this moment, when she could do no rescuing of anyone, she couldn't help but notice that the clothes were new, and the material they were sewn from was softer than the homespun Linny was used to, so this was luxury. Changing out of her birthday dress, she found again the little bag hanging around her neck.

The cat peeked out with its enigmatic silver eye from under a curled paw.

"My private business, Half-Cat," said Linny, and she shifted around to put her back in between that bag and the cat's eyes.

She was remembering the image of the girl that had come creeping into view on that card, the last time she and Elias had taken a look. The light was dim in the room already, but she could see the picture had kept blossoming, somehow, in the dark. Why, even the tiniest of cat tails was there, though in a different part of the picture, waving from behind the vase in the background. It was, in fact, a miniature version of that painting downstairs. How that could be, Linny didn't know. But it was. And indeed, right there on the bottom, letters as fancy as you might see on the front of a store spelled out a few words: THE GIRL WITH THE LOURKA.

It was an echo, a picture echo, of that painting, which was in turn an echo of Linny's own self. So her mother must have known this picture, long ago when she came up from the Plain. And then, for some reason, she had written on the back, "I will find her." Find who? The Girl with the Lourka? Linny herself?

It made Linny shiver a little, seeing a picture of herself so much older than she was, and thinking that in some inexplicable way, her mother must have called her into existence. She must have had that picture so firmly in mind, Linny's mother, that when she gave birth to a daughter, way up in the wrinkled hills, that child— *Linny*—made her mother's story come true. And then how could someone who looked so much like that girl in the picture *not* end up making herself a lourka and causing all that trouble?

And what exactly had her mother thought would happen, when Linny appeared in Bend wearing the dress her mother had made, the dress from the picture?

No, it was too much of a tangle, and it made her feel all knotted up inside.

She put that picture card back into the bag and looked at the smaller, thicker card there. Something seemed to be blooming on its surface, too, though it wasn't perfectly clear yet. A face. Perhaps even—a familiar face. Her mother's face. Yes, it was definitely her mother. And words were beginning to push their way to the surface as well: IRIKA PONTIS. Her mother's own name. Carrying this card must be like carrying your name along with you.

The Half-Cat startled Linny out of her musings with a sudden hiss. There were dizzy footsteps coming up the steps. Linny had just enough time to put the little bag back around her neck before the magician's ancient ma skittered in through the door with a bowl of porridge in her hands.

"Eat this," she said, popping it into Linny's hands. "Eat this and go to sleep."

"Tell me, please," said Linny, as loud as she could without shouting or bringing the magician back up the stairs. "What's this CAT?"

And she pointed with her spoon at the Half-Cat, just to make her question clearer.

"Ah!" said the old woman. "Special, special! All cats is special, says some, but this one extra so! Wandered in here long ago and stayed. Down from the hills, I guess, kiddie. Like you! To tell us you were on your way! Like the old stories! There's always a cat in the old stories. There's always a cat in the picture—"

And she chortled and left.

12

THE PRICE OF A FANCY BREAKFAST

Linny was awakened the next morning by bangings and hollerings in the kitchen below. The Half-Cat unfolded itself from the foot of Linny's cot, stretched, eyed her with each of its strange eyes in turn, and swished through the door and down the stairs.

"Naw, not that dull thing!" shouted the magician's old ma when Linny showed up in the many-windowed room in the plain dress the magician had brought her. "Working today, you are, kiddie!"

But there were unheard-of riches on the table: good bread, boiled eggs, and even a little bowl of jam. Linny went to work on the jam before anyone could notice its vulnerable position, just sitting out there on the table like that. It was made of some fruit she didn't recognize, purple and sweet.

By the time the magician came into the room, the jam was gone. But he was in a state of high excitement, all his colorful sashes and breeches practically crackling with energy.

"It's a big day for us, girl," he said, as he peeled a couple of hard-boiled eggs with his thumbs. "We'll be convincing a bunch of *madji* of what needs doing. So that's delicate work."

"What did you do with Elias?" said Linny. "And how am I going to find medicines for my friend if you won't let me out of this house?" Even though she tried to ask plainly, without sounding too snippy or rude, the magician gave her a very hard look.

"No sass, no nonsense," he said, waving a finger at her in warning. "It's all very serious business. You see the house I have to keep up."

He waved a hand around, marking out the cracks in the walls, his redheaded ma snoozing on a chair, and the places where the paint was peeling.

"Not that that's even the main thing, by a long shot," said the magician. "The main thing being, who deserves to run this world of ours? Not the bloodless Surveyors, I'm sure you'll agree. But then again, the *madji* can get a little excitable in their own right. You don't know that yet, maybe, but it's true enough. The *madji* need some encouragement and direction, I've found. And of course it's very encouraging to have a disorder bomb stuffed into your back pocket." He chuckled.

"But until now they've been reluctant. They need the Girl with the Lourka, so it appears, to tell them to accept that encouragement before they'll pay out coin for it. I explained it all to them yesterday, when I was handing over your dear brother. The Girl is finally among us, I told them, and she wants some changes around here. Such a piece of good luck, you showing up when you did! You see the advantages all around. You're going to get them out of a silly stuck place—they'll buy my good weapons now. And that means we can afford eggs in this house."

As far as Linny could tell, the magician's only interest in the Girl with the Lourka was as a way to help him sell things to other people. As much as she had enjoyed the eggs (and the jam), she didn't like the way they got mixed up in the magician's thoughts with his "good weapons."

"What's a disorder bomb?" she asked.

"None of your business," said the magician with a cozy smile. "Run upstairs and put on that fancy costume of yours. You will be coming out with me this morning, to meet some would-be clients. Don't overthink this game, Linnet from the hills. All you have to tell them is this: you're against the evil of the Surveyors. Time for the *madji* to rise up on your behalf. I have the weapons to make the rising possible. That's all you need to know. Go, change!"

As she was going up the stairs, he called up behind her, "And don't get clever!"

But I will *be clever*, thought Linny fiercely. *I will, I will, I will.*

The Half-Cat came winding up between her ankles, purring a little. It seemed to have taken a liking to her, for some reason.

"It's all strings and sausages around here, have you noticed?" she said to the cat. It was a saying from home, used for things that are good and pleasant in themselves, but you don't want to think too much about how they're made. "You don't know where lourka strings come from—well, never mind."

That lovely jam and those lovely eggs, paid for by the magician's awful weapons! It made her determined, all over again, to find her way out of this house.

As she was changing back into the dress her mother had made, she took a quick look inside the little sack she still wore around her neck. The card with the picture on it was there, and also the paper on which her mother had scribbled instructions for finding her mythical Aunt Mina: "315 West River Quadrant, Angleside; also called Bridge House, Bend." And more numbers after that. Well, who knew what that meant? But Linny knew what a river was.

And every hour she spent in Bend was another hour of Sayra fading away, far off in the hills.

When she went back down the stairs, the magician's redheaded ma was ensconced in her chair, watching with shining eyes as the magician moved crates up from the basement and down the front hall.

"A coach waiting!" she squawked at Linny. "Ever been in a coach, kiddie? On your way to make them fight the war, finally! So don't you be falling out or nothing!"

"HUSH, MA," said the magician from under the crate he was balancing on his massive right shoulder. Meanwhile his other hand pounced and settled firmly on Linny's arm. "Come now, girl. Got your lourka there? Wrap up in this cloak, so you don't stick out so much everywhere we go. Be quick and keep quiet. Your brother's good health is depending on you, remember. And these will be *very dangerous people* we're seeing. So be warned of that."

And he bundled her out through the front door and up into a closed box with seats inside, all bouncing slightly as the horses in front did nervous things with their hooves. It gave Linny's stomach the wobbles. This must be what his dandelion-headed ma had called a coach.

Piled in front of Linny's feet were the crates the magician had been hauling up from his ruined basement room. She eyed them with distrust. There was nothing good in those boxes, she felt quite sure.

Wait! Was that something furry poking up from behind one of the crates? Yes—the tips of a couple of pointy ears, one golden and one silver.

"Half-Cat?" said Linny in a whisper. A golden eye rose up under the ears and stared at her for a moment, before all signs of cat vanished behind the boxes.

The magician was swinging his enormous body into the coach, and the whole vehicle swayed and sagged as he did so, making Linny grab the side of the bench to steady herself.

It would have been more interesting, this first ride through the Bend side of the Broken City, if Linny hadn't been so queasy. She tried to steal glimpses through the window of the coach, to help her mind figure out the pattern of the streets in the neighborhood, but her body was unhappy about all the swaying and bouncing and wobbling the carriage was doing. It wasn't natural for human beings, who have their own perfectly fine legs and feet and everything, to be dragged through bumpy streets in wheeled boxes.

Just to make things worse, the magician kept sending grins in her direction, as if this torture were actually some very special treat.

Linny did not meet his gaze; she kept her eyes on the world outside. What's more, she did not actually lose any of her fancy breakfast, so that was a triumph right there. No jam wasted! She hung on, and made it through.

13

THE DEATH AND DOLLOP

"Ah, here we are," the magician said finally, as the coach lurched around some last corner and quivered to a halt before a sullen-fronted tavern, its windows painted black to fend off curious eyes. "The good old Death and Dollop!"

Linny was already reaching in some desperation for the door of the coach, but the magician's enormous hand got to the latch first. He wasn't going to let her out until he had had his say.

"Listen up a minute, girl," he said. "It's not complicated, the task you have here. You tell these people they need to arm themselves with the tools I have conveniently brought along. As far as they are concerned, you are the Girl with the Lourka, and you want the Surveyors brought down. That's simple enough, I guess. Otherwise, stay mum. Behave yourself, and nothing bad will happen, to you or your dear brother. Am I clear?"

He hopped out first and had a conversation with the man in front who drove the coach. Only then did he help Linny out of the conveyance, which apparently was going to wait in place for a while, with the magician's boxes tucked away in it.

Inside the tavern, Linny had a sense of tables and stools and smoke and shadows, and perhaps of curious pairs of eyes staring her way, but the magician hurried through the dim space to another room in the back, where four men and a woman around a table all looked up at once when the magician guided himself and Linny through the door.

Linny took a breath to steady herself. These must be *madji*.

They stared in silence. Linny could tell they had been talking something over in low voices and were now feeling interrupted. She stared right back at them, not wanting to seem intimidated. Pipe smoke circled lazily about the room.

"Good morning, all!" said the magician with outsized good cheer. "A pleasure to be doing business with you on such a happy occasion and such a fine morning."

"Don't know about the happiness of the occasion, Mr. Malkin," said one of the pipe-smoking men. "But I see you've brought the new stray of yours along."

For a moment Linny thought he must be talking about

the Half-Cat, and looked around to see where the animal had gotten to, but there was no sign of so much as a whisker, golden or silver, and then she realized the man was just referring to her, Linny. Which made her a little mad—that, and the fact she still felt ill from the coach and the pipe smoke.

"I'm not a stray," she said, pinching her lips together. "Strays are lost."

A couple of the others laughed out loud, and one of them punched the man who had spoken on the shoulder.

"And you're not lost?" said the man. "You don't seem to be home where you belong."

"I left home to come here, on purpose," said Linny with stiff dignity. "I'm not lost. I'm never lost. I would like to know where Elias is, though. Are you the ones who have him?"

The magician gave the back of her arm a little pinch.

"Your brave brother is proud to be doing his bit for the cause, I'm sure, my girl," he said. "For *your* cause! After all, it is your will that the *madji* finally rise up against the Surveyors."

"Well, it's true that I don't like the gray people much," said Linny. "But that doesn't mean I like the nasty things in your crates."

The pinch became much stronger then. It hurt.

"*Useful* things," said the magician, and every word

was a warning. "*Necessary* things. Sometimes you have to destroy in order to heal. Your wish is that we undo the grid of the Plain, to save the wrinkled hills."

"Um—" said Linny, and the pinch became really almost unbearable. She tried to twist her arm free from those pinching fingers, but it couldn't be done.

"The Girl is tired, of course," the magician said. "Having just come such a very long way, down from the hills. But I promised I'd show her our brave *madji.* Fighting for her."

Fighting for me? thought Linny, and her stomach twisted.

"How can we be sure she's real?" said the woman on the far side of the table. She had fiercely braided hair held back with a band; she looked like someone you would not want to run into out in the woods on your own.

"What do you think?" said the magician with an enormous shrug. "You know the painting. Look at her. We wished and wished for the Girl with the Lourka to come back to us, and here she is."

The eyes of all those people became even more like screws twisting into soft wood. Linny wanted to duck, to turn away, to hide behind a chair, but she had learned patience while making the varnish for her lourka. Varnishes can't be hastened. Linny knew from sad experience. If you got impatient and added the juniper gum to the kettle before the linseed oil was really, truly burning hot, unusable glop would be the result.

Any child of Lourka had heard the expression a million times: "Not until the feather scorches."

Linny sat tight.

Hang on, hang on, she told herself.

"Well, well," said one of the men. "She's kind of young looking, isn't she? And there's costumes and wigs these days, we all know that."

Somebody guffawed, Linny was glad to notice. Her hair might be messy, and perhaps not very clean, but surely it didn't look like a *wig*.

"They waste our time doubting," said the magician with extra-elegant contempt. "You demand action, and they quibble. You are the Girl with the Lourka. So go ahead, play them something."

Her hands were a little shaky and damp. No wonder! Anyone who has been kidnapped by a magician is liable to have sweaty palms and fingers that tremble some. But her lourka was familiar; the wood of its neck was smooth and warm.

She played them a tune she had just made up herself in her head that morning, a song about leaving things behind, about Sayra fading and her mother waiting and her brothers splashing about in the creek. It didn't have any words, but she was proud of the way she had put hints of these things into the music, all the same. The quaver that was Sayra fading came out, she thought, especially well.

There was an impressed silence in the room while Linny tucked the lourka back into its sack and slung the sack over her shoulder. They couldn't argue with that, thought Linny. Whoever she was or wasn't, this lourka she had made was the truest thing about her.

"So there it is," said the magician finally. "Enough of this dithering. There is work to be done, the Girl with the Lourka wants it done now, and I have the tools to help you do it."

Linny had to keep herself from looking around for this strong-opinioned, willful Girl the magician seemed to want her to be.

"But it's a bad idea you've been pushing, Rodegar Malkin," said a man with a dark brown beard. "And pushing it, you certainly have been, long before the stray girl showed up. Why should we mess with their water?"

"They mess with our land," said another fellow.

"They do, they do, don't they?" said Rodegar Malkin. "They won't be content before they've put every last inch of the world on their grid, and taken all the wrinkles out of everything. I see how it is. The wrinkled hills cry out to us to do something to protect them. Enough, already!"

And his huge hands made a large gesture that was a

kind of silent explosion: *KABOOM!*

"Ha!" said one of the others. "Tempting thought, of course."

"Let me remind you that I offer all you need to make it happen," said the magician. "And by way of providing a public service, as you might say, the prices for my, ahh, special tools are set, I think you'll find, at very reasonable levels."

He leaned forward with what his size made an impressive show of drama.

"Think! All that wicked waterworks machinery gone, in one sweet moment! That building that chokes our poor river now! Gone! The Surveyors would never recover from that blow."

"What does our Girl say?" interrupted the brown-bearded man, turning to stare at Linny some more.

"She agrees completely, of course," said the magician. "She is tired of waiting around for the *madji* to become bolder in their dealings with the Surveyors."

"But—" said Linny, and the magician pinched her again.

"Remember *your brother*, out there with the *madji*, trying to undo the harm of the Plain," said the magician pointedly. "Don't say anything *your brother* might not be happy to hear you say. Sometimes you have to destroy what you want to heal, you know."

"Hey there, ease up on the girl," said the bearded man to the magician, with something almost like disgust. "What I don't understand is why she would throw her lot in with a two-faced old arms dealer like you. Malkin, stay calm there, man! Just stating the bald truth, as you know well enough."

Rodegar Malkin stood up. His head almost grazed the wooden beams of that back room, and his face was beginning to flush red.

"Your long-looked-for Girl with the Lourka finally appears, you *madji* fools, telling you it's time to rise up and fight, and all you do is dither! As you wish. I can do business with a thousand other people, can't I? Just because I'm giving you first crack at the best goods doesn't mean anything much, I guess. Come along with me, Girl. We'll leave them to bicker among themselves till the Surveyors nab them all."

That was when something peculiar happened. The five people around the table all stood up, too, and somehow arranged themselves so that some of them were standing in between Linny and the magician, just as simply and instantly as that.

Linny felt alarmed. She did not trust or like Rodegar Malkin, true, but she didn't know these people any better.

"Hey!" said the magician.

"Hey, yourself," said the man with the beard. "We're

just saying, you don't get to bluster off. We are thinking over your generous offer, and we will come to a decision about it soon enough."

"We're also thinking the Girl with the Lourka might be better off staying with us," added another, darker-headed man.

The magician and the *madji* glared at each other, and Linny felt herself beginning to smoke, like linseed oil just before the test feather dips into it. She was not, she thought, another crate to be lugged around town or sold to the buyer with the most coin money or finally thrown at something and made to explode.

The feather went in; the feather was scorched!

She caught the merest flick of a cat's tail, silvery golden, back in the dark places down the hall, and without thinking a single thought more, she ran right out of that room, somehow dodging the arms of all of those *madji*, somehow even dodging the grasp of the enormous (and bellowing) magician. Quick as fire, quick as scorching, she raced through the Death and Dollop and out onto the street beyond.

14

RACE TO THE RIVER

She couldn't believe it at first, that she had managed to slip through all those angry people. Probably it had helped that she had had no idea she was about to bolt; she had just up and bolted. But this was no time to think real thoughts about anything. She hoisted the skirts of that dress safely away from the cobblestones, and she ran down the street as fast as she could go, turning off the main road once she was around a bend and out of sight of the tavern, and following what she sensed must be a slight slope downhill toward the river.

A Bridge House, near the river. That was where her Aunt Mina would be. A house near a bridge. Linny kept running.

When she paused to catch her breath, some minutes later, a faint hiss from the roof of a nearby house startled her. The Half-Cat was there, walking calmly along, all silver on this side. As soon as the cat noticed her staring at him (or so it seemed to Linny), it turned around and walked (all golden tabby) for a few paces the other way. And then it turned again. She was panting after all that running, but the Half-Cat didn't have a whisker out of place.

"Are you following me, then?" she said to the cat. "Why?"

No answer from the cat; it picked its delicate way along the roof of the house and pretended not to notice Linny staring up at it. So she shrugged and kept running, while the Half-Cat shadowed her, up above.

Fifteen minutes later, a lane so narrow that Linny began to worry it would dead-end and become a trap instead changed its mind and spat her out into bright sun—on a street that ran right along the bright sparkling blue-green laciness of the river.

The Half-Cat leaped gracefully down from the last rooftop onto the balustrade and turned its odd face in her direction, almost as if saying, "See? See? Here it is!"

"Ah!" said Linny, and even though she was running, running, she breathed it all in, the world she saw now.

This was what she had tried to explain to Sayra, how it felt for her when she climbed a tree up high enough to see the world, or got to the top of a little ridge and could look out and see the rippling earth and stone everywhere around, or that time when she had found the outcropping of rock halfway up the Middle Woods, from which you could look down on the actual village of Lourka and see all of its rooftops and alleyways and laundry lines out back. It was like some part of her was always ravenously hungry for views, for overviews, for anything that gave her a taste of the lay of the land.

"Hungry?" Sayra had said, laughing. "Hungry, like your tummy rumbling, for a *view*?"

Oh, how she missed Sayra! That brought her back to herself. There were still angry *madji* and one very enormous magician coming after her. She trotted along the side of the river, gasping a little for breath and eyeing the world that had just come into view.

How strange the buildings looked, on the other side of the water! They were squarer and shinier, Linny noticed, almost as if they had been made with metal and glass, but why would you build a house out of metal and glass? Wouldn't it be awfully sunny and hot in a house like that? So maybe she wasn't seeing things properly. She would have to cross the river to get a better look at those houses.

That must be Angleside, over there, she realized with a start. The other half, the Plain half, of the Broken City. Over on this side of the river, meanwhile, in Bend, the streets were winding and chaotic, as if they belonged to some overgrown village. Linny could well imagine the people of such different places not liking each other overmuch.

Faster, faster! Every muscle in her legs was smoldering by now, and the stones of the city streets were beating bruises into the soles of her feet.

The river was quite wide in this part of the city, she saw, but ahead it narrowed some. And there, farther yet, was a great white structure that went right from one side of the water to the other: a bridge. *A bridge!*

She wrapped the cloak around herself so as to look like nobody in particular (tucking the lourka away under her arm, out of the way), and set off at a trot down the embankment toward the bridge. The river's edge became busier the farther she went, and although her heart pounded a little as more and more people showed up on the streets or even brushed by her, she calmed down some once she realized that no one took notice of her. To them she was just a girl hurrying on some errand, not a fugitive from the *madji*. Not the Girl with the Lourka. It is a pleasant feeling, being anonymous in a city.

Linny slowed her trot to a walk, figuring that looking unhurried was as good as a disguise, and took note of everything: of the way the streets on the Bend side of the river arrived at the embankment from all sorts of odd directions, while way over there, on the other side of the river, what must be Angleside, the streets seemed to open up at quite regular intervals.

Here was an odd thing, however: across the street from

her now was a girl, a few years older than Linny, with a fancy dress on and an instrument in her hand. What was that? Linny stared. A wooden box with threads running across the sound hole, rather than strings. What kind of sound would that make? But the girl was arm in arm with a friend and heading toward the bridge. The friend pointed—almost, but not quite, in Linny's direction—and the two of them doubled over in laughter. They looked quite merry, really. Linny turned to see what they were pointing at and stopped in her tracks for a second.

Another girl, wearing something that looked like a reckless copy of Linny's dress, made of whatever scraps she had found in the rag bag. But the oddest thing was, this girl also had an instrument in her hands—an actual instrument this time, though nothing like a real lourka, with strings that looked like maybe they were perhaps even capable of making a sound, if you plucked them with enough force.

Linny could feel the hair on the back of her neck spring to attention. Who were these girls?

And then a third brushed by Linny. Her dress was a better copy—the buttons were even of metal, though perhaps not quite of silver—but the "lourka" she wore on a cord around her neck was made of something that looked more like a pressed-paper hatbox than anything else.

"Where are you going?" breathed Linny as the girl

paused to hitch up her stockings.

"Taking the long way to the fair!" said the girl happily. "Today's the day! My mother was a claimant once, said it's huge fun—and they feed you free food all the days of the fair!"

Linny's stomach rumbled immediately.

It had taken passing by a pretzel stand and then a soup merchant to inform poor Linny that she was hungry not just for views, but for a "little something," as her father used to say in the middle of a long afternoon. But she had no coin money in her pockets, and it would be foolhardy indeed to start strumming on the poor lourka when she was trying not to be found! That thought—and all these girls around her in the crowd with their odd parodies of real instruments—made her tuck the lourka away even deeper under her cloak, and while she was at it, she tucked the thoughts of food away, too. You have to be tough, when you've just made a break for it.

As she got closer to the bridge, it became ever larger, shinier, and more splendid. It was built of white stone, a rising and falling swoop of a bridge, with four great pediments reaching down into the water. A pattern was carved into the arch: geometrical on the Angleside end, it became ever more recognizably wild looping vines by the time it reached the nearer bank of the river. It was a wide bridge, too, wide enough not only for people and carriages to hurry across it, but for bright awnings and tents to be pitched in the middle of it. It seemed to be a market as well as a bridge, and over it rippled a long bright banner: HAPPY CLAIMANTS' DAY! Except that something peculiar appeared to be going on in that market. Men in gray, moving forward in a line across the bridge; people shaking their hands in the air; a man on a ladder grabbing at the rippling, bright fabric of the banner—what was that about?

And she didn't see any house at all, not right here nearest the bridge. Perhaps on the other side?

Something furry wound itself through her ankles and made the strangest sound, a low warning squeak. The Half-Cat wanted her to keep moving, apparently. There was a small commotion over there on the street to the right—Linny caught a glimpse of yet another girl in a bright dress with a child's pretend version of a lourka in her hands, this one being descended upon by a very large person, an enormous person, colorfully dressed. The magician!

Linny put her head down and slipped deeper into the crowd, grateful for the blandness of her cloak and for her own lack of height, and tried to move at the crowd's own speed, keeping large bodies and pushcarts in between herself and the side of the street where she thought the magician must be moving along.

She flowed along with the crowd to the very foot of the bridge, and there the flowing crowd was brought up short and began to get tangled. A line of men in gray uniforms had formed about forty feet up the bridge, and behind them, other men, also in uniform, were putting together a makeshift fence out of metal grates. The crowd grumbled and surged, and the uniformed men barked orders at them and pointed at a large sign hanging on the central panel of that brand-new fence. It was hard for Linny to catch proper glimpses of the words on that sign, as the crowd thickened and became (from Linny's perspective) a solid mass of shoulders.

She saw NOTICE! and CITIZENS OF BEND and something about an EMERGENCY DECREE and FALSE CLAIMANTS and DEATH. That was not very promising at all. She stood on tiptoes for one last look, and saw this: GIRLS WITH LOURKAS.

Her heart stopped for a second. Just stopped and froze and then began galloping forward again.

"What's that mean?" she said to herself.

"Means crud for news!" said the person beside her. (Linny blushed to realize she must have spoken right out loud just now. Then she looked and saw . . . yet another girl, with pretty brown curls tumbling down her back, another dark-blue vest over a colorful skirt, another box with strings dangling at her side.) "Changing the rules like that, and on Claimants' Day! And didn't I have the devil's own time putting this costume together? For nothing, I guess. Angleside killjoys! Well, may they fall right into their Plain Sea and be bored all to death!"

It wasn't just Linny listening to her speech. A few of the people closest in that crowd hooted their approval; some laughed.

"Fair has to have a Girl, though, don't it?" said someone a few feet away.

"Well, not me, not this time, it won't have," said the angry/pretty girl. Linny could see she was already trying to pull herself out of the tide of that crowd. "Not if they're going to threaten to *kill* us, the vile griddlers. 'Immediate sentence of death for all deemed impostors,' it says right there. Well then, good-bye, I say."

"Too bad!" and "Luck to you!" said a few voices, and a few others cursed the Surveyors with crunchy, furious words Linny had not heard before.

"And they're checking papers on the bridge, those gray cowards!" said someone else. "What're they frightened of, anyway? Girls with toy lourkas?"

There was the sound of someone spitting in disgust, which was not a sound Linny wanted to hear in a crowd as thick as this one. (Where was there for disgusted spit to go?)

"Someday she'll come, our true Girl, and take charge, and they know it," said another voice. "Maybe she's already come, hmm? You know what the rumors are saying—that a girl showed up in the market square, who looked real as real. Scared, that's what they are."

Nervous laughter from here and there. And bobbing above the sea of people, not that far away anymore, Linny caught sight of the magician's hat.

Well! She had no time to think what to do—she had an instrument that could be nothing other than a lourka hidden under her cloak, and no papers to show any Surveyors. So when the cat hissed from between her feet and then leaped pointedly through the crowd and toward the upstream side of the bridge, Linny blindly followed, making as little commotion as she could, though at least one woman yelled something unpleasant when Linny elbowed past her.

The entrance of the bridge was made grander by a pair of columns, rising pointlessly into the sky. Linny ducked behind the farther column, out of the way of those crowds again, and held her breath. Had the magician or the *madji* (because surely the *madji* must also be right out there somewhere) heard that woman's yelp? Had they caught a glimpse of a smallish person in a cloak of no recognizable color slipping across the flow of people here? Linny stood very still for a moment and then realized that her cloak of no recognizable color must still be a darkish blot against the white stone, if any of those people chasing her had managed to get to this side of the bridge ahead of her. No, she'd better keep moving. The Half-Cat was already padding on, covering ground fast but without ever seeming to hurry.

And as she lifted her head for a moment, to see what lay ahead of her on the upstream side of the bridge, she had another of those moments where that hungry place inside her was suddenly fed by information, by the lay of the land, by the view. The river narrowed here and grew louder. The lower parts of the city had been quite flat, but here the water appeared around a kind of high corner and then tumbled down in a series of lively waterfalls. And up there ahead of her, across the narrow liveliness of this upper river, but before the actual bend in its course, was another bridge, a much smaller and stranger bridge, a bridge that was, in fact, a house, built above the water and stretching from one bank to another.

Linny's heart did a little leap of recognition: *Bridge House, Bend!*

And that was when she heard the men's voices, *madji* voices, from back by the huge stone bridge. They were loud, and they were breathless from running, and they were shouting, "There! *There* she is! Go! Grab that girl!"

Sometimes hiding is the right solution, and sometimes a girl just has to run like the wind and hope she's faster than the angry people after her. Linny hitched up her skirts and ran.

15

THE BRIDGE HOUSE

Linny raced up the slope of the embankment as fast as she could manage, considering the fancy dress and the breakable lourka, slapping in its sack against her side. It turns out a person can skitter along a sidewalk pretty quickly when she's being chased by an enormous magician and a bunch of rebel fighters with an interest in grid-destroying weapons.

The Bridge House was very beautiful and peculiar, stretched as it was across the crashing, tumbling river, from one side to the other. Linny was running as hard as she could, so she caught only glimpses of the house's windows looking out over the waterfalls, and only glimpses of the crooked roofline of the house, steep and shingled near the Bend side of the river, but ever boxier as it crossed toward the Angleside. Linny sprinted up the sloping riverside as fast as fast, hoping very much that this really was the Bridge House of which her mother had spoken, and that her Aunt Mina really lived there.

As Linny approached the thick gates that kept the street apart from the Bridge House's front steps, the thought zipped briefly through her mind that this Auntie Mina had better not be out buying bread for dinner or what have you, because Linny really, really, really needed someone to be willing to open this house's door and let her in. It was either that or face the angry *madji*. Not to mention the even angrier magician.

She slipped through the garden gates, slammed them closed and latched them shut, and then ran up the stairs to the Bridge House's front door, as solid as a tree trunk and every inch of it carved with pictures of hills and rivers and trees and more hills—but she couldn't look at it now. The *madji* were only a few seconds behind her. She gave the door a couple of desperate bangs with her fist.

"You, Linnet!" called the enormous magician from the other side of the fence. He was tall enough that his head showed above the top of the gate, and he started shaking the iron bars with his massive hands. The latch might hold, and then again it might not. "Come back, you fool! That's the *Tinkerman's* door. You can't go in *there*!"

"Why can't I?" asked Linny, still furious about everything: the queasy-making ride in the coach, the weapons that did something terrible to the structure of the world,

163

the sliver of a room where the magician had kept her a prisoner. Plus how he had dragged off poor Elias!

Linny turned her back on the magician and the *madji*, all of them, and pounded on the door. The *madji* were shouting, too.

"Just go away, all of you!" said Linny, not even turning around to look at them, her eyes focused on the door that her Aunt Mina, her mother's sister, must must *must* be living behind. *Oh, hurry!*

Sometimes a good stare can work like magic. That very moment the door flung itself open, and a crisp voice said, "Who can possibly be knocking at *this* door? Nobody ever comes here."

No, this could not be Linny's Auntie Mina. The voice was not a woman's voice, for one thing.

"Umm, excuse me, hello!" said Linny, gasping a little for breath. "Is someone named Mina here, please? Can you tell me fast?"

"What's all the ruckus?" said the man, taking a step forward into the light. He was dressed in a black and gray work shirt and striped apron, and had a black cap pulled down over his head, and a silvery ponytail running down his back. "Why is that giant trying to break through my gate?"

"Not a giant—he's a magician," said Linny, feeling more desperate every second. "Please, *is Mina here*?"

"Magicians!" said the man, and he waved a narrow wrench he had in his hand in the general direction of the gates. "Aha! Of course! Hotheads! Know-nothings! *Go away, you lot!*"

The magician roared in response, rattling the gates so hard with one huge fist that Linny thought surely the metal would crack and give way.

Enough! Before her brain had had time to catch up with her limbs, she had already scooped up the Half-Cat and barged right under the man's arm and into the dark hall beyond the door. And then compounded her crimes by kicking the big front door shut with her foot. (The shouting outside vanished, just like that. The door must be really very thick.)

The Half-Cat made a shrill, offended spitting noise, scratched itself loose, and sprang to the ground, where it strutted back and forth for a moment, shrugging its fur back into place like a goose settling its feathers after a fight.

Linny wasn't any better. For a moment all she could do was lean forward, her hand on her knee, and gasp.

But the man with the work apron wasn't looking at her just at that moment. He had finally noticed the cat. It was the strangest thing: his whole face lit up.

"My best of all inventions!" he said. "It's my own lost kitty cat brought you here!"

"Excuse me, but why'd the people out there call you the Tinkerman?" asked Linny. What she wanted to ask was, "Excuse me, are you dangerous?" But this seemed like a way to come at the question from a more tactful angle.

"No respect for applied science anymore, is there? On the one side of the river, know-nothings, and on the other side, know-it-alls."

"Oh," said Linny. She wasn't sure whether this meant he was dangerous, or not at all dangerous. She looked around, just as a precaution, looking for other ways out.

They were standing at one end of a long, long corridor, lit by what at first seemed an endless line of windows along the left-hand side. The windows could not be all the same, though: the light was different, farther down the hall. Brighter, perhaps. The windows closest to the door she had just come in by were curtained and shuttered. Hence the shadows here.

Along the right-hand side of the hall were doorways and doors, so many of them that Linny could not count them all. A house that was also a bridge! She had never heard of such a thing. A house between places. Living in this house must be like always being on a journey.

The man had shifted his gaze back from the Half-Cat by now. He stared at the lourka sack in Linny's hands, and at her face, and then back at the bag again.

"And what's in that?" he said, pointing.

"My lourka," said Linny. "I made it."

"*Did* you?" he said, his eyes all at once waking up and focusing. "A *lourka*? So you're here for the fair?"

"No," said Linny. "I never heard of the fair until I got to the city. I'm looking for someone named Mina. Does she live here?"

"Oh, Mina!" said the man. "Mina hasn't been here for years."

"But I thought she'd be here," said Linny. Disappointment, thick as a blanket, settled over her. Now what was she supposed to do?

"Did she go somewhere?" she said.

"Her sister got herself lost in the wrinkled hills," said the man. "Mina wanted to follow after."

"She went into the hills?"

"She tried, all right, but the hillsickness stopped her. You can't just waltz up into those hills, you know."

Linny certainly knew that. Her mother had been almost sick enough to die when she had first arrived in Lourka. But then she had gotten better.

"But if Mina didn't go into the hills, where'd she go?"

"She got ambitious, that's what. Started working on a cure for hillsickness—an antidote for magic. Then she could go looking for her sister, couldn't she? But the Surveyors heard what she was up to, sure enough, and so they nabbed her."

Linny was having trouble following the story. Mina

wasn't here, though; that much was clear.

"The Surveyors took her away? Because they didn't want a cure for hillsickness?"

The man barked with laughter.

"The other way around! The other way around!" he said. "They want a cure for hillsickness so much they shiver to think of it! Imagine what they could do then— how they could finally map every nook and cranny of those hills and tame all the wild places. So when they heard what she was up to, of course they whisked her right off to a research hub at the plainest edge of the Plain Sea, where I suppose she's been stirring and mixing ever since. And she'll be kept there until they get what they want. And who are you, you young person with all these odd questions?"

"My moth—I mean, Mina's sister, Irika, told me Mina might know about medicines. My friend is sick. That's why I came down here to the Plain. For medicines."

"Did you just say *Irika*?" he said. "So have you seen her, then, the child of my wife, my almost-daughter Irika? We lost Mina to the Plain, and Irika to the hills. There's symmetry for you. Where are you from, that you've been chatting with my Irika?"

"From the hills," said Linny.

"Oho!" said the man. "A girl, down from the hills, with a lourka over her shoulder! That's a news item, right there. I'd better run a quick scan."

"What's a scan?" said Linny.

The man had already darted over to a chest of drawers against the wall and was rummaging around in them for something.

Linny shrugged off her cloak. She was hot and sweaty after her mad dash up the embankment. Though then she remembered all the ribbons and buttons on the dress she was wearing, and she made her face very tough to compensate. Just because she was wearing ribbons didn't mean anybody should take her for a fool.

The Tinkerman swung around, brandishing a double-pronged wiry fork that he had dug out of that drawer.

"Found it!" he said, and he darted forward and back, holding the wiry fork thing out toward Linny and watching its wires vibrate and hum, as if they were strings being played by some entirely invisible musician.

"What's that thing?" said Linny. "What are you doing?" Like most people since the dawn of time, she did not like having sharp things pointed at her.

"Measuring the magic in you, as scientifically as I know how," said the Tinkerman. "I'll have you know this is wrinkled technology, which is something new. Something quite special. Cat's whiskers and wires. And you, young lady, are registering very high on my meter here. Unbelievably, impossibly high. You've been far up in the hills, I'm guessing. Especially your right pocket. What's that in your pocket, impossible girl? And where does it come from?"

"Would you mind putting down that big fork?" said Linny, making an effort to stay polite. Of course she knew perfectly well what was in her pocket. Her hand quickly checked, and it was still there: Sayra's present.

"But where oh where have you been?" said the Tinkerman, putting the fork thing behind his back even as he leaned forward some. "And why oh why has an impossible creature like you come all the way here?"

"I told you—I had to," said Linny, feeling increasingly desperate. "For medicines. To save my friend who's fading. She's trapped in Away, and now Mina isn't even here!"

"Oho!" said the Tinkerman. "Around here they like to say Away doesn't exist."

"Does so," said Linny.

"How do you know that, girl?"

"Because I was *there*!" said Linny. "Well, almost. I'm pretty sure my right hand was there."

"The hand in your pocket," said the Tinkerman shrewdly.

Linny pulled that hand of hers out of the dress's pocket and hid it instead behind her back.

"And how did your right hand get into Away?" said

the Tinkerman. "I'm very curious about that—I have a theory about the place, you see."

"I played a song," said Linny.

"A song!" said the man. "How delightful! Well! When they hear about these readings, they'll have to admit how right I've been all along. Complexity, like water, flows downhill. Oh, don't look so puzzled! Complexity's just the scientific word for wrinkledness, for magic. Run some nice wires from Away down to the Plain, and it'll power all our lamps eventually, that's what I've been saying. All we need is for Mina to get that antidote finished. And she must be nearly done by now. Oh, they'll just have to agree to send us, once they get a good look at you. Come this way!"

It made her feel a little shy. Perhaps it was because of the *things* all around her here. This part of the house, she now saw, was full of *things*, the shelves absolutely crammed with dead animals, filled up with stuffing so they'd look real and staring at Linny through glinty glass eyes. There were even pickled creatures in jars, not to mention other things that weren't creatures at all, neither pickled nor stuffed, but carved toys or dolls made of twigs or polished rocks.

"Here we are," said the Tinkerman, stopping short in front of a series of shelves and reaching up for his notebooks. "This, this, I think, and this—"

171

When a crashing din interrupted, coming from much farther down the hall. A pounding on the walls, a shouting, a banging, a raucous metallic ringing.

"What's that?" said Linny, jumping around in alarm. Her mind had gone immediately to raging *madji* and enormous and unhappy magicians.

The Tinkerman seemed as surprised as she was.

"More visitors!" he said. "But nobody ever comes to that door, either!"

It was true—the noise was coming from the other end of the house. The Tinkerman was already speeding down that long hall, with Linny behind him, because she didn't know what else to do, and also because she did not much want to stay, all alone, at the end of the house that held those staring creatures in their jars. The Half-Cat padded along beside her, keeping its own counsel.

"Coming, coming, coming," muttered the Tinkerman under his breath.

On the left-hand side of the hall, the line of windows gave Linny glimpses, through a light mist of water spraying from the tumbling river, of the larger bridge downstream, of the river widening out below, of the two cities spreading out on either bank: chaotic pointy roofs on the left, rectangular blocks of shiny rectangular buildings on the right. Under other circumstances, not involving her having to race along after this muttering old man toward absolutely horrible crashing sounds at the far end of the hall, Linny would have liked to stand at one of those windows for a while, just soaking up all that information about the world.

The noises were getting louder and more alarming. There was a whirring, whining sound added to the mix now that made Linny want to cover her ears and hide. The Half-Cat yowled. The Tinkerman broke into an actual run. And suddenly the whole far end of the hall filled with smoke or dust, and a half-dozen men in gray came striding in through the cloud, while the Tinkerman ran forward, waving his fists and shouting in rage.

Without thinking anything over, Linny ducked through the nearest doorway, into a room that was something between a kitchen and a workshop, all incomprehensible machines and white walls. Her eyes assessed it in one second, and she bit her lip. There was no place to hide.

"What have you scoundrels done?" the Tinkerman was wailing, down at the far end of the hall. "I was on my way to open the door! We were coming to the blasted court ourselves."

"Noncompliance with search order," said some gray voice while boots came stamping down the hall, one two, one two. "Harboring illegal persons. You think we don't keep an eye on this house? Transport of aliens. Reckless disregard of immigration laws. That's plenty of trouble, Arthur Vix. Smuggling dangerous impostors across the river! Better hand her over now."

That cat outside wouldn't budge! And in any case, there really was, no matter how hard she looked, nowhere in this room to hide.

Plan B, she thought to herself. *Time for a backup plan.* But there was no backup plan that she could see.

Outside in the hall, the Tinkerman was almost babbling, he was so angry. He was sputtering about warrants and property damage, and the gray voice was saying, "Hand her over. Hand her over."

Sometimes if you cannot hide, the worst thing of all is being found. So it was not a plan, exactly: it was instinct—it was not wanting to be found—that made Linny step right back through that doorway now, to stand as tall as she could next to the hissing Half-Cat and face down that crowd of gray men in the hall.

"There she is!" some of them shouted. But she held her ground and stared unblinking into their grayness, and for a magical moment they fell into the silence that means there's been a rewriting of the story.

For the length of that moment, at least, they had not found her.

She had found *them*.

16

THE FIRST SURVEYOR

Then they arrested her anyway.

The gray uniforms came and surrounded her and pointed down the hall, to where they had made a dusty mess of things by knocking down the Tinkerman's Angleside door.

"You'd better run away," whispered Linny to the Half-Cat, but it had parked itself on her toes and was practically throwing off sparks as it glared at the men in gray all around, so in the end she had to pick it right up. It was like trying to lift a very awkward, prickly, hissing sack filled with sand and molasses.

The good thing was, having the angry Half-Cat in her arms helped disguise the awful shakiness that was spreading through all her limbs.

It is hard to stand tall and pretend not to be afraid when your arms insist on trembling.

The other distraction, as the gray men marched her

down the hall and through the dusty hole in the wall that had once been a door, was the angry Tinkerman, who darted around the edges of the gray men, yelping and protesting. They were interfering with his research work! And stealing his inventions! When the regent heard about this, he would—

"It's the regent's own orders," said the gray man who did the talking. "Take it up with him."

And when the Tinkerman wouldn't shut up, they arrested him, too.

But by then they had emerged onto the (damaged) porch of the Bridge House, and for a moment Linny's mind soared far away from all these arguing men and her trembling knees and the sagging weight of the Half-Cat. As she stepped across that threshold, the other half of the Broken City, the Angleside, spread itself out like a strange feast before her. Her first impression was of straight lines and fire. Every corner so sharp you could cut yourself on it, and the sunlight rioting between all those sheets of metal and large glass windows.

It was so very different from anything she had seen before. She loved the undulating, shifting hills, but these angles also satisfied some kind of longing in her that she hadn't even known she had.

And, anyway, it was such a relief to be out of that narrow hall, even if it had to be a crowd of Surveyors hustling her out. "You're such a squirrel in a tree," Sayra had said once. "Running from burrows. Climbing up, climbing up! Anything for a view!"

Oh, Sayra!

Linny sent some hold-on-I'm-still-coming thoughts fiercely in Sayra's direction, shifting the Half-Cat in her arms.

The Surveyors hurried her (and the Half-Cat and the still-protesting Tinkerman) into a strange wheeled cart, made mostly of metal, but lacking horses or donkeys or even goats to make it move. Apparently on this side of the river, the lack of horses and goats meant nothing. One of the gray men pushed a red button, and the cart started moving forward, entirely on its own. All the man had to do was shift a lever one way or the other, and the cart's wheels turned, as obedient as could be.

"I thought they didn't have wrinkled things over here!" said Linny, forgetting herself.

"Hush, hush," said the Tinkerman. "There's nothing wrinkled about it; that's *electricity* it's running on. Still scarcer than it should be, electricity, but you know what we've got planned about that."

And when Linny didn't respond to the significant look he was giving her (because she had no clue what he was talking about), he leaned closer to her and added, "My theory! My plan! To tap into Away. Think! Think! We *could* convert all that dense antientropic complexity into so much power we could all have carts of our own—"

It sounded slightly menacing to Linny. He spoke of Away as if it were an old maple tree you could bore into to catch drip-drops of sweet sap. She turned her head to the side and looked instead at where they were going.

A broad street led away from the Bridge House and the river, past a long line of buildings that were almost too glaring in the sun. Some kind of thin stone had been used to pave walkways on either side of the street, but it wasn't as though there was a lot of muck in the street itself, to warrant such caution about walkways. It was an eerily clean street, to tell the truth.

They buzzed along in the cart-without-goats, Linny feeling too warm in her dress. The sun glared and glittered around them, all the buildings being so flat and shiny. In Bend, the streets would have been filled with people, but at first Angleside struck her as empty, inhabited only by straight edges and bright surfaces. Then she looked more closely at the wall nearest by, and she gasped: people were looking at them, right through it. She had never heard of a wall like that before. It was very smooth, as well as transparent. A wall made of glass!

After that came a truly grand building, dark and windowless. It seemed to Linny a silent, secret place. It had tall columns of stone in front of it, and no glass walls to speak of.

The man in the cart pushed his button again, and it came to a stop.

"Out," said the gray man, opening the door.

It wasn't the building that started Linny's knees shaking again, though. It was the brass engraving bolted over the front entrance of the building: a brass image of a girl holding tools in her brass hands—a flat triangle with measure marks carved into it, and another pointy angular thing. The girl was just lines etched into a plate of metal, but the extra knobble in the elbows, the little mole on the cheek, the determined, no-nonsense nose looked all too familiar to Linnet.

"What's *she* doing over here?" Linny whispered to the Tinkerman. "I thought the Girl with the Lourka belonged to the wrinkled side."

"Haven't studied much history, then, have you?" said the Tinkerman. "She set things in order everywhere. Over here they remember her as the First Surveyor. By law, the regent's job is officially temporary, just ruling until the next true Girl shows up, crown in hand. Except until now she never has shown up, has she? And the crown was lost ages ago. By now the whole thing is just a foolish tradition, dragged out and dusted off every ten years for the fair."

"So you don't think I'm real?" said Linny.

"Real! Of course you're real! But that doesn't mean the legends are real. Legends are legends—useful things

179

for keeping the wrinkled side in line. You're a girl, and you happen to have a lourka. Good! But that doesn't make you *the* girl with *the* lourka. That's my line, and I'm sticking to it. You're too important to science to be wasted on politics!"

"Enough out of you," said a gray man rudely to the Tinkerman, and they marched their arrestees (plus one cat) up the great stone steps toward the entrance of the blank-faced building right here—not so blank, after all, of course, because right there above the engraved shadow of the First Surveyor, there was a pair of grand words engraved into the stone:

SURVEYORS' COURT, said those words.

Stand tall and pay attention, Linny told herself sternly.

The first thing Linny noticed as they entered that building was how astonishingly light it was, despite the complete lack of windows: a different kind of light, chillier than sunshine.

There was a hall leading deeper into the building, and off that hall opened doors and even windows, though the windows looked only into other rooms and not outside. It was more like a street than an interior hall, Linny decided, and she shook her head to help it settle down. She was not used to spaces being so large and grand.

The Surveyors took their prisoners upstairs by means of a metal box, also run, Linny guessed, by electricity. It slipped from one floor to the next in that huge building, and every foot it moved gave a person more information: how tall this place must be, how much distance between one layer of rooms and the next.

Then the Surveyors ushered Linny and the Tinkerman into a large cube of an office, where a man was sitting behind an enormous black desk almost exactly the same deep black as the man's hair. Both the desk and the man's hair gleamed a little in the strange light of this building. His face was all angles.

"Regent!" said the leader of the group of Surveyors. The rest of the gray men had stayed out in the hall. "Bringing you the criminal, as you requested. The impostor—and Arthur Vix. He obstructed justice, so we had to take him, too." He sounded almost apologetic about that.

The angular man's eyes narrowed at the sight of the Half-Cat and then fixed on Linny's face, until she had to blink and look away.

"And a cat?" said the man, still staring. "I don't remember asking for a cat."

"It's not just any cat!" said the Tinkerman. "It's the cat I improved—"

He was all a-bubble now with his story of the Half-Cat, how his lost almost-daughter Irika had found it in the hills, and he had improved it, how it was the start of a whole new era of wrinkled technology, and so on and so on.

The angular man put up his hand to make him stop.

"Arthur Vix here, whom they call the Tinkerman, has long-winded theories about everything. But let me jump ahead to the interesting questions," he said to Linny. "Did you think you could just sneak in to cause trouble without anyone noticing?"

"I wasn't sneaking *or* causing trouble," said Linny, while the Half-Cat hissed quietly in her arms.

"No?" said the angular man. He pointed at Arthur Vix, who stuttered a little. "There's a hole in this man's house. That strikes me as trouble. And you are, this very minute, wasting my time, and that's more trouble."

"Your Surveyors blew up his door, not me!" said Linny. She never liked to be blamed for things that weren't her doing; there were enough things, as it was, that *were* her fault.

"Because you were there, hiding," said the angular man. "Don't go messing with cause and effect. A false claimant to the crown, holed up in the Bridge House! An impostor! We couldn't let that go unpunished, could we?"

"Oh, dear," said the Tinkerman. "Now you're completely missing the point. This is a girl who has actually been to Away *and can lead us back*, once the antidote's ready and all. You should see the readings from my scanner! She's not one of your claimants; she's evidence. Here, take your hand out of your pocket!"

That last line was aimed at Linny, and it made her jump.

The Half-Cat had hopped down to the floor a few minutes before, and Linny's right hand actually had been in her pocket, just at that moment, making sure Sayra's present was still there. The Tinkerman was brandishing his metal fork.

"Show him! Show him!" he said encouragingly to Linny. She didn't follow his logic, but she held out her hand, and opened it.

There were little gasps in that room, from the Surveyors standing close enough to see.

On her palm lay the silk rosebud that had been pressed into her hand by whatever part of Sayra had been taken off to Away.

Even here in the Plain, it was oddly transparent. Vix's fork trembled and hummed.

"Do you see that? Do you see that?" he said triumphantly to the regent. "That's not just some wrinkled knickknack brought into town from the near hills. *Those* things lose their magic by the time they get as far as the Plain side of the river. But this hand! And whatever that thing is there, that the hand is holding! They are the real deal. And anyway, why do you think a girl like this even exists?"

Linny twitched in her skin. She was being stared at very hard, and she didn't like it one bit.

"If Away can produce *this*," said the Tinkerman, making a sweeping gesture that incorporated all of Linny from head to heels, "a copy accurate down to the last curl and second mole, just think of what else it can do!"

"I'm not a copy," corrected Linny. "And I wasn't produced by anywhere."

"Quiet," said the Tinkerman. "I'm explaining the energy implications of Away. It takes huge, enormous, vast amounts of energy to make something as impossible as you—an exact replica of the Girl with the Lourka. That's my point. But if that's what can happen, up in the wrinkled places closest to Away, imagine what we could do if we went right to the source. Light bulbs shining everywhere!"

"*You* misunderstand *my* point," said the regent, honing the edges of each one of those words. "We *cannot* have *replicas* running around. It is a threat to public safety, not to mention stability. Light bulbs are extraneous."

The men were glaring at each other now, across that table.

"Wait," said Linny. As far as she was concerned, their whole conversation had gone seriously astray. "I am not

184

a copy of something or a scientific theory. I have nothing to do with light bulbs, whatever those are. I don't want crowns or powers—I want medicines to save my friend who's fading, who's trapped in Away."

"A touching story," said the regent. "But when I hear about some Girl with a Lourka being paraded in front of the *madji*, in order to encourage unlawful, violent, dreadful behavior, am I supposed to ignore that? That was *exactly* what the court was worried about, late last night, when they passed our sudden new law. So now we see they were wise."

"What's he talking about?" said the Tinkerman, looking over at Linny with some anxiety.

"Are you saying you passed that awful law because you had heard about *me*?" said Linny. It was a strange thought.

"It was a sensible precaution," said the Chief Surveyor.

There was a period of heavy silence in that room.

"So," said Linny, remembering something someone had said on that crowded, jostling bridge. "What happens when the actual Girl with the Lourka shows up for real?"

"I think we can safely consider that impossible," said the Chief Surveyor.

It was a strange thing that happened to Linny at that moment.

Suddenly, in this bare room without windows, with those cold, sharp eyes digging into her skull, she found herself remembering Sayra's room, so different from this one, with those curtains at the window that Sayra had covered with embroidered birds, perched on their tangle of embroidered vines, all sewn with such bright threads that they seemed about to leap from the linen and fly around the room. And Sayra, no, the shell of Sayra, curled up in her bed, her hair smooth and gold and fading, her hand unmoving by her thin face . . . so familiar, and fading . . . her fingers, which were always so nimble and busy . . . still, and fading—

"*Sit down!*" said the angular man. Linny must have jumped to her feet again without thinking. She had forgotten everything but Sayra for a moment. After all, why was she here, really?

"The actual, real Girl with the Lourka could just ask for medicines, I guess, and you'd have to give them to her?" said Linny. "Since she would be ruling the whole place? And she could come and go as she wants?"

"What?" said the Tinkerman. His voice was rising; he was beginning to sound frantic. "What's all this about? Don't get them mad. They'll ruin our expedition. Science is the only thing that really matters, so don't go messing everything up. They're wily here."

"No," said Linny. Everything was becoming clear

in her mind now. "The only thing that really matters is Sayra waiting for me to bring those medicines. So yes, then I'm a claimant. Not a prisoner: a claimant! Why not? I know who I am."

The Tinkerman let his face fall into his trembling hands.

The regent was more reserved, and the expression in his eyes was guarded. You could not read his mind from his eyes.

"That's official, then," he said, standing up slowly, like a shadow rising over a faraway hill. "You heard her yourself, Arthur Vix. Nothing for you to do now but go home."

"I thought I was arrested," said the Tinkerman sullenly.

"I'm unarresting you. Go away and invent something that actually works. But the claimant stays here. No shortage of beds in the dormitory, since this impulsive child is the only claimant this year. We wanted zero, but we have one. We will adapt. Oh, and we'll keep the cat, I think. Let the real lab men see if there's anything to your wrinkled technology."

And the room was suddenly bursting at the seams with people, some of whom were in Surveyors' gray and some who wore blindingly white coats and carried nets and a cage.

Linny reached down in alarm for the Half-Cat, but it was already gone from under her chair. Yowling and hissing, it was being shoved by men with enormous white mitts on into a metal cage.

"Stop that, you awful people! Give that cat back!" she shouted. She tried to get a hand on the wires of that cage, but the men in white coats were too quick for her. Someone grabbed Linny's own arms from behind her back, and the men in white coats went out again through the door.

"What are you *doing*?" asked Linny, trying to yank her arms out of the guards' hard grasps.

The regent rapped on his desk.

"Enough," he said. "Far too late for such fussing. You, claimant, should have thought about the consequences, shouldn't you, before you broke the law and came over the river. Well, the matron takes you now. *My* heart will not break if you don't pass your tests, little girl. And, by the way, no claimant ever has."

And he waved them out of his office with his thin and angular hand.

17

STRONG TEA

The guards steered Linny out of the regent's office, while the Tinkerman followed, moaning and groaning his disapproval. At that point Linny's impressions of everything around her were all a terrible jumble: there was a bell chiming quietly, somewhere overhead, and people in gray were moving through the halls at great speed, as if this were the official hour for running all errands. The faintest echo of a cat's yowl, from down that hall there. She paid attention to that wisp of a clue.

The guards were turning her to face a middle-aged woman with short, pale hair and a pained expression on her face. *Time to look like a harmless lamb,* thought Linny grimly, and she let her shoulders slacken some and blinked her eyes a few times, just to soften them.

"Let go of her, please," the woman said to the guards holding Linny. "The girl comes with me now. No, not you!"

That was directed at the Tinkerman, who had made a step in the woman's direction.

"Go home," she said to him. "You know the rules. No aiding and abetting. Only claimants in the claimants' dormitory. Good-bye."

"But it's not fair! It's a waste!" said the Tinkerman. The gray men, the Surveyors, had him encircled now. "She's supposed to be my guide, up to Away!"

The matron snapped her fingers with her free hand (her other hand had a firm grasp on Linny).

"This way, claimant," she said. "Come along quickly."

"Please, where are we going?" said Linny, using her lost-lamb voice while her eyes and brain soaked up the pattern of the halls as best they could. "And my poor, poor cat! It was so unhappy! Where'd they take it off to?"

"That's the lab men's concern, not yours," said the matron, and Linny filed the term away: lab men. "You and I and these guards here are going along to the claimants' dormitories. Turn here, please, and no nonsense out of you."

A sharp turn to the right and then another one of those magic boxes; it took them about as far down as they had come up before, but Linny could tell they were deeper within the mass of that building than they had been in the regent's office.

Keep talking, Linny said to herself. *But pay attention all the time.*

"But you know there's been a mistake. I don't even want to be a claimant. I just came down here to find medicines for my friend who's fading. But they said they're going to punish me if I don't pass their tests. The man back there said as much. Please—"

"I'm afraid I'm not supposed to let you chatter," the matron said. "If you don't want to be punished, then you just have to do your best to pass the tests."

"But the man back there said *nobody* passes them."

The matron had no response to that.

They turned the corner into another corridor, which ended in a door. The matron pushed a card into the slot, and the metal door slid open. Behind it was another door, an old-fashioned one made of wood, and this door the matron opened by fiddling with a latch.

"In the old days, it would have been all a-bustle here, the day before the fair, but this year we have nobody. Well, almost nobody, of course. This is the claimants' dormitory, right in here. All cleaned up and so on last week, before we heard about the new law. Gracious, look at you; you *are* young, aren't you? Well, it is what it is."

Linny was trying to figure out what had just happened, when they stepped through that pair of doors, so different from each other. The whole feeling of the building changed. She was quite sure the walls around her were suddenly made of old things, wood and stone, and not the whatever-it-was that the Anglesiders used for walls, ceilings, and floors.

There were actual thick beams running across the ceiling in here! And whitewashed plaster in the in-between places!

The matron saw her gaping and laughed.

"The girls always make a face when they first come in," she said. "Now, don't go damaging anything, claimant. This is the historical record, in here, and not just any old dormitory."

"It's a completely different building," said Linny, looking back at the doorway. "Right next to the big new one?"

"*Inside* the Surveyors' Court, child. You won't have seen such a thing before. They kept the old hall—built by the First Surveyor herself, you know—and constructed the new grand structure right around it. The historians had some clout in those days! Of course, the wiring in here's completely new. And the desks and the bunk beds, all replaced now and again as they age. A thousand claimants have passed through this place, I guess, over the years."

Bunk bed after bunk bed, all the way down that long, narrow room. They must have expected many people to come stay in this dormitory, perhaps in other years. Simple worktables and matching chairs stood under the windows. A blank, glassy picture in a frame standing on every table, and a window above, but those windows looked out not on the world, but through a second wall of glass (because the new building had swallowed up this old one), and then, across a space of some kind, at a hundred other, Plainer windows in other Plainer walls.

Apparently the Surveyors' Court had been built as a square around a courtyard, and all its windows faced in. But even the first layer of windows, the ones that looked like they had been transported over here from Bend, didn't budge when Linny wiggled them. And beyond them was the second skin of glass, which looked like it might put up a pretty good fight if you tried to break through it.

That worried her. It's always better to be in rooms you can get out of easily, if you need to.

"What's that door over there?" she asked. It was a solid old thing, absolutely bristling with locks and latches. "I guess not the way to a privy."

"Privy's down at the other end," said the matron, pointing. "If you want to use it before we get started. Hurry up! It's cartography first."

Whatever that was.

Linny followed the pointing finger and found a tiny

room, behind a sliding door, with two metal basins in it, set at different heights. It must be quite a recent addition to this ancient building. Porcelain and metal, and with water that came rushing out of spigots at a touch; this was what a privy looked like, apparently, on the Angleside. An outhouse, indoors! Linny splashed the sink water on her face to wake herself up.

Think! Think!

What did she still have with her to help? She had once had a cookpot, and Elias, and then eventually a Half-Cat. And she had lost them all.

"What do I do?" she asked the blank wall above the basin. The wall said nothing, but as Linny dried her hands on her skirt, she felt the comforting lump that meant Sayra's birthday present was still there, despite everything, in her pocket.

That half-visible silk butterfly-rose was the only thing in the universe, apart from Linny's own right hand, to ever have traveled into and out of Away. Just to show it could be done.

All right. Too bad Sayra wasn't here to save Linny this time, so that Linny could finally get to work saving *her*. Surveyors were miles worse than wolves.

How stupid she had been, to think she could just wander into the Broken City and find whatever it was Sayra needed to come back from Away and be alive again properly.

You better wait for me, she told the ghost of Sayra's butterfly-rose. *You better hang on. I'll show them all. Somehow I'll pass these unpassable tests and make them bring me all the medicines in the world—*

There was a brisk knock on the sliding door.

"Are you all right, claimant?"

Linny put on her sweet-as-a-lamb face again and stepped back out into the dormitory room.

"Sorry I took so long," she said. "I just got to worrying again—about my friend, you know, and my cat."

She was laying it on a little thick, she knew, but the matron patted her on the shoulder.

"There, now. You'd better let go of such distractions. The cat is gone. Things that go to the lab men to be studied don't come back alive. No, don't look like that!"

Because all of Linny was caught up in one awful thought:

What?

"They're going to hurt my cat?"

"No, no, they won't *hurt* it. This is a civilized place, what are you thinking? They'll make the beast comfortable, claimant, while they take it apart. It won't feel a thing."

Linny had to try so hard not to scream that her whole face felt like it was twisting into knots.

"Oh!" she said. "No!"

"Calm yourself, calm yourself, please!" said the

matron. "If you want to pass your tests, you need to focus."

The matron slapped two things on the table: a plain brown box and a roll of paper.

"Cartography!" she said. "You won't know that word, coming from the backward hills, but it means the science of maps. It wouldn't be a proper test, without maps."

"Because of her being the First Surveyor, not just the Girl with the Lourka," said Linny. She was watching the matron unlatch that box with a brisk twist of the fingers.

"Correct," said the matron, giving Linny a sidewise glance. "Sharpish, are you? Why did you blunder across the bridge, then, in such an inhospitable year, and such a young thing as you are?"

While she spoke, she was setting metal instruments out on the table, and then she unrolled a sheet of paper—fancy thin stuff, with little squares marked off very faintly all across it.

"There you are," said the matron. "The trainer will step you through it. I imagine it will all seem unusual to you, coming from so far off the grid as you do."

"I've seen a map before," said Linny.

The matron shot her another one of those pointed looks.

"Have you, then?" she said. "Odd girl, indeed. But good for you."

Linny remembered too late that she had not only stolen a glimpse of the Surveyors' map, but actually burned down their camp in the process, and blushed. She lowered her head quickly, to keep the blush private, and started examining the metal tools the matron had just finished setting out.

"What are those things?"

There was a hum in her brain when she saw them, like the hum that came over her when she worked on a lourka. A map might not look much like a lourka, but it called to Linny as a lourka did.

"The cartographer's kit," said the matron. "Compasses and rulers and suchlike. Some of what's necessary, to make a map the old-fashioned way. And they are to be treated with respect, the instruments, claimant. Maps are a serious business. Well, now you've only an hour to work, so off I go. Here are a few biscuits to help you focus. The trainer will set the questions for you. Tap the screen when you're ready for the next."

The matron flicked her hand against one of those glossy screen surfaces that had been pretending to be a blank picture in a frame. Apparently that screen was the trainer she kept mentioning. Linny had one of the biscuits and slipped a couple more into a pocket for later.

"Any questions?" said the matron.

Well, yes, many questions, but none of them were the

kind that the matron was likely to answer.

"I'll leave you to it, then," said the matron. "You still have fifty-seven minutes. Use them well, claimant."

And she left, locking the door very carefully behind her, which showed that trying to seem as harmless as a lamb only went so far, on this side of the river.

Fifty-seven minutes turned out to be not very much time. The trainer showed pictures of the tools on its glassy screen and explained how they might be used. It set little tasks: "Here's a tiny part of a make-believe city. Use the cartographer's kit to transfer the picture of it onto the grid-marked paper."

It woke up her brain, like drinking a mug of very strong tea. This was what the world looked like! And yes, of course, you could make that picture echo not only in your brain, like it did when you looked out from the top of a tall tree or suddenly got a view of the river and what was beyond the river—no, if you worked carefully, you could put that picture down on paper. No wonder those Surveyors had been so intent on their work, up in the hills!

Linny kept forgetting to breathe, her mind got so caught up in the three-way dialogue between her brain, her fingers, and the metal tools of the cartographer's kit. And every now and then a little silver bell would ring out, from wherever it hid behind the glassy expanse of the screen.

Then suddenly she looked up and realized the matron

had come back into the room without her even noticing.

"Well!" said the matron, examining the screen of the trainer. "That's quite extraordinary. I've never seen that before."

"Seen what?" asked Linny.

"The trainer claims you've actually passed that section! Did you do something to this machine?"

Linny shook her head.

"Must be a fluke, then," said the matron. "Never mind. A healthy bedtime snack for you now, and then sleep. Tomorrow's the rest of the tests, and then the fair."

Linny blinked at the instruments in her hand, at the matron setting down a not-very-interesting plate of something on her food tray. So it really was like being in her workshop in the woods, way up in the wrinkled hills: maps and lourkas, not so different in flavor, if you were Linny. For a long moment, a very long moment, she had actually forgotten everything else in the world.

"I advise you to sleep now and not to fret overmuch," said the matron. "Fretting blurs the brain. Put it out of your mind for the night. After all, in recent times it's always been a lark for the claimants to come over here and eat their biscuits and parade about the fair for a bow and a laugh."

"A lark!" said Linny, trying to fight back the shiver of anger that rose up in her. "If I fail, they want to kill me. That's what they said."

"Not a lark this year, no, of course not. But we must put everything into its historical context, mustn't we? Long ago it was also very serious, the judging of the claimants. Deeper and darker. I've heard the historians speak on the subject, how the girls went into the dark and didn't come out—"

That wasn't turning into the comforting speech the matron had probably had in mind. She stopped in the middle of a sentence, peered closely at Linny, and shook her head.

"It all seems very hard, I must say. Well, good night and good luck to you. Whatever happens, I suppose we've done what we could."

And out she went through the doubled door, the old and the new, and the doors both slapped shut behind her.

For a few desperate minutes Linny just sat there, trying to think her way out of this box with no exits. She did not yet really believe there was no way out. Linny had always been stubborn that way, about not giving up. There are ways forward, and then when those ways are closed, there are other ways around, and when the trail breaks off or fades out, there are still other secret ways, always. That was Linny's approach. But this place right here had the most walls and closed doors she had ever experienced. Even without wolves or snakes, it was horrible.

As awful as this room was, however, she figured it had to be better than being cooped up in a tiny cage, like the poor Half-Cat. It was better than fading away to nothingness, up in the hills, like poor Sayra. It might even be better than having to run around dangerous places with the *madji*, like (as far as she knew) that lummox Elias was having to do. Those three thoughts braided themselves together: she would have to have courage. That was the only way.

All right, she thought. If she sat here like a good girl, maybe she could pass their stupid tests, whatever they were (and maybe not), and maybe if the tests went well, they would bring her medicines when she ordered them to in her bossiest queen-of-the-world voice (and maybe not)—but the Half-Cat couldn't wait. She would find Sayra's medicines somehow and sometime. She would. She had promised. But first there was the Half-Cat to save from the murderous lab men, if it hadn't yet been taken to pieces.

She took all the tools in the mapmaking kit, and she took the little carving knife from her lourka bag, and she went over to take a closer look at that other door, not the one she had come in by, and not the door hiding the indoor privy, but the mysterious, much-bolted old door at the other end of the room.

18

LOCKS AND LATCHES

Locks and latches were no match for someone with as many years' training in pilferage and lourka making as Linny had had. She used the mapmaking kit's sharp compass to jimmy open the simplest locks and whittled herself a key from a sliver of the door itself to get herself through the last one. It was a comfortable bit of work, almost like being at home and breaking into her father's workshop for the thousandth time.

But what she found beyond the door and all its latches was not like any workshop she had ever seen. As her eyes grew more accustomed to the dim evening light, she saw that the room, quite large, was filled with blocky cabinets, each holding a number of long, flat drawers, stacked one on top of the next. She slid open one of those drawers, and large sheets of paper lay there. She thought for a moment, running her fingertip over the old paper: this was the room that had belonged to the First Surveyor. It was hard to see anything properly, but these surely must be drawings or diagrams. Or maps.

What to do about the light, though? That was another thing Linny knew well enough. You can't take your winking candle into a space with windows and not expect someone in the village to notice. All the windows across the courtyard . . . they were sort of the Plain version of a village, Linny figured. Here it wasn't really question of a winking candle, because light came on when you pushed the round switch by the door, but to hit that switch would be like shouting her presence in this room to all lingering Surveyors who might be looking across that courtyard for some reason.

She scooted over to the outside windows and looked out for a moment at the second skin of more modern glass and all the ripply rectangles across the way. She was beginning to think she might have to carry each of those maps, one at a time, into the other room to look at them, when a string brushed against her cheek and turned out to be attached to thick curtains, rolling down and down. Somehow she had missed them in the dark. So she lowered the blinds, turned on the light, and got to work.

There was some sort of system to these drawers, but she didn't understand it. She did find that maps of one area or one type of place seemed to be filed together, so a glance at whatever was on top was enough to disqualify a whole drawer at one go.

Faster, she said when she started feeling tired.

There were maps with rivers on them, and maps of farms, and maps of structures she did not understand, but it was not until the twenty-seventh drawer that she finally found drawings of a building with an empty square place in the center. She took that stack over to the floor right under one of the brightest lights and went through it, sheet by sheet, doing her best to stack those sheets in order.

There were spaces marked LABS on the highest floor. She took very particular note of that. At the bottom of the stack were sheets much older than anything else she had seen, and with a simpler diagram. She looked at those pencil marks, looked up at the walls and windows around her, and her heart gave a little bounce of excitement: she was looking at the plans, the drawing—the *map*—for the very room she was in! There was the door into the other room, which had been turned into the claimants' dormitory all those years later. There was the unused fireplace over there, and the closet on that other wall; everything was here in this picture, once you knew how to read it properly. Now she went back a sheet and studied that one, and there it was, yes, the old building embedded in the new.

She looked at those sheets for what seemed like a very

long time, tracing all the important edges of things with a finger so that the memory would sink deeply into her brain. Then she put those maps away, slung her lourka bundle across her back, shut the old door between the map room and the dormitory, and crawled into the fireplace.

Linny knew that back home in the village, the oldest, largest houses had fireplaces with narrow toeholds in their chimneys, so that the lucky boy sent up to clean out clumps of soot would not be always "slipping down into supper," as Elias's mother liked to say. (Elias's house probably had the second-largest chimney in Lourka, after that of the floury baker.) This old, old house that the First Surveyor had built back in the distant past and that had been swallowed whole by the glass-and-metal Surveyors' Court later—it was almost like Elias's house, back in Lourka, wasn't it? And indeed, when she reached up with her hands into that chimney, she found the toeholds waiting there for her.

Thank you, she said to the First Surveyor, who had looked so much like Linny herself and who had also, to judge from her various portraits, loved a peculiar, wrinkled cat.

Still, it took an extra couple of seconds to gather the courage to start that climb up the dark chimney. She had to tease herself into it. *So silly to be afraid!* It would be just like climbing a tree, probably—only inside out.

That made her smile, and before the smile could leave her, she flung herself upward and started scrabbling for finger- and toeholds. A piece of good luck: the top of the chimney had only the flimsiest piece of wood covering it. It was no trouble at all pushing that up and away, so that she could scramble out of the chimney into this strange, strange space that the plans had suggested must be here.

There was a kind of crawl space—dim and shadowy, but not (thanks to the outer shell of windows) completely dark—between the roof of the swallowed-up old building and the next floor of the new one. The chimney had disgorged her right near the highest part of that roof, where it came very near to the messy underside of the next floor, and she clung to the ridge for a few moments, fending off two fears at once: the fear of being too high and too precarious, on a surface that sloped too steeply for comfort to either side, and also the fear that comes over a person when the ceiling of a cave lurks too close to her head, because up here on the roof ridge, the next floor was very close indeed.

But that's good, she reminded herself, and in the workroom of her mind she brought out all the maps she had just studied and looked them over until they blended perfectly with this bizarre place she found herself in. And then she found she could move again, and quite fast.

This next part was the trickiest, of course. Linny scooted along the roof ridge, eyeing the ceiling above her, where according to the maps, there should be a weak spot somewhere—there!

It was an old-fashioned hatch, just a square cut into the ceiling, presumably so that workers could reach this very space Linny was now in (though why would they ever need to?). She inched closer and then pushed up at the square with the palm of her hand, and to her relief, the hatch's cover shifted easily. No locks here! A moment later she had pulled herself into that next, much darker space, where she sat for a while, letting her heart stop pounding and clearing her mind again so that she could find her way properly. She was in the new building again now. Sitting where she was, she would never have guessed there was an old-fashioned house hidden beneath the floor if she hadn't just scrambled up through its chimney herself. She felt around that space, and yes, her hand bumped against the bottom step of a small staircase. Good. She slid the cover back over the hatch and started climbing the stairs, counting the levels as she went. The fifth level was the one she wanted. That's what the drawings had told her.

There was a door out of the stairwell that led into some kind of abandoned supply room, and a second door at the other side of that. She was just beginning to ease it open when light and sound stopped her. On the other side of that door, people were arguing as they wrestled with something—something that hissed and yowled and made scratching sounds.

"Strap it down!" said one voice.

"You think it's so easy?" said the other, and then there were more shouts and some swearing and the slam of a wire door.

Then a short pause.

"Well, how are we going to plug it in and get readings?"

"Sedate it."

"Readings won't be any good. *You* know that. And tomorrow morning they carve it all up. There won't be anything left."

"Do you know what time it is now? We should be home sleeping, not wrestling with monsters just because someone upstairs gets a sudden clever idea."

Another silence.

"Oh, just wrinkle it all," said the second man again—and that was something Linny had never heard before, "wrinkle" used as a curse! "Give me the lab book."

Scribbling sounds. A gasp and a smothered laugh.

"They'll figure out you faked it."

"No way. I told you, the cat's being carved up tomorrow. How will they ever know?"

"You're nuts. I'm leaving. And you know what? If anyone ever asks me, I left already ten minutes ago—"

And then there was a flurry of hurried sounds, more bickering, and the light went off (except for a faint green glow), and doors were slammed farther away, and everything was still again.

Linny waited in her hiding place, breathing in and breathing out twenty times, to be safe, and then opened the door and pushed through a bunch of lab coats on hooks, right into a room filled with glowing machines, an ugly-looking table, and a cage with a lump's worth of cat in it.

"Hey there, you," she said quietly as she sprung open that cage, and the Half-Cat stepped out with the dainty nonchalance particular to cats, even cats who have just come very close to being strapped down, plugged in, and (Linny shuddered) eventually carved into pieces.

She pointed to the door she had crawled out of a few minutes earlier.

"Come on, let's go!"

They needed to get out of there right away. They needed to scram!

And in fact a door opened or closed, somewhere not nearly far enough away. And Linny heard footsteps.

She didn't wait another second. She stuffed the Half-Cat through the door into the little staircase area, and (sudden inspiration) grabbed one of those lab coats off its nail to take along.

"Now upstairs!" she told the Half-Cat, and gave it a push in the right direction. It sprang to the side, not wanting to be shoved, but then it trotted up the stairs at a good pace.

One . . . two . . .

The staircase ended in another small door, just as it was supposed to, according to those maps, and this door, without even a latch to its name, led out onto the roof.

They were supposed to sneak quietly across the roof to another, slightly larger staircase, and Linny felt a little foolish as she put on the stolen lab coat and picked up the Half-Cat, just to be cautious, but halfway across, the roof suddenly became a much louder place than she had expected. Alarm bells! Sirens! Emergency lights!

"This way! This way!" huffed Linny as she started to run.

And then the door into the second staircase wouldn't open! That was a bad moment. Linny had to drop the cat to fiddle with the latch. Her hands felt suddenly as clumsy as paws, but she twisted and jiggled, and to her infinite relief, the latch popped open. Not locked, after all—just a little bit rusted, like a latch on a gate back home.

She picked the Half-Cat back up and ran down this other staircase, which was larger and brighter and went down and down and down, all seven levels to the street. As she passed the doors, she could hear people pounding on them and generally making a racket, but she had no time to worry about anything but going down those endless stairs. At the bottom of the staircase was an actual exterior door, and when Linny poked her nose out, she saw the most wonderful thing: an empty street, and no one nearby. It was amazing. It was incredible.

The Half-Cat jumped from Linny's arms, and Linny followed it out into the square shadows of Angleside at night.

19

ESCAPING INTO THE DARK

Linny was moving so fast at that point that she was several streets away from the Surveyors' Court before she realized that the Half-Cat was no longer padding along at her side. It had sprinted off somewhere, she guessed. Linny felt a little pang of hurt, and then set it aside. You couldn't expect gratitude from a cat. And at least nobody would be carving it up in the morning. That was definitely the main thing.

While she leaned her head against the nearest wall and caught her breath, she noticed how quiet the world was on this side of the river. True, there was a faint jangle from the Surveyors' Court alarms, already far behind her. But apart from that, stillness.

At night in Bend there had been noises: people laughing, people singing snatches of rough music, cats or dogs or men fighting, something icky being thrown from some window into the street with a squelching *squerch*, shouts, whistles, rumbles. . . . But here on the Angleside, even with the quiet jangle of the alarms in the distance, it was quieter than the village of Lourka in the middle of the night, where at least there were the calls of night birds and the snuffly noises people and animals make when they rest. But these Anglesiders! They had maybe even figured out how to sleep without snoring.

She almost laughed at that thought, but at that moment a small shadow jumped out at her and hissed.

"Oh, *now* you're back!" she said to the small shadow. "You made me worry!"

At that very moment, a bigger shadow loomed up out of the darkness behind the small one.

Linny was already running away when she made sense of the thing the big shadow had just whispered at her: her name.

She whirled around, and the two shadows came up to meet her, the larger one not as silent as a person should be when sneaking around a woods or a Plain or a town at night—just like a clumsy oaf.

"Elias!" said Linny, remembering to say it very quietly.

"Oh, Linny, thank all goodness, I found you!" huffed Elias, and then it was as if the many words he'd been saving up since the magician dragged him away just came spilling out—a hushed flood of words, like a creek slipping past in the dark: "I heard you'd been taken! They saw something from the other side of the river! And I was crazy with worry, and they wouldn't tell me much, but then I volunteered for something they needed doing over here so I could come rescue you. And look, now I've done it! I've done it! Linny, you wouldn't believe how you have them all sweating nails, back on our side of the river. They said you walked into a trap, going into that Bridge House! But I've got you now! How'd you get that white coat thing? I almost didn't recognize you. That cat popped out of nowhere a minute ago and was showing me how to go—"

The smaller shadow preened a little in the dark, and the diffuse light that the moon made when filtered by the clouds glittered silver in one of its eyes and golden in the other.

"Oh!" said Linny. "The Half-Cat is the cleverest cat I ever saw. I bet it caught your scent in the air. I didn't even know cats could do that. But how did *you* escape?"

"I told you. I'm not escaped. I'm on a mission. But first I came to rescue you. Which I guess I've done!"

"No, you did not," said Linny, in a slightly louder whisper. "You keep saying that, but if you want to know the actual truth, I rescued myself."

The Half-Cat gave an impatient whistle and started padding off along the street.

"Where's it going now?" said Elias.

"I guess it wants to get us somewhere where we'll be safe. It seems to know what it's doing."

"Don't know about safe," he said. "But we need to get you well out of here. And then across the river somehow."

They were moving deeper into Angleside now, the river somewhere to their left side and rows of square buildings all around them shining slightly in the misty night.

"I can't go back yet," said Linny. "I don't have the medicines. My Auntie Mina's being kept in some research hub, deep in the Plain. I've got to find her so I can get the stuff for Sayra."

"On into the Plain? Don't be ridiculous!" said Elias. "After I went to all this trouble to save you? Listen, it's the start of the fair tomorrow morning. There will be all sorts of crowds here. It's perfect. You can just blend in with everyone else, and then wander away at the end of the day, simple as simple, back to the hills."

"Not me," said Linny. "For one thing, I can't blend in anywhere. But Elias, that's maybe what *you* should do. To get away from the *madji*. And then I'll go on to Mina and get the medicines from her—"

"You can't trust Surveyors," said Elias.

"Right. But Auntie Mina doesn't count. She's my mother's sister. Mama wouldn't have sent me to her if she thought—"

"They're all evil," said Elias. "You don't know how

215

things are. They're trying to ruin the whole world. I have to do what I can to stop that. I promised. It's bigger than just what we want. They'll put the whole world on their grid and undo every last wrinkle. You know how bad it feels, on this side of the river."

Linny was taken aback. Did it really feel bad, over here? Certainly being locked in a room had felt bad, but then that had been awful on the other side of the river, too. Elias had that suffering look on his face, though—a more intense version of the suffering look he had had ever since they came down out of the hilliest parts of the hills. Unwrinkled places made Elias unhappy. But apparently Linny could travel through wrinkled and unwrinkled places, and feel just fine anywhere.

"*Nothing* feels right over here, on the Plain side of the darn river," he was saying now. "We can't let them ruin the whole world. That's why I went with the *madji*. That's why I volunteered today. What happens to Lourka, if the Surveyors ruin everything everywhere? Don't you see? It's Sayra I'm thinking of, back there. And everybody."

Linny found herself feeling oddly embarrassed; she missed the trees and birds and so on, but the bitterness in Elias's words right now was almost an accusation. Did he love the wrinkled country more than she did?

No, thought Linny first.

Maybe, thought Linny, a moment later. If hating the

Plain meant you loved the wrinkled places more. He was much better than she was at hating the Plain.

But mapmaking feels a little like making a lourka, she thought. Your whole mind and body, focused on the details of things: carving this bit just exactly so, making the map's lines meet up just exactly there. She couldn't settle the question, so she sidestepped herself away.

"It's not like you had a choice about going with the *madji*," she said instead. "What do you mean by 'volunteered'? And where the heck is that cat taking us, anyway?"

They had been following the Half-Cat for quite a while already. The sky was beginning to gray up in the east; even this long night would eventually end. Now, however, the cat was climbing a street that went up a little hill. Just because it was the Plain side of the river didn't mean that everything over here was flat. Linny and Elias followed the Half-Cat, and Elias huffed and puffed a little extra loud, to make the point that that he couldn't answer difficult questions while he was working so hard.

At the top of the hill was an area with grass and little square benches made of stone and larger rectangular shapes made of hedges that had been forced with scissors and clippers to abandon the ordinary wild shapes of growing things. This was the Angleside idea of a park, Linny guessed. But she was not wasting too much attention on the brick-like hedges, because the hill dropped off, past a geometrical balustrade, and there was one of those views of the broader world (though all in grays and shadows still, it being so early in the new day) that filled the nooks and crannies of Linny's hungry soul.

They had come quite a long way from the Surveyors' Court, apparently, for there was yet another bridge across the river, a bridge that Linny had not seen before. The river ran a little narrower again here, and the bridge spanning it was very old and massive and thick—no lightness to it at all—as if a baby giant had built it thousands of years ago, using giant-size blocks. Each foot of the bridge was surrounded by a large space, cluttered with wagons and little tents and displays and fountains.

The Half-Cat purred.

On long days in the woods, back when they were younger, Linny and Sayra used to make little villages together out of twigs and bark and leaves and flowers. From this hill, that's what the spaces on either side of the bridge looked like, with their wagons and tents and displays—two miniature worlds blossoming along a curve of dark water.

The world on this side of the river had more right angles to it, and the glint of glass here and there responded to beams of bright light from hand-carried lanterns. On the far side of the river, everything was dimmer in the gray, but specks of candlelight flickered like distant stars, and the paths between the booths were so twisted as to be more or less invisible, while extravagant shapes (trees? balloons?) loomed here and there.

Dark shapes wandered through the cluttered spaces, holding lanterns or candles or lamps, depending on what side of the river they were on, and those dark shapes were people, setting things up and testing things and even calling out to each other.

"It's the fairgrounds," said Elias.

No kidding, thought Linny.

They had already slipped down low behind the balustrade, to keep out of sight.

"There's the Bend side and the Angleside of the fair," said Elias. "The *madji* explained it all to me. Once every ten years it happens, and they open up the bridge there, and people come and go freely across it. See that old platform thing halfway across?"

There was a kind of stone house or stage sticking up in the center of the bridge, but you could see the nighttime ghosts of people walking back and forth across the bridge on either side of it.

"That's where the Girls with Lourkas—not real ones, of course—usually do their funny puppet-maze thing. They told me about that, too. It's all part of the fair."

Linny looked at him, but his face was lost in shadow.

"What funny puppet-maze thing?"

"It's like a joke almost, I think. They have pretend Girls with Lourkas who pretend to do some sort of pretend test. Getting a puppet through a labyrinth? Sounds pretty dumb, right? I guess it all used to be more real long ago. But now they just do silly stuff, and everyone laughs."

"Not this time," said Linny with grim satisfaction. They wouldn't be able to say she had failed their stupid tests! No, she was *gone*. "Nobody for them to laugh at this year. They made it against the law to wear one of those costumes, so the girls will all have stayed in Bend. And I ran away. And I hope the fair is boring for everyone—serves them right. Hey, what's that?"

Out ahead of them, the river made its second great curve, this time away from the wrinkled hills and toward the Plain. Moreover, just beyond the fairgrounds and to the right, the water ran right into what looked like a great metallic wall, stretching all the way across the river.

"Waterworks," said Elias, and he said it with great disgust. "That's where they ruin all our water, before it heads any deeper into the Plain."

"Really? They ruin water?"

Linny was trying to think how water could be ruined. You could drop something very nasty into a well, of course. You could make it undrinkable that way. And for an icky moment, she imagined workers dropping garbage into the river, behind that sleek and daunting wall.

"They unwrinkle it," said Elias. "They take the magic and the flavor out."

"Oh," said Linny. "So water in the Plain hasn't got any flavor?"

She felt sorry for everyone living in the Plain, if so.

"They don't *like* things to have flavor. They're hardly like real people at all. That's just part of their awful plan, though."

"What awful plan?"

"They mean to put all of the wrinkled country on their horrible grid and unwrinkle us. And we can't let that happen. *That's* why I'm—"

The Half-Cat gave a sharp hiss. Some of the lights below them were now turning to cast their beams up the little hill, at the balustrade Linny and Elias were hiding behind.

"Don't move," said Elias in a murmur that was quieter than a whisper. He didn't have to say anything, though, because Linny had already frozen, very small, behind one of the thicker pillars of the balustrade.

The light came spilling through the slats of the balustrade, washing back and forth, and Linny could hear the voices that belonged to those lights: "Did you see that? Something's up there."

Her heart pounded.

The Half-Cat had leaped back, away from the light, and now it was scratching away furiously at the part of the little hill closest to them. There was already more light in the air. The hill was a darker, more complicated tangle of grays against the paler gray of the sky. And where the Half-Cat was scrabbling at the hillside, there was now a patch darker even than the rest of that dark hill.

"Nuts," said Elias. "They're coming up. They can't find me. I can't have them find me."

"*You!*" said Linny. Here she'd almost gotten used to thinking of Elias as a reformed human being and much less of a selfish lummox than he used to be back in the hills.

"If they find me, they'll just kill us both," said Elias, and for a second he pulled the flaps of his jacket back, and Linny saw the magician's disorder bombs, tucked in rows along the inside of his jacket. "I'm on a delivery run."

"Oh, no," she said. The wrongness of those canisters! "What are you *doing*?"

"You hide yourself, Linny. I've got to go, or the whole thing will be spoiled."

And he didn't wait around for Linny to ask more questions or to see her find a safe place to hide, or anything. Suddenly he just sprinted away into the deeper darkness.

There were shouts from the people with the lights, and Linny heard them start to run up the slope.

The horror of everything—of the horrible canisters Elias was carrying around with him, of the gray people coming up the hill now to capture her again—was a hole as dark as midnight, and Linny was teetering at the edge of it. If she fell in, she would never be able to climb out again, or maybe even to move—that's how she felt. But even on the edge of hopelessness, Linny felt the swift, sharp urge to run away spread through her like fire. To run away and hide! She looked around to see where hiding might best be done.

That was one of her wrinkles, hiding.

The Half-Cat meowed at her. Where was it? She couldn't quite see where it had gone, but as she scanned the small hill over there, she thought she saw, peeking through the tangle of vines, a suggestion of midnight darkness, a hollow in the side of the small hill, as dark as despair.

That was enough. Linny sprinted across the grass, back away from the balustrade toward what was left of the hill. She stayed very low to the ground, which is an awkward way of running, but the voices called out again. They had seen something—Linny at the balustrade or Elias scooting away. Linny stayed low and ran.

She caught glimpses of things she hadn't noticed

before, as she hurtled toward the hollow in the little hill: stone carvings crawling up the sides of the hill, all somewhat obscured by vines and plants, but obviously old. It hardly looked like something that belonged in Angleside at all. And then she was flinging herself backward, right into that hollow that the Half-Cat had discovered. She slid her legs in first and reached out afterward to pull the vines loose again, so that they hung down over the entrance to her hiding place, at least as much as could be done.

She lay there very still, willing her breath to slow down and become less noisy, willing the people coming up the hill to go another way. Trying not to think of Elias, not right at this moment, because if the horror came back and swallowed her while she was hiding in this hole, she did not think she would be able to keep from crying, and crying is noisy.

20

DEEPER AND DARKER

Thank goodness the hiding place had turned out to be deep enough to hide the whole of her! As the sounds of hurrying feet and dabs of bright un-candlelight came nearer to her, she scrabbled backward a little deeper into that deep—surprisingly deep—hole in the hill.

Then a boot came right up to the entrance of her hole. She could see the heel of it, filtered through those dangling vines. Linny's heart threatened to drum itself right out of her poor chest.

His boot's pointed sideways, she told her frightened heart. Linny knew you had to be very stern with yourself sometimes, when fear starts threatening to take over. *Sideways, so he can't see me hiding.*

"Must have been *madji*," said a voice, and there was the unpleasant sound of someone spitting in disgust. "They're everywhere, these days. Like rats."

Linny kept backing away from the entrance, a stolen,

quiet hand's length at a time.

"Rats on a rat hill," said another voice. "Just look at this place! Don't they clear out rat nests anymore in this part of town?"

And to Linny's horror, that booted foot came crashing right through the screen of vines. Keeping her stomach low, she snake-scrambled her way backward roughly enough that the rocks scraped against her legs and elbows.

"Hey, look!" said the man. "There's an actual rathole here. For extra-large rats, to judge from the size of it."

Linny's heart thudthudded so loudly she thought it must be audible to all of them. *Back, back, back!* The man was bending down, you could tell from the sound of his voice. Any second now he would take that unnatural, unforgiving light of his and shine it right in through those vines, and Linny's hiding place would have failed her—

But at that moment something warm and furry came racing forward across Linny's back, and before she had time to scream out herself (those men had been talking about rats! She was being walked on by *rats*!), all possible noises were drowned out by the mewling yowl of an angry, spitting Half-Cat flinging itself right into the bright light ahead. So it was the younger man with the boot, and fortunately not Linny, who broke the general hush by shouting out in surprise. And then the other man laughed, not very nicely (and all the while Linny scooted herself back, back, back—it was amazing how far back this hole kept going), so that there was a distracting muddle of sounds from outside: shouts and curses and laughter and those awful noises a cat can make when it's angry, like a demonic child screeching and hissing in the night.

"*Cats*, not *rats*!" said one of the men outside. "Hoo, what a spitfire! Weird looking, isn't it? Come here, you wildcat. . . ."

This was the moment when the ground vanished from under Linny's feet. Since she was more or less lying on her stomach in that tunnel, she didn't fall right away. She waved her legs about, feeling for the slope of the tunnel, and she felt around with her hands for outjutting rocks to hold on to while her legs looked for solid ground to rely on.

But a half second later, when the Half-Cat came plunging back into the tunnel and unsettled Linny's arms, which should have been holding on to those rocks for dear life, she started slipping backward like nobody's business, and the ground gave way under all of her, and there was the loudish noise earth gives when something heavy is sliding down it, and she was actually falling now, into some deep hole in the ground—and she fell and fell until she hit ground again, with a thumping wallop, and then, for a thin slice of time, she knew nothing at all.

Nothing.

Time started again. She opened her eyes and saw . . . more nothing.

That was perhaps the worst moment of her life so far, to be buried in darkness that way. She had never liked being stuck in dark places, not places where you couldn't see the lay of the land or figure out where you were. Panic surged through her. She flailed her arms around and immediately discovered one or two important things:

—She was on her side, resting in what seemed like a tunnel with an earthen floor.

—There was enough room around her for her to flail her arms around in. That immediately took the screaming edge off her fear. She was not *buried* in earth. She was simply in some unknown underground space. (She told herself these things with as much conviction as she could possibly muster.) She was still, after all, able to breathe. And (she kicked her legs out a little) her bones were not broken, despite the fall she had just had.

But there was a third important thing, and that thing was now purring and pushing its soft and furry back under her hand and licking her cheek with a very rough tongue: the Half-Cat was here with her. *Thank goodness.*

"Thank goodness," she said again, right out loud. She felt so shaky in her relief that the words wobbled all around. And then she understood from the way the out-loud words wobbled that there was more space here than she had thought. She reached a hand straight up, as high as it could go, and ran into nothing but air. *Aha!* She pulled herself into a sitting position, and instantly felt much better; panic backs off a little when your head is above the rest of you. Now she knew where up and down were. That was a good first step. But she kept one hand on the reassuringly warm fur of the Half-Cat all the time.

She blinked her eyes and squinted, but the dark stayed dark.

"Ugh!" she said aloud. "What I need is a candle! I need light."

And that was when the Half-Cat *turned on one of its eyes.*

The sudden beam of light was so shockingly bright in that unimaginably dark place that Linny squawked in surprise and covered her own eyes with her hands. But only for a second, and then she peeked, amazed, at the transformed darkness, at the tunnel walls now appearing around her, at the Half-Cat with its impossible, glaring, brilliant eye.

It was its silver-side eye that had turned into a spotlight; Linny could just make out the faint glimmer of the golden eye beside it.

How could a cat cast a beam of light with its eye?

It was not the sort of light a creature in the wrinkled hills would have anything to do with, either. Linny had seen mushrooms glow red or orange in the middle of the night, in the woods around Lourka. She had caught glimpses of night birds with flaming chests sailing like jewels across the sky. She had certainly watched lantern fish swim figure eights in the creek in summer. But there was nothing wrinkled about this light. It was harder and cooler than anything you'd find up in the hills. It was more like the light in some of those rooms in the Surveyors' Court.

"Is that one of the things he tinkered with, the man in the Bridge House?" Linny said to the cat, and touched its head shyly, with one outstretched finger. The Half-Cat did not flinch.

Linny was waking up again, finally. She looked around at the tunnel she was in—so much larger than the rathole she had first hidden in. This tunnel looked like something people had made, and it went along into the dark in two directions. Above her head was the hole in the ceiling she must have tumbled out of, a few minutes earlier, and right there on the ground near her was the poor lourka, still cocooned in its bag. She picked it up quickly and took a look. There were some little scratches on its sides, but considering the tumble it had just experienced, the lourka seemed to have come through even better than its maker. So that made her happy. She twanged a couple of strings, to encourage herself, and then slung the bag over her back, heaved a sigh, and started looking around that dark place, assessing the situation she was in.

At first glance, that situation was not so great. Linny could see no way to climb back up the way she had come falling down, for instance. Even if she stood right up, her head would be a little lower than the opening of that hole. She was going to have to try the tunnel she was in, in one direction or another. Linny stood there for a moment, looking first down one direction of that tunnel, then down the other, and let her body and brain tell her which way she was looking: one direction ran back under the little hill; the other went toward the steep slope that led, eventually, down to the fairgrounds.

Linny crouched down and went that way.

All too soon, there was another choice to make. The tunnel she was in bent sharply to the left, skirting an inky-dark hole in the ground. When the Half-Cat poked its head helpfully over the edge for a moment, Linny caught a glimpse of metal bars running down the side of that hole—a ladder of sorts, she guessed. Linny looked down the tunnel to the left and looked down the tunnel with the ladder, and although the top several layers of her mind wondered why anyone would ever go *farther* underground, given the choice, there was something about how the air smelled in the tunnel to the left that she didn't care for. The slightest whiff of something moist and decayed came from that direction. Air that had never heard of the sun.

Whereas, kneeling by the hole in the tunnel floor, she thought she sensed a liveliness in the air, as if it were coming from somewhere in particular. Maybe even the outside? Could her mind be playing tricks on her?

It took more courage than she really felt, but Linny turned right around and reached with her leg for the first rung of the ladder.

This was maybe the way through this nightmare, and she needed to get through, because Sayra was still waiting for the medicines to save her, somewhere far away. *Sayra!*

The Half-Cat gave a little yowl and leaped down onto Linny's shoulders. *Oof!* It was pretty miraculous she didn't just fall down into darkness again right then.

She steadied herself and started climbing down that ladder, being very careful never to put all her weight on any one of those rungs, because who could say how old they must be? And down she went, with the cat making her shoulders ache and the bag with the wrapped-up lourka in it bouncing along on her back.

Down and down and down. The first few minutes were frightening but tolerable. After five minutes, though, she began to get nervous. How far down could this ladder go? Another ten minutes, and her hands were trembling, not to mention her brain rebelling some. She was quite sure she must be below the level of the plain she and Elias had looked out at from the balustrade edging the park. She had a moment of horror, imagining this climb never ever ending, her hands and feet reaching for new rungs in this ladder forever and ever.

But as she paused to shake out her tired hands and feet (one at a time), she took a few breaths and again got that sense of fresh air somewhere far ahead, and again thought she must be going the right way. And then her foot could not find another rung, and when she looked past her feet, she saw the vertical chute was ending, and it was time to drop down to the floor of another tunnel.

"Here we go," she said to the Half-Cat, and the cat jumped off her shoulders and down to the tunnel floor with a solid *thump*.

Linny dangled for a moment and then followed suit.

It was nowhere as long a fall as her first tumble had been, and again immediately there was another choice, right or left (Linny sniffed the air and decided left, because the air there smelled a little bit more like the outdoors, like a river), and after that a whole series of choices, as more and more tunnels opened out from the main one.

Only once Linny did not use that inner sense of hers

to decide which way to go. She overruled it and turned to the right, because the tunnel looked smoother, somehow, or maybe just to be foolish. But as she crouched and crawled down that tunnel, the Half-Cat following her, the darkness outside the Half-Cat's one beaming eye grew darker and heavier with each of her steps, and panic began to rise up in her—and, strange to think now, all this time since the very first terrible moment after her fall, she had not felt fear like this, despite being so far underground and in the dark. She forced herself to keep going a few more steps, but the feeling grew more and more oppressive, until she stopped and fell to her knees, panting while her fingers scraped at the ground in front of her.

Which was not a good idea, because there was a puddle in the ground.

Water, greasy.

No, not just water—something foul and slimy. Something her hand sprang back from automatically in disgust.

That was enough for her. She turned around and made her way blindly back to the main tunnel, trying not to let her panic show, because it seemed to her the darkness behind her might at any moment become so thick it took on a life of its own, and if that darkness came to life and came after her, she was pretty sure it would have sharp claws and dull, grinding teeth.

Once she got back to the tunnel she'd come from, she had to crouch very small and let herself tremble for a while. She had had no idea how close she had been to horror, all this time, and now fear had gotten its fingers into her.

The Half-Cat pushed its nose into her hand, and that helped clear her mind.

"We need to get out of here now," she said to the cat, trying to get her courage back. "No more nonsense."

After that, every time Linny found herself at an intersection, she let her body tell her which way faced the river, so that she knew where she was, and then she tested the air in each of the choices, to see which smelled best. If it was really "smelling," what she was doing.

All she knew was that each time some of the choices smelled bad. They filled her with horror. Even when the Half-Cat turned its shining eye down those tunnels, they felt dark to her, darker than dark.

The roof of the tunnels was getting lower again, though. She was on hands and knees now, trying not to feel the weight of the earth above her, trying not to think about what would happen to her if there was no end to this journey, if she were really buried underground.

Another one of those intersections came, and this time for a horrible moment she had no idea which way to go.

Maybe a dozen tunnels came together here: tunnels, tunnels, all around, and at first none of them smelled right. It was the thoughts getting stirred up in her head that were distracting her, Linny figured. She made herself stay very still and quiet, counting to one hundred under her breath and then holding on even longer, not counting. Finally she found it: the thinnest possible thread of freshness, coming from an opening so small that her mind had tried to skitter right by it.

The air coming from that narrow gash of a tunnel smelled just the tiniest bit like a river, or rather, like the banks of a river. She crouched by the entrance for a while, testing the air and weighing her courage. It was so dark and so small!

A few moments later, a puff of air came through that hole that actually lifted Linny's grimy hair from around her forehead. *All right,* she decided. *This must be the way.*

It was an awful thing, though, entering that tunnel.

She had to slither on her belly, if she didn't want the poor lourka on her back scratched or damaged. Already she was so grimy from tunnel dirt that a little extra mud could hardly cause any trouble.

But it was still hard to lie down and scrabble her way forward. Human beings are not earthworms, and Linny was even more not an earthworm than most human beings: she liked being outside, perched in some tall tree, looking across the bright green world. . . .

She sighed. The world was still out there. She just had to be brave and keep moving and not think about the undergroundness of everything.

"Come on, cat," she said. "Here we go."

She had a brief but terrible moment, as she flattened herself out against the muddy ground, of imagining the cat turning around and walking off, as cats will do, taking its warmth and its tinkered eye away, leaving her forever in the dark.

But the Half-Cat purred and followed her into that low and narrow place as if there were no more natural place to be, for a girl and a cat, than in a tiny, damp, gloomy, earthy, miserable, horrible tunnel underground.

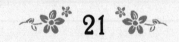

21

DOORS AND KEYS

The only way Linny managed to push her way into that dank tunnel was by stopping thinking altogether, just at least until she was well into it and moving along, propelled by muddy elbows and toes. The Half-Cat purred at her side, and its radiant search-beam eye made the way ahead brighter than the darkness behind, and that was another thing that kept Linny moving. That, and the air, which there seemed to be more of, the farther Linny crawled. That was really the secret to being able to crawl ahead in the dark at all. She kept gulping in great dollops of that air, testing it. If the air began to feel scarce, she just knew the panic would burst out of the tight corner in her chest where she was keeping it all locked up. That would be it for her. She wouldn't be able to go forward or crawl backward or do anything but hide in the dark mud and—

The Half-Cat squeezed itself between Linny and the

238

tunnel wall, nipped her ear, and hissed.

Oh, right! Linny realized she had stopped moving for a moment. That was no good. When there is darkness all around, you have to keep moving. That is key.

A couple of minutes later, the light from the Half-Cat's eye hit something ahead and scattered. For one dreadful instant Linny thought she had come to the end of the tunnel, and the end was a stone wall. But then she raised her head a little, and saw what might be a broad step carved into the stone. And when the Half-Cat jumped over her arm and walked ahead a few paces, illuminating the place as it turned its half-golden, half-silver head from side to side, Linny realized that the dreadful wormhole she had been slithering through was spilling her now into an open space, very large in comparison with the wretched burrows she was coming from—more like a room than a tunnel.

She crawled out from the narrow hole in the ground and took a few very deep breaths in relief. For a moment she had her face buried in her grimy hands, and her breath was coming and going in sobs. Then she was able to open her eyes.

Right before her was a wide but quite low-ceilinged stairway, made of stone. In fact, the whole tunnel ahead stopped looking like something only earthworms and moles could appreciate and became a thing built by actual people. Built with care, even.

She was already standing up on what turned out to be a pair of very shaky legs. She put a hand on the stone wall beside the staircase, just to convince herself it was really there and to steady herself, and all the while her mind was taking a kind of inventory of the spaces surrounding her: registering the dampness of the air, the smell of old rivers, all the twists and turns and plunging drops she had just made her way through.

"Where are we, kitty?" she turned to ask the Half-Cat—and then she started shaking again, because what she saw clearly when she turned around was the awful little hole she had just crawled out of. No human being should ever be in a hole like that. Linny couldn't imagine—she could not understand—how she had ever, ever, ever managed to enter something as dark and narrow as that hole. She must have been crazy there, for a moment, she thought. But one thing was clear: she could never go back that way.

She started climbing the stairs.

The stone roof above kept threatening to graze the top of her head, and Linny was not particularly tall. It all felt very old and massive and silent, and as she climbed, the weight of the air in that place changed. Linny paused to make sense of the difference—she no longer felt so buried underground. Was it just the relief of being on an actual staircase again?

The people who had built this place long ago also liked

to carve things into their walls. Linny hadn't noticed right away, because her attention had been on the stairs she was climbing. But along the stone wall on her left side ran a set of straight carved lines; on the right, a complicated stone tangle, which must have been quite difficult to carve.

Linny climbed up the stairs, letting her fingers run along the carvings on the walls, first the tangled lines, and then the straight ones. It was so lovely to have something more solid under her hands than earth. And lovely to be climbing up again. And lovely beyond description not to be in that horrible tiny wormhole of a tunnel anymore.

The stairs started steep and then flattened out. Then the Half-Cat blinked, and out of that quick dip into blackness something—someone—seemed to jump into focus on the stairs ahead. Linny heard herself squeak and felt herself wobble, but when she had steadied herself and looked up again, she felt glad Elias wasn't there to call her a fool.

It wasn't a person. How could it have been a person, as silent and white as that?

It was not a person but a statue, its pale stone head almost grazing the stone ceiling, and the straight lines on the left and the tangled lines on the right ran from the walls across the tunnel ceiling, only to dip down into the statue's shoulders, becoming something like a pair of endlessly long and mismatched wings, tangled and angular, wrinkled and Plain.

The statue had a stone lourka slung across one shoulder and a sheet of stone paper marked with lines and numbers draped across her other arm. She had Linny's hair and Linny's nose. And she held out her stone hands almost beseechingly, one cupped in the other, and from the hands dangled something that wasn't made of stone at all.

It was a medium-large ring of some kind of silvery metal that apparently did not tarnish, even when left in tunnels for hundreds of years. From it dangled an old-fashioned key, not very large and (unlike the ring it hung from) dark with age, and another little strip of nubby metal as shiny as if it had been born yesterday, covered with odd lines and raised dots.

She ran her fingertip over those bumps and then lifted the key ring right off those stone hands as easily as she might have grabbed a coat from a coat hook.

"This means there's going to be a door!" she said cheerfully to the Half-Cat. She ducked around the statue and looked up the stairs. A surge of encouragement had lifted her hopes.

Then she stopped.

In front of her was not one door, but two. Nearly

identical and side by side, and above them were two words chiseled into the stone. They weren't too hard to read. They said, WHICH WAY?

Linny snorted. *Which way?* She didn't care which way, as long as it led out. And she had the key in her hand, didn't she? One of those doors would have to answer to that key. That's how stories work. If there's a key, and a door, then the key *opens the door*. Anything else would be ridiculous.

The doors were almost exactly the same: stone doors with a keyhole where a more ordinary door might have a knob. The blackened key slipped easily enough into the keyhole on the right, but it refused to turn. But the other door's keyhole, just a smidge closer to the edge of the slab, was formed very differently and wouldn't take the key at all.

Linny was not an idiot when it came to locks and doors. Keys don't necessarily have to look like keys. So she tried the bumpy, shiny piece of metal in the left-hand door, and there was a glorious moment when it slipped home, smooth as silk. That was where it belonged.

But it wouldn't turn either!

She spent a long time moving from door to door and jiggling keys in locks, trying to catch whatever balky part of the mechanism was refusing to recognize its own key, but nothing came of that. Then she brought out the few small tools she had nabbed from the cartographer's kit and tried to pick those locks, first the one on the right, then the left, but these doors would have none of that. A long time later, she had tried all the tricks she knew, and by the end she was exhausted, and the doors were as closed as ever.

She went back down the steps a little ways and rested for a while with her back against the back of that statue. What the heck was going on with those stupid doors? How could you hand someone a key—no, *two* keys—and then not make sure the keys even worked?

Maybe the old mechanisms in those locks had rusted to pieces. Then she was doomed. Because she would not, she could not, go back into the earthworm tunnel. She could not go back.

The Half-Cat rested with her awhile, wandered up to sniff the doors, returned to Linny's side, roamed off again.

Linny watched it come and go, and she was so tired her eyes sometimes saw one cat and sometimes saw two cats in front of those doubled doors.

The doors were so like each other. They were really as like as could be. When Linny tried the eye-crossing trick with them as she slumped back against the statue, they shivered toward each other, ran into each other, clicked into focus as *one* door, denser and more mysterious looking than either had been on its own.

She let her eyes relax back into the usual way of see-ing: two doors. The Half-Cat rubbed its head against her elbow and started up the shallow stairs again.

Her heart was pounding as if it thought she had fig-ured something out.

She sat up taller, clenching the key ring in her hand, and tried it again. The world blurred; the doors slipped toward each other, closer, closer—and snapped into focus. One door. One extremely doorlike door, deeper and denser than any ordinary door, and with, she saw now, two keyholes, flickering a little, side by side.

It was an illusion, but it was all she had.

She stood up carefully, not letting her eyes lose their new focus. One door. Two keyholes.

She walked up the steps, taking it slow. And at the edges of her vision, the Half-Cat walked beside her.

Here's the strange thing: there was only one door now, not two, but the Half-Cat had doubled. Linny was quite sure she saw the shadowy gray echo of a cat on her left, and another, brighter shadow trotting along on her right. She had to will herself not to look away at the Half-Cat, to see what the trick was, because if she looked away, she would lose the door. And she was feeling, more and more, that *this* was the door she needed. This impossible door.

Even quite close to it, the illusion persisted. She held the keys on their ring out in front of her, and without looking directly at either keyhole, she used both of her hands to slip both of those keys into the keyholes right next to each other, in this impossible door.

And the keys turned.

And the door swung open.

Here everything became strange for a few moments. She stumbled through the door, not letting the keys out of her hands, and on both sides of her, the Half-Cat strode through, too, as cool as can be: a cat gleaming golden on one side of her, and a cat as silver as a mirror on the other. She felt right, and she felt peculiar, and then the cats flowed into each other and became one cat, and behind her the door closed with a bang, and when she jumped around to look, she found herself facing a blank wall, with no doors visible in it at all.

But that didn't matter, because all around her now was everything a person could ever have wanted from the world: sweet, unburied air.

22

THE GIRL FROM UNDERGROUND

She breathed in great, greedy gulps. So much air! And noise! And, most amazing of all, *light*!

There was another little set of stairs not far in front of her, very steep, leading up out of the sunken holding area she was now in. They jutted out from the side of the wall like a series of embedded bricks.

Someone was giving a speech. She thought she recognized the voice, but she wasn't sure. Some Plainish trick—some dreadful tinkering—was magnifying that voice and making it so enormous that Linny's bones shook with it. And not just her bones, but the bones of whatever building she had just dug her way into.

That voice was saying, "Greetings, citizens wrinkled and Plain!"

Linny was still a little dizzy, finding herself so suddenly out from underground. What was all the noise she was hearing? She was clearly—the air told her that—very near the river. She had kept enough sense of direction, through all those winding worm tunnels under the earth, to know that the river must be quite close by.

"In other years," said the great huge magnified voice speaking to the world from somewhere at the top of those stairs, "we would have had claimants willing to play the labyrinth game for our amusement and to fulfill long tradition. But time moves on, and worlds, like children, must finally grow up—"

She almost almost *almost* had that voice placed.

"I assure you, if a claimant had managed to pass our preliminary tests, she would be here—but as you can see, there is no one. That shows it is time to face the truth and let go of this legend. There never will be another Girl with a Lourka. No one will ever find that lost crown or claim the powers it used to symbolize. That was a fantasy, and fantasy is beneath us. We must be governed by logic, and yes, I mean by that that even the wrinkled places of the world must submit to reason, and to the wise rule of the Plain—"

The Half-Cat hissed. And the crowd's shouting became uglier and angrier, though some voices were cheering.

She recognized the voice now, in all its angular hatefulness: it belonged, of course, to the regent.

No Girl with a Lourka? What part of Angleside's

plotting did that lie feed, anyway? It was time to go up that last little flight of steps and see what was going on out there at the top of them. But first she stripped off the ripped and tattered lab coat, since it was much the worse for all those tunnels. *There!*

Her lourka, protected in its sack, had come through all the underground slithering amazingly well. Sure, there were a few new dings along its edges, but really, considering what it had just been through, that wasn't too bad. There were probably more than a few dings along her own edges, too, she figured.

The Half-Cat meowed. It seemed impatient.

"All right, all right!" said Linny.

The key ring was too big for her pocket, but she wasn't about to leave it behind. Keys are to be collected, not abandoned.

The voice was still booming, not that far away.

The Half-Cat squeezed itself to one side to let her pass, and the two of them, girl and cat, climbed up the little jutting-out steps. Linny kept one hand on the stone wall on the right, because that steadied her.

"Time for us all to open our eyes and go about our business!" said the booming voice. "Why did we think we needed Girls with Lourkas, all those years? It was always just a fairy tale and a dream. Wake up! Wake up! We have tolerated nonsense for far too long!"

That was when Linny and the Half-Cat reached the top of the stairs. A breeze blew into Linny's face, and she could almost have cried from the wonderfulness of that breeze, and also from the world, the structure of the world, flooding and feeding her starving eyes.

Had those tunnels brought her close to the edge of the river? Well, yes, you might say that. In fact, as she stepped up onto the rim from the stepping-stone stairs, she saw immediately where she was: she was standing not just *near* the river, but at the very center, the apex, of that great stone bridge that crossed the river, that joined the two fairgrounds, the wrinkled and the Plain. The tunnels had brought her to the very foot, the root, of the Angleside end of the bridge, and then the staircase had led her up *inside* the heavy-bellied bridge itself. It was remarkable! What a clever way to build a bridge, not to mention a tunnel!

She smiled at the thought of it—and also because it was the late afternoon out here, and the light was golden and liquid and beautiful.

And there were people everywhere. Some of those people were on the bridge itself, on either side of her, but held back by temporary fences.

And they were all, the ones on the banks of the river and the ones on the bridge, looking up at her. Well, sort of at her. At a man standing in front of her now. She could not see his face, since he was in front of her, but she could see how he leaned forward to speak into a round metal can on a tall stick.

"So there is no Girl with the Lourka this year, and will never be in any year to come. That is the way of progress," the regent was saying into that metal can, and every word he spoke became, by some Plainish trick, immediately huge, gigantic, enormous, overwhelming:

PROGRESS

Linny shook herself and stepped forward to get a better view of the crowds everywhere, of the fairgrounds to the right (where the crowds were mostly in grays, dotted with colors) and the fairgrounds to the left (where the crowd was dressed in every imaginable color, and then dotted with the occasional Angleside gray), of the river rolling ahead and then to the left, of everything so beautiful because it wasn't under the ground, because it was bathed in late-afternoon sun. She had never seen anything so lovely as this world unfolding in front of her eyes, which had been starved for a view like this for what felt like a very long time.

She took another step forward, out from the shadows, right into the light.

That was when the noise changed.

It had been an angry and complicated roar: angry on the left, where the wrinkled side of the fair was, and complicated on the right, where the Plain's half of the fair was laid out. Nobody on either side seemed particularly happy. But when Linny stepped into the light, the sound of both of those crowds swelled for a minute and then fell away.

The regent turned around from his tin can, saw Linny standing there, and spluttered.

In fact, as soon as he saw her, all of his angles seemed to sharpen, and his skin grew paler, and his eyes narrowed in displeasure.

"You!" he said. (He was facing away from the crowds and the tin can, but the word still echoed in the air a little, like the faint ghost of something large.) "What are—how did you even get here?"

"From underground," said Linny. Her words became very large, too. What's more, now she saw that on the Angleside bank of the river, there was a very large flat surface set up, like a giant picture, and in that picture was a moving image of Linny herself, at this very moment, only many times larger than she actually was, with the simply enormous key ring swaying back and forth in her hand. Enough to make you seasick. And the regent was up there, too. *Oh, horrors.* Linny tried to keep her eyes away from the thing. She still wasn't comfortable with pictures of herself.

"What did you say?" said the regent, blinking his

narrow eyes. Behind him the river rolled around its corner—and then ran into the blank wall of the water-works. And between here and there, so very many people, crowds on both sides of the river, balloons, flags, everything holding its breath.

"I came through those tunnels," said Linny, and she pointed to the bluff over there, where her underground adventure had begun. "All the complicated tunnels, like a maze, underground. I got pretty muddy, see?"

The lab coat had done what it could, but still.

The regent looked like someone trying very quickly to reprocess shock into disdain.

"But you shouldn't be here . . . we didn't bring you here . . . you don't even have a puppet," he said, and his eyes flicked ahead and down.

Now that she had moved this far forward—and when she leaned over the edge a bit—Linny could see what he was looking at: a steeply tilted stage, with raised lines running and swirling across it.

"What's that?" she said.

"The labyrinth, you foolish girl."

A pretend labyrinth for puppets that dangled from strings. Wasn't that what Elias had said? In the past, real girls had tried to get puppets through a labyrinth. How silly was that?

It was so much unlike the true labyrinth, so far from

being in endless darkness twisting through wormholes underground, that Linny laughed right out loud.

"Look at this!" she said, and held out her still quite muddy hands, one of them holding a now somewhat muddy key ring. When she did that, the Half-Cat jumped up very elegantly into her arms. "The Half-Cat and I came through the real labyrinth, the actual labyrinth, the horrible dark one that runs under the ground and up through the bridge, and it brought us all the way here."

The regent looked more surprised than Linny had ever seen a grown person look. His jaw was open. The crowds were not just murmuring now; they were beginning to shout, especially the crowd to Linny's left, on the wrinkled side of the bridge.

"The Girl with the Lourka!" they were shouting. "The Girl with the Lourka! Lourka! Lourka!"

"Hush!" said the regent to the crowds, but they didn't hush. Now he was waking up from the surprise and getting angry, Linny noticed. He turned to hiss at her. "Do you think that's all you have to do? Just waltz up here like that? What about the tests? What about the question? What about the lost crown? A know-nothing child can't pretend to be fit to rule a whole world!"

That made Linny jut out her chin.

"I am not a child," she said. "I'm already twelve. And you just said if a claimant had managed to pass your tests, she would be here. And I'm here. I didn't even mean to come here, but here I am. So I guess that means I passed."

She was quite proud of having come up with such a good argument on the spot, and the crowd seemed largely to agree. There were roars of approval from the wrinkled side of the river, and even some applause from the Angleside.

All the sharp edges of the Chief Surveyor's face became even sharper. He looked like one of the twins when the other twin had just stolen his nice toy horsey away.

"Don't you try to play logic games with me, little girl," he said.

The crowds were pointing and shouting many different things by this point. Most of the people out there, even the ones on the Angleside, did not seem very happy about the way the regent was conducting things. Some shouted for the question; some shouted for the lourka; others just shouted without particular words at all, they were so caught up in the thrill of the thing.

"What question do they mean?" said Linny, turning back to the regent.

"Someone who passes the preliminary tests properly is asked a question. She receives the question in an envelope after the tests are graded, and then she comes and answers it here, at the fair, in front of the people. If you think I'm going to make things easy for you, little girl, by just *handing* you the question—"

"Oh, I know what it is!" said Linny, interrupting.

Because all of a sudden she did. She was remembering the stone staircase, and the statue with the lines like wings.

"Enough!" said the regent. "You can't possibly know what the question is, because I wrote it out myself this morning."

Linny shook her head. Everything was so clear, so clear, all of a sudden. It was the sunlight that did it. Or maybe the view from this bridge. It was spread out before her now, plain as plain, how everything fit together.

"Oh, I don't care a fig about *your* question," she said, somewhat carelessly, perhaps. "I know what the real question is, the labyrinth's question—"

Half the crowd was jumping and shouting; the other half was hushing the first half and leaning forward, holding its breath.

"It's written over the doors, down there underground. Here's what it says: 'WHICH WAY?'"

Linny spoke right into the tin can when she said that, and on one side of the river the Plainish machine made the words as huge as giants, while on the other side of the river the words rolled through the crowd like the tide, passed from neighbor to neighbor, on and on.

And as that question rippled outward through the crowd, the people fell silent, waiting for something. It was a question, apparently, that had the power to change the world.

23

THE THING ABOUT CROWNS

Linny heard the enormous words hovering in the air, and she remembered how small the earthwormy tunnels were, in the underground places she had had to travel through to get here, and a laugh bubbled up in her.

Which way? Which way?

"I guess when you think about it, it's the kind of question a maze *would* ask," she said into the tin can. "It had me crawling through a lot of mud, looking for the right way to go, but the real answer was in the doors at the end."

"This is absolutely not the correct question," said the Chief Surveyor somewhere behind Linny's back, but she didn't care what he had to say anymore.

"Two doors," said Linny. "Side by side. And two keys on the key ring, one wrinkled and one Plain."

She held the key ring out to the crowd. On the Plain side it appeared, as huge as could be, on that screen high above the crowd. On the wrinkled side of the river, the wave of rumor spread across the crowd again, a growing murmur of excitement.

"And the answer was *both*. Both doors at once. Both keys."

Both halves of the world. Both sides of my Half-Cat.

"Don't tell us stories," said the regent scornfully. "A person can't go through two doors at once. That's impossible."

"Well, I don't know whether it's impossible or not, but that's what I did," said Linny.

The crowd was getting louder and louder. They were looking up at the huge image hovering there, of that enormous Linny holding out her enormous hand with the enormous key ring, and they were shouting another word, which Linny didn't understand at first, until the Chief Surveyor stepped down closer to her and tried to grab the key ring from her hand.

She dodged out of his grasp right in time.

"Give me that," he said. "It's not for you."

The crowd gave an enormous shout.

The word they seemed to be shouting was—

"Crown?" said Linny into the tin can. "What crown?"

There was a great chaos of jumping and yelling as thousands of people tried to explain something to her all at once.

While she was trying to make sense of the noise, the regent leaped forward again and grabbed her wrist.

"I'll take that now, thank you," he said, through tight lips, and he pried the key ring—*the key ring!*—out of her hand. "For safekeeping."

Linny hardly had enough time to say, "Oh!" She was filled with two kinds of surprise—not merely the unpleasantness of the regent's grasping, bony fingers, which had probably just left bruises on her poor wrist, but also, at the same time, the shock of understanding that something you thought was one thing had actually been something quite different all along.

The ring holding those keys was so large (for a key ring) because it wasn't actually a key ring at all. It was silver, it was graceful, it was round. Of course, of course: the long-lost crown! The crowd had recognized it before she had herself. She had had the crown in her hands, only to let it be stolen away by the regent—who now snapped the keys into position (how had she not noticed that the keys snapped together, into a silvery-black X), and twirled the crown thoughtfully in his own thin and greedy hands.

From both sides of the river, people were now raging and surging toward the bridge, shouting *at* the regent and shouting out *to* Linny.

At the wrinkled end of the bridge, the line of fences temporarily holding people back was being overcome by a surge of bodies. And at the forefront of that crowd was an enormous and colorful mountain of a person. That magician!

The regent had seen him, too. He drew in his breath with a hiss. For a moment he turned his sharp-boned face around to look at the howling, angry crowds on either side of the river. Linny could feel the gears in his cold, angular brain making some quick adjustments to his calculations.

He reached forward, pressed a switch at the base of the tin can, and turned around to Linny, his hand held up to hush her.

"Listen to me, little girl," he said. The words stayed very small and did not travel anywhere. "And listen fast. You said it yourself—you did not come here for crowns and powers, but for medicines for your poor, fading friend. Or that was all a lie?"

Linny shook her head, so angry she couldn't think of the right words to say. This man was the liar, standing here before her.

"Not a lie?" said the regent. "Then the truth is, this key ring is better off with me. We both know that. And on the subject of medicines—"

Out of the corner of her eye, she saw the magician, striding now up along the bridge, pushing gray Surveyors aside as if they were rag dolls or the merest folds of gray draperies getting in his way. The regent's voice had softened to a shadow, icy and urgent:

"I can find you something, little girl, that should work against wrinkled ailments. Against all magic. I have just such a thing in preparation, hidden well away somewhere. You leave this silver trinket with me, and I can find that something for you. Your friend could still be saved, despite all the time you have wasted causing trouble here."

"I could find the medicines myself," said Linny, but even to herself she sounded less than perfectly certain.

"Really?" said the regent. "I don't think so. You overestimate yourself, and you definitely underestimate me. No. Here's what you will do. When it comes time for you to have this crown put onto your far-too-young head, you will hand it back to me instead. That will make me your continuing regent, and all will be well. The crowds will be content, order will be maintained, and you will be free to go back up into your hills. With the antidote, yes. Oh, and then, of course, the other part of our bargain: *you will not come back*. But why would you want to?"

Her bones were being replaced by icicles in the shapes of bones, that's how she felt just then. Why had she ever spoken of medicines to the Chief Surveyor? Now he just had that to use against her.

Could he block her from finding those medicines? She thought he probably could.

Could he actually get his hands on that antidote? He probably could.

Did she really want to stay here, with some crown on her head, trying to make this messed-up place better, while people like the regent pinched bruises into her?

In one very secret hidden-away cupboard of her heart of hearts, the answer welled up: *Not really. Not so much.*

"I just want to go home," said Linny, without realizing she was speaking aloud.

"Exactly," said the regent. "Then I think we're agreed—"

But that was the very moment the magician swooped back into the picture.

"What are you doing to our Girl?" he said to the regent, huffing and puffing a little from his quick ascent of the bridge. "Back off. Keep away. She's ours."

"*She just wants to go home,*" said the regent to the magician, triumph bubbling in his voice. "But thank you for coming. The symmetry is so beautifully improved when a barbarian joins the ceremony."

And while the magician sputtered, the regent reached down and switched that tin can of his back on.

"We have a claimant"—the words thrummed hugely into the air—"and we have a crown."

Absolutely vast amounts of noise from every part of the crowd! Cheering, sobbing, waving of ribbons in the air! A thousand people seemed to be chanting "Girl with the Lourka, Girl with the Lourka," while a thousand other people (mostly on the Angleside bank of the river) shouted words that sounded a lot like "No more regents!"

So even in the Plain, they don't much like this regent, thought Linny. She was glad to find that out. He had been cruel to her and had tried to be cruel to the Half-Cat, and that probably meant he had been cruel to a lot of people before.

But then, on both sides of the river, the sound simply flooded over everything and everybody and drowned out all coherent thoughts.

In fact, the noise was so thick and so large that a person could almost have walked right out on top of it and not fallen into the river.

The sun was already just a hair's breadth above the horizon and sinking fast. Its light came angling low across the fairs and the river between. Linny shaded her eyes to get a better look. The sunset light made all the wonders on either side of the river stand out as if carved from air and varnished fifteen times with the garnet-red stain made from the tears of the dragon tree: on one side, shining contraptions that jumped or flew or played music or showed pictures on their sides; on the other side of the river, miniature orchards of miniature trees, wax candles growing like weeds into tall towers of silver and gold, jesters, kites, and satin banners—all on fire in the setting sun.

Linny looked at all of this, and something in her melted a little. If people at fairs could wander among Plain and wrinkled marvels, why couldn't that be true all the time?

One display, on the wrinkled side of the bridge, did strike her as particularly strange: a rectangle marked out on the ground, like a large plot of kitchen garden, filled with all sorts of wrinkled things, twinkling and murmuring and unfolding themselves, piled around what even from this distance Linny could see was another statue of the Girl with the Lourka, whether made of plaster or pale stone, Linny couldn't quite tell. Men in gray uniforms pounded metal stakes into the ground at the four corners of the rectangle.

That seemed a little odd, but there was mixing between the sides of the Broken City on a day like this one, of course. To judge from the sprinkling of gray in the wrinkled part of the fair and the colors among the gray on the Plain side, people must have been streaming back and forth across this bridge all day, before they had put up the barricades on either end of the bridge, for the regent's speech.

"Claimant!" said the regent. "This is the moment where you do or do not accept this crown, so ancient and so lost to us for so long, and all the responsibilities that it represents."

He reached forward with the crown, tucking it into Linny's wild and (she realized) exceptionally muddy hair. It was that enormous image of her on that enormous screen that reminded her how wild and muddy her hair was, after her journey underground.

The crowd shrieked its approval. The sound went on and on. Loud waves of joyful, hopeful noise broke over Linny's head, a flood of excitement and happiness. Even the people in gray were cheering, Linny saw. They too had felt the brokenness of their Broken City. They wanted to step outside their old fears and live ordinary, joyful lives. *Why not? Why not?* It made her gulp a little, even her, Linnet, who never cried.

Then the regent interrupted all that sound:

"What?" he said, as if Linny had spoken up in a voice too soft for human ears. "You have something, claimant, that you want to say?"

And his knobby finger poked her in the back, reminding her. He was waiting for her to hand him back that crown.

"You are so young," he said into the tin can, prompting her. "You want to go home."

"Wait, what is this about?" said the magician, suspicion rippling through him.

At Linny's feet, the Half-Cat wrapped its tail around one of her shins, which was oddly steadying.

"Of course I do want to go home," said Linny, and her words spread out over the fair. "And I also want to do the right thing."

"Yes," said the regent, and on the huge screen she could see him stretching his hand out, expecting her to reach up right this next minute and pull the crown off her head. And hand it back to him.

Then she would be free, he had said, to return to the hills, with the antidote in her hands, and never come back.

But there was a problem with this plan. Linny could not see how handing a crown to someone as cruel as the regent could ever be doing the right thing.

Oh, Sayra, she thought. Everything had seemed so simple, long ago. And now nothing was simple.

"I don't know what to do," said Linny.

A moment of silence passed through that crowd, as if a thousand people had sucked in their breath all at once.

"You know perfectly well what to do, claimant," said the regent.

"I don't," said Linny. "It's 'Which way?' all over again. I don't know which way this world should go. I don't even know yet which way I should go. All I can do is try my best, because wrinkled things are wonderful, wonderful—and so are maps and compasses and machines. All of you—"

There were so many people out there, and all of them hanging on to her every word.

"All of you will just have to help me figure out how we can do this impossible thing together, and go through both doors—"

Because she, Linny, was like this world. She was always going through both doors at once, wrinkled and Plain. She didn't have the words to say this properly, but there are more ways to speak than words.

She swung her lourka off her shoulder and held it out to the crowds.

"See?" she said. "The whole world is in here: measurement and magic, both at once."

And she shook the stiffness out of her fingers and played that for them as a song, simple and sweet.

24

UNWRINKLED!

The hush after the last note seemed itself to be part of the music. A pause as the world peered around a corner and glimpsed something wonderful there.

And then that silence turned into noise, enormous noise—tumultuous cheers and hullabaloo!

Linny could feel the regent's eyes digging angry holes into her shoulder blades. He said, once the noise had abated a bit, with his frigid voice, "I see. You will regret this, sooner or later. But on with our program now."

He pointed. In front of the tin can on the stick, there was now a table with a lever machine, connected to many wires heading off to the right; a long wick, leading off to the left; and a flickering candle.

"Two sides to every world," he said. Those were ceremonial words, apparently. He said them with such a flat voice, almost as if he didn't believe what he was saying. But Linny knew the flatness hid anger.

He put the candle into Linny's hand and pointed at the wick, and a moment later fire was racing quietly down the long fuse and along the balustrade of the bridge, where the wick string was cleverly held up by a series of little metal rings.

The sun melted at the horizon line, became a molten puddle of gold, and was gone, leaving a sky as brilliantly rose and gold as the belly of a wrinkled trout.

As the sun vanished, the Angleside half of the fair sparkled into light, all at once. Small globes of glass were strung like drops of dew on a spider's web, a web of beaded glass that ran around the booths of that fair and on high poles along its paths, and when Linny pressed the lever the regent pointed to, a miniature star began to shine in each one of those little glassy spheres. In places, whole clusters of lights drew pictures in the air, of towers and trees and flying machines, and some of the strands of the lights were colored green and blue and red and purple and yellow—like strings of jewels, only brighter than jewels ever could be.

And just as Linny was smiling at the bright, jewel-like Angleside lights, the long fuse she had lit with the candle reached its endpoint, and there was a screaming cacophony of lights and thunder as fireworks blossomed over the wrinkled side of the fair. The fireworks exploded in every possible fiery shape and pattern, and the last of the rockets released a great flock of tiny paper lanterns that flickered as they drifted down from the heights—flickered and then floated, hovering and bobbing, just above the heads of the fairgoers on the Bend side of the river.

Linny saw children—not just children, no, grown men and women—jumping up into the air to try to catch one of those pretty peach-colored flames in paper, but the lanterns bobbed gently out of reach each time. They were wrinkled lanterns, and did not care to be caught by human hands too soon, but each time they swam a little ways out of reach, they made a pretty little sound, like a ringing bell.

Some of the fireworks settled on the head of that statue of the Girl with the Lourka, over there in the square the gray men had been marking off with their spikes, and a fountain of sparks danced into the air now from her head, like a feathery crown made of fire. Worlds of light on both sides of the river! Linny's eyes soaked up the beauty of it, of all of it, the electric brightness of the Plain side, and the wilder lights dancing over there on the wrinkled side of things.

There were *ooh*s and *aah*s from the crowds on either end of the bridge, not to mention the people now crossing the bridge itself (the barricades must have been trampled right down). And Linny could not have said which display she liked better, the one on the Plain side made possible by machines and glass, or the wrinkled mystery of the other fairground's bobbing, chiming lanterns.

The regent tapped her on the arm.

He had switched off his tin can again.

"I will ask you one more time. Will you be sensible and responsible, and put this crown into my care?"

"But I don't think I can," said Linny. It was that business of doing the right thing.

"The choice is on your head, then," he said, and he switched the machine back on that made voices so large.

"One more remark, if I may—"

"Hey," said the magician, in mild protest, from Linny's other side.

"One more remark, I say, before we go about joyfully stuffing food into our happy, happy mouths—"

His voice boomed out over everywhere, an inexorable tide of sound. Linny shrank back an inch from that over-size sound, but there was nowhere soundless to shrink into. She could sense the whole crowd shrinking with her, as if they were all, all the thousands of them, children who had been caught red-handed, who had smiled when they had not been given permission to smile.

"We must keep clear minds even as we rejoice. A successful claimant has come down from the wrinkled hills—that is very good news. But it should not blind us to facts. Only a child or a fool would argue that the halves that make up our world are the same in worth or value. Why, even here, at the bridge that crosses our river, we cannot help but see the past on one side and the future on the other."

The cheers had died off, and the crowds shifted nervously from foot to foot, waiting to see what this man who had been regent so long, whose eyes and hands still radiated power, would say.

"The future lies with those who have the power to reshape the world. To help us all keep that in mind, we have set up one last display on the Bend side of the fair—there!"

He pointed at that odd, small rectangle filled with wrinkled things—with floating books and growing miniature trees and singing flowers and toys that could walk or dance or laugh on their own, thanks to their wrinkled natures—that crowded patch of wrinkled ground, with, at its heart, the statue of the Girl with the Lourka still streaming sparks from its hair.

"A representative assortment, as you can see, of the most wrinkled things we could find. And we have marked out that rectangle by means of a set of grid stakes linked to the waterworks, just by way of experiment and example. The wrinkled hills have stayed backward so long, because hillsickness hobbled us and kept civilization limited to the Plain. But I tell you now, we are on the brink of a new age, when wrinkled places will no longer make anyone sick. We have found an antidote to hillsickness, and the antidote will allow us to cure the deeper disease. And now our newly found claimant will do us the honor of pressing this other lever here, so that the lesson may be made clearer. The power behind the cure. A new beginning for us all."

It was something glittering in his voice, something eager in his eye, that made Linny shake her head.

"No," she said. "What are you doing?"

"Oh, but you will," said the regent, glittering more sharply. "The lesson is about why it is important to keep one's bargains. It is about who is really in charge, in this world. So I'm afraid it does have to be you who pushes this lever."

And before Linny could move away, he took her hand and forced it right down on that lever—she shouted out, but that did no good, and the magician had shouted, too, and was lunging toward them. She felt a surge of energy pass through the various wires, enough so that her hair stood straight up on the top of her head, and over there on the wrinkled side of the river, the rectangular patch of ground where that little plaster statue was went dark. Its lanterns and fires and glowing things just plain winked out, all at once.

Something bad had happened there. But what? Linny

pushed the regent to one side, dodged the shouting magician (who himself was being tackled by a bunch of Surveyors in gray), jumped off the old stage in the center of that bridge, and began running, as fast as she could, down toward the Bend side of the river.

The crowds let her through. Most of those faces were simply puzzled (everyone asking his neighbor, "What just happened?"). But many were upset and beginning to grow angry.

The feeling that bit into Linny now was grief. A gap had just been torn into Linny's soul. Something had been lost.

And then, oh, miracle, Elias was there beside her. Elias! She was so relieved to see him, but so horrified by the dark patch of ground where the statue had been that the relief vanished into the air, almost as soon as it appeared.

"Why?" he was saying. "Why? Why? Why?"

"*What was that?*" Linny asked him. She didn't stop running, though.

"Their grid," he said. He tried to say more, but Linny was dragging him off the bridge now and through the fair. Everyone around seemed to be shouting and surging in one direction or another, but the crowds fell back to let Linny pass, because she was the Girl with the Lourka, and she still wore the crown.

There she was then, facing the ruined patch of the fair, the breath in her painful and making her pant. The little statue was still there; the plaster girl's eyes looked dully down at Linny. But sparks no longer sprayed forth from its head, and lanterns no longer hovered in the air, not in this part of the fair, and the flowers in their pots had wilted, and much of the color had vanished from everything there. It had been a display of everything wrinkled, and now it was a rectangular patch of ordinary ground, covered with broken things and junk.

How had they done this awful thing? They had put real power into their grid, and they had found a way to mark off a part of Bend, filled with everything wonderful—and then they had *unwrinkled* it.

"The dirty griddlers! The buzzards! The rats! The foul, foul pigs!"

That was Elias, cursing and crying at Linny's elbow.

"And they made *your hand* push that button thing that did this! We'll show them. Oh, I'll show them if I can—"

He turned and shouldered his way through the crowd, heading back to the bridge, where the magician was fighting with a sea of men in gray. Linny looked at all the broken things in this rectangular place, and then she remembered (her brain was moving slowly, it seemed, as if it had lost some essential part of its own wiring) what Elias was carrying under his jacket.

Those awful canisters, full of destruction, that the *madji* had asked Elias deliver to someone. What was it about this miserable city? The Plain side unwrinkling things; the magicians making disorder bombs to undo the very bones of the world . . .

"Elias, wait!" she shouted, and then took off after him.

"Is it war?" said a man's voice, not far away. "Is it war, Lourka Girl?"

"Stop him for me," she said, pushing the crowds away with her hands as she followed Elias back to the bridge. "Stop him. Please stop him. He mustn't help them do anything terrible."

"War! War!" said voices from the crowds—and the ordinary people in gray, the ones who moments before had been laughing and smiling at the displays on the Bend side of the river, like everyone else, were now taking alarm at what the voices around them were beginning to say. The gray people were trying to get back to the bridge, too, back to their side of the river. But it was slow, moving through those crowds, even though people still gave way before her, before Linny. But some small part of her brain could hear voices crying out, not so far away, and fists thumping and perhaps even vases or bones being crushed.

Bad things were beginning to happen. The crowd was still mostly just murmuring, but soon there would be nothing anywhere but bad things.

She ran as fast as she could, pushing her way through the people around her, and soon she had her hand on Elias's back again, and he was swinging around, fists flying, not knowing who it was.

Linny ducked.

"Elias, please don't," she said to him. "Come away with me, so we can talk."

"There isn't time to talk. I have to get the weapons where they need to go. You know it's only fair. We can't let them get away with *that*."

No, they couldn't just get away with that, with unwrinkling a part of the world.

They were at the edge of the bridge, pushed up against the stone railing. The crowds were milling and struggling around them, and some large percentage of that crowd was probably watching them.

Linny tried to hang on to Elias, tried to whisper into his ear.

"Please stop. Please think. Those bombs the magician makes—they're bad, too. Maybe even worse than what just happened, than unwrinkling things. The magician's bombs destroy whatever's there, they ruin space—they make places wrong. Elias! *They don't fix anything.*"

"I think a place without any wrinkle to it is already as good as destroyed," said Elias. "Can't you feel that? Why can't you feel that? On the Angleside, it feels horrible all the time. And they want to do that to every part of the wrinkled country. That's what they're planning. It's too late to talk about fixing things. Let go of me, Linny!"

He was scrabbling at the railing now, trying to climb up it; he was so eager to get out of her grasp.

And Linny was hanging on to him tooth and nail, with all fingers and both hands.

"Stop it!" she was saying. "Stop it! You idiot! You'll make things worse. You'll get hurt!"

She remembered what even those tiny pea-sized disorder bomblets had done to people in the market, when the magician had thrown them. And Elias had huge sticks of that stuff tucked into his vest. She had seen that.

"Let go of me," said Elias. "You don't understand anything. You never understood anything. All you cared about was yourself."

In both fairgrounds, people were shouting at each other. Things were falling apart. And the people around them were shouting, too.

"Let go," said Elias, and Linny held on as tight as she could.

She could be stubborn. She truly could. Maybe he was right, and that was selfish. But she would not let him go. He was perched on the railing now—he had swung his legs over somehow, and Linny hung on to him as tight as she could, not letting go. If she hung on long enough, he would rethink his craziness. That was her hope.

It was at that moment that a screech of laughter came dancing along the railing itself: red hair and bright clothing, dancing on the railing as if it were a line painted on the floor, not a thin band of stone high above a river in which it would be all too easy to drown.

"Need help, laddie?" that voice shrieked. "Why won't you let him loose, Lourka Girl? Haven't you maybe done enough, pushing their wicked buttons for them?"

It was the magician's old ma, her brilliant red puffball of a head glowing slightly in the dusk. She was wearing a ragged parody of Linny's own dress, rough stripes in many colors running down the skirt, all old and worn and fraying.

"Go away," Linny said, and to Elias she said, "Don't do *their* work, Elias. The magician just destroys things and makes money on it. That's as bad as the gray people. What if something happens to you? What do I tell Sayra then?"

He opened his mouth and started to say something. But what that something was, Linny didn't find out, because the shrieking fireball that was the magician's old ma kept coming in her wild dance along the railing and flung herself on them, while the magician himself shouted out and wrestled with Surveyors up higher on the bridge. *Oof!* Pain shot up Linny's poor arms, and the old woman with the dandelion's worth of bright red hair was shouting even louder.

"With me!" she shouted, and in one awful leap, she wrenched Elias out of Linny's hands and right over the edge of that bridge.

No no no no! Linny scrambled back to her feet, grabbed at the bridge's railing.

There was a great splashing in the water, down below, and that splashing commotion was being pulled down the river, away from the bridge, as fast as the water could flow.

Linny couldn't see exactly what was happening. Those were Elias's arms thrashing around, weren't they? Was that crazy old woman trying to drown him?

No no no no!

Elias was gone.

25

DISASTER

"What's going on down there?" the regent was saying, somewhere behind her back. Even he had been fighting, apparently, or wearing himself out by ordering others to fight; his voice was ragged and harsh. "Why don't those guards take control?"

Linny was leaning over the railing, her knuckles white. She could see splashes that must actually be people drifting over to the right side of the river—but they were already headed around the bend. The river water Elias was maybe drowning in ran into the gray wall of the waterworks there, not so far away now, not far enough. What happened to the water then? And to the water-logged bodies it was carrying when it splashed up against the waterworks wall? What would happen to them?

When the river turned the bend, it became impossible for Linny to see what exactly was going on with Elias in the water.

Please don't drown!

"That was someone you knew who fell in the river?" said the regent, now so close to her she could see the welt on his cheek where someone must have punched him. There were gray Surveyors behind him now, and others, slightly farther away, still trying to subdue the magician.

"You!" said Linny, furious. "You unwrinkled that part of the fair!"

"The only way to make barbarians behave is to show them what kind of force they're up against. That's a message they can understand. The rest is all nonsense."

Linny whirled around, finally angry enough to look away from the river.

"And you used my hand to push that horrible lever! You had no right!"

"That's enough—" said the regent.

And at that moment, there was a horrible noiseless shock, an explosion that shook through every mind in that place on some peculiar frequency ordinary ears couldn't hear much of, though it shook Linny's bones: an awful, enormous *whooooompf*, coming from behind her back, from far away, down the river, and sucking all the air out of the world for a moment.

A silent thunderclap. And then people started screaming. One thought drowned out everything else in Linny's head as she spun back around and grabbed the bridge's railing with both her hands.

Elias!

Something had gone wrong with the river. Linny's first impression was that the twilit water there beyond the bend had suddenly tilted off the usual axis, as if the river were a board someone had kicked aslant. Then she noticed the sickening clots of smoke, thick, greasy, and greenish gray, rising up from one end of the waterworks. Oh, no. Oh, no.

Elias!

"What have your insane *madji* done now?" The regent was gasping behind her, but Linny was already pushing her way down the bridge toward the Angleside fair, because it was on that side of the river that the smoke was rising. "Take her! Take her! Hold her, you people there!"

"Don't you touch me," said Linny when she felt a hand on her shoulder. "You let me by."

A pair of rough-dressed *madji* had popped up on the other side of her, with the magician looming behind them. Their shirts were torn, and they glowered at the gray Surveyors behind the regent.

"Stop," said the *madji*. "The Girl with the Lourka is ours. She'll come with us."

One of them took Linny's sleeve. So now there were two hands on her, claiming her as theirs.

"Let go," she said. "I don't want to go with you, either."

"She's ours," said the regent to the *madji*. "Take your filthy wrinkled hands off her."

They were pulling at her now, the Surveyors on one side and the *madji* on the other. And as the quarrel heated up, both sides got angrier with each other and, for a moment, remembered Linny that much less.

The Surveyors and the *madji* frowned and shouted and pulled, while the regent and the magician followed along on the edges. They were surging down to the Angleside end of the bridge, the little knot of *madji* and Surveyors pulling at Linny and yelling at each other. Linny, fighting to keep her balance, kept grabbing swift looks out over the bridge and the river, trying to take the measure of where she was.

"She comes with us! That crown is ours!"

"You fools! They're ours! Ours!"

And so on and so forth. Meanwhile, all around them was another knot of people, watching and not knowing quite what to make of what they were seeing. But Linny saw that the frowns on those faces were deepening as the men shouted more loudly at each other and pulled Linny back and forth. The people watching shouted warnings at the men who had Linny in their grip—at all of them, the Surveyors and the *madji*.

"Stop it!" said Linny.

The ones pushing and pulling ignored her, though.

"Murderers!" shouted the *madji*.

"Barbarians!" shouted the Surveyors.

"Let me go," said Linny, but they were too preoccupied with their quarrels to pay any attention to her. "Let me go, *so I can go home*!"

The regent turned to look at her, and the *madji* turned, too.

Linny had grabbed the crown from her head already, not wanting any of these fighting men to have it. And then there was a moment when she was pressed against the balcony of the bridge, so near its Angleside foot that the bridge was already arching over land, not river, and looking down through the twilight into a hundred or a thousand shocked and frightened faces, not that far below her.

"Here!" she said suddenly, loudly enough that the nearest dozen could hear her, even without a Plainish tin can to help. *"All you people!* Keep this safe for me—keep it out of their hands. *Pass it on!"*

And she threw the crown itself right down into the crowd, where it vanished. There were roars of anger and surprise from behind her—the regent shouting orders, the magician howling in rage—but she could hear a rising murmur from the crowds below. Her words were being passed back and back, spreading like a ripple across the sea of faces. And somewhere below the surface of that sea, a crown was being handed from person to person. On and on and on.

That was when one of the *madji* actually took a swing at a Surveyor, and the Surveyor swung back.

Everything changed in that fraction of a second, because some of the hands on Linny fell away for a moment, and with a shrug and a twist, she was free.

In another half moment, the crowd had opened, just the tiniest amount, to let her fling herself through, and then closed itself up again behind her. Linny could hear the shouts of the *madji* and the Surveyors change, as they realized they had lost now both the crown and her. People were pulling her through the crowd, handing her back, from person to person, and some of the hands moving her along were in the gray sleeves of Anglesiders, and some of them were dressed in the bright colors of Bend.

"Run fast, Lourka Girl," said voices around her. "They mustn't harm you. You'll come back when it's safe and set things right. Promise us you'll come back."

"Promise!"

Promise.

"I will, I promise, I will," said Linny as she pushed forward out of the crowds. They shifted in turn to make a vast wall of themselves in front of the men who must be chasing her. She kept moving and moving, past the displays with their little robot toys and their lights, and nobody could catch her, because there were crowds in the way, and there was smoke, more and more smoke.

All she wanted to do was get to the place where the smoke was rising up, to find Elias.

The smoke got thicker and thicker as she ran toward the river. And it was getting dark.

No Elias anywhere.

She kept wiping the tears and smoke out of her eyes, and running on a few steps, and then pausing to cough and blink, and then she was standing on the edge of the broken river, looking out toward the wall of the waterworks, which now had a ragged bite taken out of it on the far right side. It made Linny feel ill, looking at that gap in the waterworks wall. Where was Elias? Some of those bombs had gone off here.

But there was no Elias to be seen anywhere. This was where Linny chose one of two responses possible, under the circumstances. She could either sink to the ground and cry miserable tears until the Surveyors or the *madji* finally caught up with her, or she could keep going. Keep going forever, perhaps.

Because she thought maybe there was too much pain everywhere for her to stop. She had an idea, now, of what her mother had been thinking when she left the city behind and went way up into the wrinkled hills. She had had it with this place, where only horrible things seemed to happen.

It was because of Linny that Elias had come down to the Plain, where he had suffered so much. And it was because of Linny that Sayra had been lost, up there in the hills. It was fatal, really, to be a friend of Linnet's.

When she looked back she saw (through the darkness and the haze) those enormous crowds, still holding steady, still being as strong as stubborn people can be, so that the *madji* and the Surveyors were slowed down too much and could not come right after her. That stubborn crowd was the only tiny bit of hope she had left in her, but it was enough to keep her going, to make her turn and slip away from all the commotion, the pleading and crying and shouting, the smoke and the chaos.

She went around corners and down streets and kept running, and at some point she looked down and saw the Half-Cat keeping pace with her, with the nonchalant step of a cat not even in a hurry. Even when she had to lean against a wall in the dark and gasp for breath, the Half-Cat sat calmly, licked its paw, and then walked a few steps farther and jumped into the front basket on one of those power-driven carts they liked to ride around in on this side of the river.

It flicked its tail against the rim of the cart's basket, and that clearly meant "Come quick!"

Linny hesitated. It hadn't looked too complicated when the Surveyors had been driving the cart. Push the button and off you go. Something like that. There were definitely buttons here. There was a red one, too. Right there.

Presumably you could go farther in something like this than you could running on your own two legs.

When the sound of the tumult behind her changed and began to come closer, she stopped all that extra thinking. She jumped onto the seat, pushed the button, and held on tight to the handle that turned the wheels—as the cart started moving, faster than a girl could move, faster than a cat, down the Angleside street.

She had announced she was going home, and maybe she was. But there was something she had to do first, and that something meant going farther away from everything she knew, and deeper into the Plain.

26

INTO THE PLAIN

Even though everything had gone wrong since Linny's birthday—no, not just since her terrible birthday, but pretty much since she had talked her way out of the tether and started making that lourka of hers, or maybe since the first time she had ever heard the sweetness of music teased out of sheep-gut strings, or maybe since the day she was born. Even so, even faced with disaster all around, Linny found herself feeling a sense of relief as she left the Broken City behind and struck out into the Plain. She was swooping along a long, straight road, with the Half-Cat tucked up comfortably in her basket and her lourka bouncing on her back. It was dark, so she couldn't see much beyond the lights of the cart itself, but there were streetlamps along the road, even out here beyond the edge of the city. The dots of light ran ahead of her, on and on and on, and if she turned her head to either side, she could see more dots of light marking out other roads far away. All in all, it gave the impression of being a galaxy of extraordinarily well-behaved stars.

And the world grew very quiet, except for the *rumble-whoosh* of the engine and the wheels speeding along the smooth surface of the road.

At first she had been just running away from the turmoil of the fairs, and away from the magician fighting the regent, and the terrible sound of the disorder bombs going off in the river, and away from thinking about Elias and what might have happened to him when the corner of the waterworks became unmade, but after a while, moving along the long road in the dark, she began to feel her thoughts detangling themselves and becoming simpler.

Sayra needed her. That was still the truth at the bottom of all truths.

And she could not—she would not—fail at this, too.

She could not. She had not hung on to Elias hard enough, and the river and bitterness had swept him away. She had let the crown go, at least for now. But she was determined not to go back to Lourka with her hands empty.

When the burst of energy that comes whenever you run away had begun to wear off, Linny began to feel tired, and just a little cold. She had found that if she pulled the guide lever back, the cart slowed down to almost walking speed. Up ahead and to the right, a clot of lights might mean a building of some kind. She wanted to get off the road and more or less out of sight, in case those gray Surveyors came zipping along this way, looking for her.

She turned down the side road and trundled past lines of low glass houses. Too small for people to be living in them, but when she stopped the cart (which involved running off the side of the path into a ditch, but fortunately the ditch was shallow, and the cart had been going very slowly when she started trying to figure out how to make it stop) . . . anyway, when she had climbed out of the cart, she saw they were greenhouses, with plants growing in them. And there was a door that was not locked!

Inside the greenhouse, the air was warm and heavy and sweet-tangy, because this one housed tomato plants. Even in the dark, it was an easy thing to let her fingers find a tomato ripe enough that it came off the vine with only the slightest of tugs. She wiped it on her skirt and took a bite. She was so hungry! It tasted sweet and dense, as a good tomato will. Full of life. And all that without the slightest wrinkle in it, that she could taste.

She offered a tomato to the Half-Cat, but it declined.

Things did not have to be wrinkled to be astonishing. She had learned that a few times over since coming down from the hills.

She went back outside and hauled the Angleside cart

right into the greenhouse, so that it wouldn't be too visible for anybody passing by. She pushed it in between those tomato plants, and then stopped to catch her breath. She was tired.

There were some sacks piled up in a corner of the greenhouse. Linny made a little heap of them and fell down on top to sleep for a while. She could feel the sleep coming for her almost as she let her head sink down. She was so tired her bones hardly knew how to hold themselves together anymore.

When she opened her eyes, which was just at the point where the gray morning was beginning to chase the night away, she remembered immediately the horrible feeling of Elias falling out of her grasp, and the *whoompf* of the awful thing that had happened to the waterworks, the explosion taking Elias out of the world. The night before, she had been too numb from fatigue to know what that meant, but now she opened her eyes, remembered everything that had happened the day before, and began to cry. Linny didn't cry often, but when she did, she made a thorough job of it. She cried now right until the rising sun splashed itself, sparkling, against the glass panes of the greenhouse. Then she wiped her eyes on her sleeves and gobbled a couple more tomatoes as breakfast.

Enough moaning. Elias would want her to save Sayra. That much Linny knew for sure. He would have wanted

Sayra saved almost as much as Linny wanted to save her. And Sayra was fading away, every hour a little more. How much time had Linny wasted in these greenhouses, just because she was tired?

She ventured out into the morning brilliance, blinking her eyes and wrapping her arms around her body to ward off the chill. The cluster of lights she had seen the night before must have belonged to the buildings just a little farther down the road. The farmhouse, Linny guessed, if you could call these rows of glass structures a farm. Nothing here smelled enough of sheep dung to count as a real farm, to Linny's way of thinking.

Out that way, past the "farm," the world got flatter. And if she squinted a little, she could see the morning sun flaring up as it hit something large out there in the flatter parts of the world.

"I wonder where the hub thing is," said Linny to the Half-Cat. "With the medicines hiding in it somewhere. But also with Surveyors."

She didn't trust Surveyors.

It seemed safer to leave the cart behind. The cart was faster than walking, but it was hard to hide in something like that.

Anyway, it was peaceful, walking down the road. The Plain felt large and unhurried and quiet. There was a thin mist hanging over the fields, and it glowed in the new sun while the surface of the road whispered under her feet.

In half an hour's time, she saw another clump of buildings off to the right, larger and more imposing than the greenhouse farm where she had spent the night.

Far, far to the left, the horizon was rippling in a way that Linny had never seen before. A trick of the mist? It was all very flat, and that in itself was something new, for a girl who came from the wrinkled hills. The world had unfolded itself, all around.

It made her feel a little strange inside.

Not bad strange.

A little clearer and emptier. Like she used to feel long ago when she was little, and her mother would empty buckets of water over her head and scrub her hair perfectly clean.

The building was very large and very square and surrounded by a low wall: a Plain building.

"This is it," said Linny to the Half-Cat, after squinting to help her eyes read the words on the sign by the gate. "Okay. Let's see what we can find."

She crouched down behind the wall, out of view of anyone watching from those smoky-glassed windows, and started around the building, looking for weaknesses in its defense. In Lourka, every building could be counted on to have a weakness of some kind, a loose window frame or a place where a thatched roof left a gap between itself and the wall.

Here it would be harder to sneak in, no doubt about

that. But of all the people in the world, Linny was pretty sure she was one of the sneakiest.

And the Half-Cat padded along silently beside her. (Cats don't have to work at it—they are by nature sneaky.)

As she rounded a corner of the building behind the fence, she heard a faint metallic clapping sound that made her ears sit up and take notice. She peeked over the fence to see what it might be, and smiled: a back door, not quite latched, banging gently against the sill in the breeze. That was lucky!

"Wait for me," she said to the Half-Cat.

She ran forward along the wall until she reached the dark edge of the building's shadow, because fences should not be jumped in bright sunlight, and then, before anyone could have counted to five, she was over the fence, across the gap, and easing herself, soft as a ghost, silently in through the door.

Where she stood very still for a moment, sorting out the sounds (murmurs of people, hums of machines) and the gray outlines of that place.

She must be in a workshop of some kind, she thought. It felt familiar, that way. There were tables and machines around her, and shelves lining the long back wall.

When she had taken the measure of this room, and satisfied herself that the human sounds were still some distance away, she slipped closer to the shelves.

What would medicines look like?

Here she saw tubes and spoons and cubes of metal and complicated twisty things that might be tools but were nothing you'd ever see in the hills.

At home, her mother kept dried leaves and roots in jars, to make tisanes when the twins had sore throats. But there were no dried leaves here. It wasn't that sort of room. *Pause for a heartbeat; steady yourself; move on.*

She crept to the door at the end of the room and held her breath while she turned the knob, as if that would make the hinges think twice before squeaking.

She could tell by listening, before she even looked with her eyes, that this next room must be large. But when she put her head around the edge of the door to look, her heart got dizzy. She had to look at the ground again for a while, just to reclaim some sense of balance.

All the windows were narrow and high, and the artificial lights were off. Linny's first impression was of a twilit cave. The room went on and on and on, vanishing ahead of her into the gloom. And up and up. And all of it, as far as Linny could see, was rows of shelves, and on those shelves, everything. Bottles and boxes and vials and orderly white sacks.

The thought that flooded her then: she had been such a fool.

How could she ever hope to find the medicine that

Sayra needed among all these thousands of shelf-dwelling jars? She didn't even know what she was looking for, not really.

What an idiot she had been! She had been so focused on finding this place that she had forgotten that part of the problem. She had just assumed she would somehow recognize the powder or herb or whatever it was that she needed. *Fool! Fool! Fool!*

Things could not possibly get worse—but then they did.

The room exploded into lightning-white light, and a hand took firm hold of Linny's arm.

The hand was very strong. Linny couldn't shrug her way out of its hold. And while she was trying, a voice that went along with that hand shouted words at her: "intruder" and "thief" and "papers" were some of those words.

It was the end, then. She had been caught. All those years of sneakiness had come only to this, a rough hand nabbing her, maybe only a few feet away from the medicine she had come so far to find. Sayra's medicine! Elias was gone, and now she would be gone, too, and who was left, then, to find a way to bring Sayra home?

Oh, she was worse than a fool. She was a failure.

27

ABOUT SURVEYORS

While Linny did all that silent shouting at herself, the strange hand was shaking her arm, demanding answers. Linny looked up and saw dark hair, angry squinting lines where eyes would ordinarily be, a plain gray smock.

"I . . . um . . . I . . ."

She remembered to stammer a little. It was good to stammer, when you'd been caught. It gave your brain an extra second or two to think something up.

"Well? Who are you, anyway? And what in the name of all the sciences are you *wearing*?"

The man slapped his own ear, for some reason, and began to talk to somebody Linny could not see. "Hey, Five, you said they were exaggerating about all the terrorists? Well, guess what? There's a *madji* intruder in the fourth storeroom. Yes. Yes! Caught in the act. Yes, I'm waiting for you calmly. Hurry, though. Got to assume it's armed. Yes. I'll ask again. Hurry."

The man gave Linny another shake. "Papers? Identity papers? Showing who you are? No, don't move!"

Linny had been thinking as fast as she could, under the circumstances.

"C-can't," she said.

"Can't what?"

"Can't show you papers without moving," she said, straightening her spine as much as she could.

The man made an angry sound.

"So you can talk! Well, are you here with a gang? Or just destroying things on your own?"

"I'm not destroying anything," said Linny, offended, and at that moment another person in gray popped through the doorway. A woman, with short dark hair.

"You didn't say she was a child!" she said to the man.

"I'm *twelve*," said Linny, offended all over again.

"Let her go," said the woman to the man. "What's come over you? She's just a child!"

"Don't you check the newsfeed ever?" said the man. "Child *madji* terrorist on the loose, dressed up like one of those girls with banjos. Single-handedly destroyed the waterworks, just last night. And then ran away home to the wrinkled hills. Only apparently not, on that last bit, because here it is."

"Lourkas, not banjos," said Linny. "And it's completely not true. I didn't destroy anything."

"We all know the newsfeed is sometimes not as plain as it should be," said the woman calmly. "Who are you, then?"

That was a use of the word "plain" that Linny hadn't heard before. And what was a newsfeed? What could news possibly have to do with food?

The man grumbled before Linny had a chance to figure out what she wanted to say.

"Says it has identity papers."

"Do you?"

"You mean one of those cards showing a name? One of those? Yes," said Linny.

It wasn't precisely a lie. And it did seem to be an emergency. She twisted around to reach into the little bag around her neck with her free hand. That made the man nervous, she could tell—his grip tightened—but she had the card out before he could protest.

He bent his head to squint at the card she was holding.

"Irika Pontis?" he said. "But that's—"

The card was out of Linny's hand before he finished his sentence. The woman in gray could move very fast, apparently.

She no longer looked very calm.

"Go call the Surveyors," she told the man. "We'll hold her until they come. I've got her now."

He let go of Linny's arm and went trotting from the room, while Linny tried to figure out what had changed in the woman's face, why the grate there had suddenly plummeted down and shut everything out.

And then she took a closer look at the woman questioning her, and her heart bobbled like a duck on a rough patch of water.

It was the way the eyebrows angled up and down, always a little surprised.

The eyes were the same color, too—brown with a ring of green around the pupil.

And there were similar little patches of wrinkles at the corners of the eyes, born of laughter and worry.

Right now, however, the eyes were angry.

"I don't know how you got this card," said the woman. "But I do know you are not Irika Pontis. Irika Pontis is my sister."

And Linny said in a whisper, "Auntie Mina!"

They stared at each other.

"What have you done to Irika?" said the woman, but there was more doubt than anger in her now.

"Nothing! How could I do anything? She's my *mother*! She sent me to the Bridge House to find you, but you weren't there—"

"She's alive? But the *madji* took her."

"No, they didn't. She wandered into Lourka, somehow, hillsick as could be, and then she just stayed. You can't get back if you leave, so she stayed. She's my mother. I told you, she sent me to find you! Auntie

Mina, she said, in the Bridge House."

"But you don't look like her at all. You look like—"

"I know," said Linny, feeling quite tired of all of it. "I just look like an old painting. That's what happened. My mother came looking for the Girl with the Lourka, up in the wrinkled country, and boom, here I am."

"'Boom' implies suddenness," said Linny's Aunt Mina. "And I haven't seen my sister in more than twelve years. I dispute the boom."

And the wrinkles crinkled up a little around her eyes, so Linny saw she was almost laughing. That little bit of warmth undid Linny's caution.

"Oh, please. I need you to help me!" she found herself saying, all in an incoherent rush. "You can't let the Surveyors get me. If I don't get back home very soon, Sayra will fade away for good. I promised I would find medicines and come back to her! I *promised*!"

"Who's Sayra?" said the woman. "You've lost me. Oh, no!"

She slapped her own ear lightly, the same gesture the man had made.

"Ten! Wait! No, I'm all right. I'm fine. Wait on that call. What? Blisters!" They liked talking to invisible people, here in the Plain.

Mina looked distressed now, as she turned back to Linny.

"Explain very fast indeed. The Surveyors will be on

their way by now. Why do you look like a painting, who is Sayra, and did you say you went to the Bridge House looking for me? And what's your name, child, anyway? Quick."

"Linnet," said Linny, and she did her best with the other questions. When she explained about the Bridge House, where she'd met the Tinkerman, the woman groaned.

When Mina groaned, she looked a lot more like Linny's mother.

"Oh, that awful man! Practically stole the Bridge House from us. Married our mother very late in her life. Irika and I used to whisper to each other that he wanted to marry Mother's research collections, not her herself. And he has some very strange theories about Away."

"He wants me to take him there, to go looking for power, he said."

"Oh, no," said Mina. "Very bad idea. Quick, come along this way while we talk. The Surveyors will be on their way. He's wrong, though. We should be trying to understand the wrinkled places, not trying to use them, abuse them, destroy them. Destroy ourselves, maybe."

"What do you mean?"

"Listen. It's a physics problem. Quite a tricky one. We have scientists here studying it as hard as they can, and they say our world, our wrinkled/Plain world, is a peculiar anomaly. In fact, it shouldn't really even exist. 'Soap-bubble universe,' that's the word. And fragile, fragile. Who knows? If that Tinkerman ever brought his great experiments and his wires to Away, all of everything might go *pop* like a bubble, and that would be the end of us! Through this door now, Linnet, please."

"What?"

How can a world go pop *like a bubble?* Linny's stomach went cold from the very thought of it. They were in another supply room now, as vast as the first, and still Linny's Aunt Mina was hurrying them along.

"When impossible things exist, you have to keep the opposite ends of them far away from each other," said Linny's Aunt Mina, as matter-of-factly as if it were an explanation for why three birds plus another three make six. "Otherwise, they can short-circuit, and then it's all over. But never mind that. No time now. Explain fast about your friend."

But as Linny explained, Mina kept shaking her head.

"A girl's mind taken off to Away—that's not the sort of thing we deal with, here in the Plain. Our medicines are meant to cure fevers and poxes and skin rashes, not wrinkled curses. Irika would have known that."

"But she was *hoping*," said Linny. Meaning, secretly, that she, Linny, had been hoping. Was still hoping. Would hope as long as she possibly could.

Mina looked at her thoughtfully.

"There's one thing," she said. "But I don't know. See, what you have to understand is, when Irika got lost in the hills, I was so sad I hardly knew what to do with myself. On the wrinkled side of the world, I guess you might say my heart broke. But it didn't really break. I was just so lonely without her. And I thought, *I have to go find her, my lost sister.* But I couldn't. We get hillsick, you know."

Linny nodded.

"Mama almost died," she said. "But I don't seem to feel sick, no matter which side of the world I'm on."

"Well, some of us get it worse than others," said Mina. "And I get it so badly that already in Bend—in Bend! Within sight of the Bridge House!—the world starts spinning and the nausea rises up in me. Irika wasn't like me. She could go much farther afield than I ever could. Maybe that's why she became a Surveyor."

"What?" said Linny. "What? Mama's not a—"

"Hush, we don't have time right now. What I'm saying to you is, when she left, I decided to follow. And to follow, I needed to concoct a remedy for hillsickness. So I started that work. Twelve years ago already. And here's the thing—"

"The antidote to magic," said Linny. "They say it's almost ready. So they can go marching up into the hills and ruin things. And, by the way, Mama doesn't ruin things. So she's not a Surveyor."

Mina shook her head.

"But that's why she left, don't you see? She had become a Surveyor, back when she was young, because she had a talent for maps. Such a funny thing—she always seemed to know where she was!"

"Oh, me too!" said Linny, her heart melting a little.

"Nothing wrong with liking maps. It's only under this regent that Surveyors have warped into something ugly. Irika wanted to stay a good person, so she left. And I wanted to follow her so much I started working on that antidote, and that's when my trouble started. The Tinkerman let it slip to the Surveyors, what I was working on, and the Chief Surveyor had me hauled away out here, where I'm not allowed to go beyond the back wall there. See this?"

She showed Linny the metal ring, clamped tight around her ankle.

"It sets off a blasted deafening alarm if I cross any of their boundaries. Cheaper than soldiers, and just as effective. They don't want to *hurt* me. They want me to make that remedy, so they can, as you say, march up into the hills—"

And ruin things, thought Linny, finishing that sentence for her.

"The funny bit is," said Mina, with an unreadable

expression in her eyes and the corners of her clever, clever mouth, "that although I had made such huge strides in this project before they imprisoned me here, my progress since then has been very, very, very slow."

She guided Linny through a door. And through another door. Her words were easy and relaxed, but her movements were exceedingly awake, alert, and quick.

"Would an antidote to magic, to hillsickness, help my friend in Away?"

"I think it might," said Mina. They were in another great huge room now, filled with shelves. "*If only* it existed. *If only* I had somehow managed to secret away a single dose of it, before it became clear what the Surveyors had in mind for its use."

She was ushering Linny down one of the aisles now. Linny opened her mouth to ask another question, but Mina shook her head in warning and put a finger to her lips: "hush hush." Then she reached her hand up, up to one of the higher shelves.

"Because my brain has become very fuzzy," she said. "Since they put the shackle on my ankle. And since I heard about those plans to unwrinkle the wrinkled places. I have found chemistry very hard to focus on. It's sad, isn't it? After my sister, Irika, chemistry was what I used to love most in the world."

In her hands was a crystal-glass vial with a stopper.

In it, several grains of some green powder. There was a label on that vial that said only ADD THREE DROPS WATER FROM PLAIN SEA.

Mina took Linny's hand and curled her fingers around the vial. Then she wrapped both her own warm hands around Linny's, and there was such courage and affection in her hands and her voice that Linny almost couldn't stand it.

"They come all the time, demanding and shouting," Mina said. "But what can I do? I work all day, and then something happens, I drop something, I spill something, so every day it is as if I must start over. They will never have their antidote, I'm quite sure. Indeed, I have a feeling that today all my remaining notes will be accidentally destroyed. And the apparatus, too. Too bad."

There were voices being raised in some other part of that building.

"Apparently it's time for you to go," said Mina. She had already hustled the two of them over to another one of those outside doors. "I won't see my Irika again, I guess. But I have seen her daughter, and that is a wonderful thing. You must kiss your mother for me, when you find her again. Oh, and about the Plain Sea—"

The door was open; the wind came and sputtered in their faces.

"We can't even get near it. It does something odd to

our brains. But you, like your mother, seem to have a knack for getting to places others can't reach. *Even so, don't let the water touch you. Use this—*"

It was a long, curved glass dropper.

There was more noise from the other side of the building.

"Go, go, go," said Linny's Auntie Mina. "I will do my best to distract them. I haven't done much with my life, perhaps, but I have gotten lots and lots of practice in delaying Surveyors."

She bent forward and kissed Linny on her wild and messy hair, and then gave her a gentle shove out the door.

Linny looked back at her, something strong and warm bubbling up in her.

"Auntie Mina!" she said. She was looking for the right words. She had never wanted to find the right words so badly as she did right now.

"Time to run away very fast," said her aunt, with a last quick smile, and she stepped back in through that door.

"Auntie Mina, you're, I think, you must be a—"

The door swung shut.

So the right word came a little too late that time, but maybe that didn't matter.

The right word, by the way, was:

"Hero."

28

THE PLAIN SEA

The Half-Cat was waiting for her behind the back wall.

"We've got to hurry now, sorry," Linny said to it.

There was a siren blaring; she didn't care much for that sound. It probably meant the Surveyors had found out she had been there and then gone. In another second, they would surely come spilling out of all possible doors.

Before they could nab her, she had to get to the Plain Sea, where the water for Sayra's antidote was waiting.

So she ran.

For the first fifteen minutes or so, she ran with her mind full of fretfulness about what might be happening back at the research hub, and whether her Auntie Mina could really distract and delay a bunch of Surveyors. But the world was growing quieter and quieter all around her, until even the sound of her breathing began to seem like an intrusion, and she slowed her pace to a quieter lope.

On either side of her stretched a great plain of yellow grass, rippling in the breeze. She was on a path forward, through that endless yellow field, and there were no hills or trees or houses anywhere. Once or twice she had to stop and shake her head, because the sameness of everything made a person's head a little dizzy.

Dizzy was not the same as frightened or upset! She felt, in fact, strangely calm, for someone the Surveyors were after. But none of that mattered much, out here.

She thought nothing would break the beautiful monotony of that yellow grass, but then something caught her eye, down the path ahead of her—a pole or a toothpick (since distances were so hard to judge) sticking out of the endless yellow. She walked toward it for fifteen minutes, watching it grow taller, and when she arrived at the thing itself, she saw it was a simple sign, stuck on a pole.

AREA CLOSED. USE EXTREME CAUTION AT ALL TIMES.

The Half-Cat meowed, which was a strange sound in that quiet place, and sat itself down at the foot of the sign.

Caution, thought Linny, without tasting anything particular in the word. It went floating, simply, through her head and moved on.

The Half-Cat didn't follow, but that was all right, too. It meowed again, already from distinctly farther away.

The world was flattening out. She quite liked the feeling, actually. It was restful. The yellow grass sighed a little as the breeze brushed through it, and somewhere ahead was another faint roar of a noise, and her feet walked forward, step after step after step.

Eventually she noticed that the yellow grass was thinning out. She could see the sandy soil it somehow grew in. And after another very long time, the sound her feet made on the path had softened to the faintest *swish swish swish*, because the path was made of sand, sand was all around her, and ahead, where the sand seemed to darken a little and grow glassy, was the sea.

That must be why the cat had stayed behind. Cats, she remembered vaguely, did not care for things like lakes or puddles.

She looked to her right and her left, and again it was all more or less the same, everything she could see. Wonderfully peaceful, truly. A step later, her feet tripped on something, but even that little jolt didn't bother her much. Her hand reached down and picked up the thing her toes had stumbled over, and she saw it was a bone, but again her mind registered the fact without alarm.

The sand was beautifully flat, and the sea came rolling in, and it, too, was flat and lovely. And every now and then the sand was dotted with bones, which would become part of the sand in time.

She sat down to watch the water come in. It licked its way up the sand, in arcs and curves and parabolas, and

313

then it shrank back into itself. And it did that again and again and again.

She could sit there forever and not be tired of it . . . the water moving in, the water moving out. The plain sand and the plain air and the Plain Sea.

Some quite long stretch of time had passed before she remembered that a Plain Sea used to mean something important to her. Maybe not so important that you would have to do something about it, but still, important. Her mind felt cluttered with those thoughts in it. She preferred not to have a cluttered head, so she pushed them away, but that mental effort woke her up a little more, and she looked down at the long, narrow curve of glass in her hand and remembered it was a dropper.

For collecting drops.

Her mind thought about drops for a while, about the curve and roundness of them, about the equations you might make up to describe them, all of which in turn reminded her of the push and pull of the lovely sea.

It was not until somewhat later that she looked down and saw the crystal vial in her other hand.

She thought about how much nicer the little bottle would be if it were empty, if she just dumped those green grains into the sand. In fact, she had gotten as far as pulling the top out of the vial when something stopped her. It might have been the greenness of the grains, which would have been jarring, maybe, against the pure yellow sand.

Whatever it was, she stood there quite awhile, with the glass dropper curving forward from one hand, and the almost empty vial in the other.

She was supposed to put water in the bottle, but she couldn't remember why. She looked at it and looked at the sea, stared at each of them for a very long time.

And then, to her own surprise, she found herself standing up and walking forward, to the place where the sea lapped at the sand, and she leaned forward with her long curved dropper and squeezed water into it, and then put three drops of that Plainest water into the crystal vial.

One.

Two.

Three.

The little green grains fizzed and bubbled when the Plain water hit them. The fizzing turned them into a teaspoon's worth of liquid, as green as spring leaves.

It was as she was pushing the rubber stopper so snugly back into the vial that the watery edge of the Plain Sea washed right up over the toes of her shoes and for a while cleared her thoughts utterly away. She had been too active for this quiet place, poking at the sea with the long curve of glass. She stood watching the water come forward and recede, come forward and recede, lapping at the sand and her toes and the patient, quiet heaps of bones.

The light around her (on the sand, the sea, and the bones) changed color. She did sort of notice that. But nothing had to be done or could be done about that changing light.

She stood there and was empty and free and plain.

If you waited long enough, time would become as flat and plain a thing as the yellow fields or the sand or the sea, going on and on forever without end. And this was that endless moment for her. She had reached the end of the world.

Everything has an end, even worlds. Ends. Everything has ends.

That reminded her of something:

"Yarn's like life—two ends and a tangled middle."

A tremor ran through her. Someone used to laugh and say that, when the yarn got away from her. Who was that? When was that?

Someone who was also, she seemed to remember, at an end of the world, also fading, because worlds, like tangles— like lives—have two ends, as anyone knows.

After that long, long moment of ending, she was beginning to see things again—the water at her feet, the vial in her hand, the liquid in it shining leaf green, like something she couldn't remember, something she really wanted to remember—oh, that was it. *Like Sayra's eyes.*

She took a great gasping breath and stepped back out of reach of the water.

Then something stung her on the back of the neck. And again.

Someone was apparently throwing pebbles at her.

And calling her name.

"Linny! Linny! Come away from there."

Although this wasn't a place where she could feel angry, she did feel mildly bothered. The plainness and quiet had been so perfect, before the pebbles and the shouting! She turned around to see what was going on and saw an extremely bedraggled, grubby, dirty, unhappy face looking at her from the top of a rolling dune. A familiar face! If she had a little more time, she might even have been able to come up with a name to go with it.

"Quick," said that person. "Quick, hurry, come away from here."

He had a cat in his arms. Linny was pretty sure she had seen both of them before, the cat and the person.

"Darn it, Linny!" said the irritating person. "Didn't you even notice what was lying there all around you? Look!"

A hand shook something in front of her eyes.

Sand falling from grubby fingers, and clenched in those fingers, a bone.

A bone. Was that bad?

For the first time in a very long while, she felt a twinge of unease.

"Bones all over! Cursed place!" said—

Wait! The grubby person had a name!

"It's *Elias*!" said Linny, and in remembering his name, she also remembered her own. She remembered a lot of things, all at once. Her mind snapped back from plainness and became all wrinkled and complicated again. "But you drowned! Or exploded!"

"*Almost* drowned and *sort of* exploded," said Elias. He seemed almost proud of it. "I remember being in the water and that magician's awful ma pulling at my jacket. I guess it came off at some point. I don't know. I don't remember anything else until I washed up on the river's bank, way down this way. Then that cat of yours showed up, so I knew you must be nearby. Come on! Don't stand there! We have to get away—it had you trapped, until I rescued you."

"Rescue me! You did not," said Linny. It was almost like old times, arguing with Elias. "I had just remembered Sayra, all on my own. I got the antidote, see?"

She waved the little bottle before his nose.

They were walking away from the sea now, step after step. It was becoming almost normal to be walking again, though she was sorry to leave the quiet curve of the water slipping up the sand and back again.

How miraculous that Elias was actually here.

"I thought you were dead," she said, a little shyly.

"Nope. But *you* soon would have been, if I hadn't been

318

there to pitch pebbles at you. That's a deadly, horrible place, that beach. Oh, don't look at me like that. Did you see all those bones everywhere? Ugh. People go there, and they *die*."

It was definitely, actually Elias, that lummox! She had really thought he was gone. But here he was—and to her surprise, Linny found she had never been so glad to see anybody in her life.

29

BACK TO THE EDGE

They were walking through those long fields, heading away from the Plain Sea, and as tired and as hungry and as wobble headed as they felt, they were both filled with an extraordinary feeling: with hope. It made them want to tell each other everything, the past and the future, which for the first time looked less than totally black (if you kept your eyes studiously away from the dark spots in the picture). Linny talked about the leaf-green antidote, how she hoped it would cure Sayra of the magic that had sickened her, how she would carry it up to Away, where Sayra's spirit was, more alive than the faded shell of her body back in Lourka, and Elias told his own story over and over again: the dandelion-haired woman grabbing at him, the jacket slipping off, water filling his lungs—

And that was the point in Elias's description when they came over the top of a little swell of land in that otherwise flat world—and found the Surveyors right there, waiting for them.

They had a sand-colored wagon that blended into the grass of the field. There were four of them waiting, with their gray uniforms on and circles of black glass hiding their eyes.

"Oh, no. Run!" said Elias, his voice hoarse, but it was too late for running, because the Surveyors had already jumped on them, from what felt like all sides. Linny and Elias were already being led to the wagon now by all those rough hands, and the Half-Cat was emitting muffled meows from over to the left, as if it was being stuffed into a sack and didn't like it.

"Well, that was easy," said one of the Surveyors to Elias. "Like tracking a clumsy bear. And now we've nabbed you and the girl, as well. Why didn't you go home, girl? That's what we thought you'd done—lit back out for the hills."

"Two for the price of one!" said another one of those Surveyors. "Hey, don't you start struggling. Won't do you any good."

The Surveyors were bundling them into their wagon. There was no way to wriggle out of their grasp. (Linny did try, and the hands on her shoulders just became tighter and heavier; over to the right of her, she could hear Elias trying to shrug off one of those hands and failing.)

It was a large wagon, much bigger than the cart Linny had driven out of the Broken City. Linny and Elias, their hands tied, and the dangerous-looking sack that contained the Half-Cat, were dumped into the back seat. The lourka in its sack was at Linny's feet. Her mind, meanwhile, was full of skittering panic but couldn't come up with a coherent thought, much less an actual plan. She was still dazed from her time at the edge of the Plain Sea, and dazed from the happy shock of finding Elias again. And now dazed all over again from the sudden hope suddenly being ripped away.

And she was hungry. She hadn't eaten in ages, it seemed like to her. Not since those juicy tomatoes. And tomatoes only go so far.

The road the wagon took went right by the research hub, where the blank walls gave no clue about what had happened to Aunt Mina after Linny had left.

The thought of Mina was bad enough, but then a worse thought caught up with Linny: *she gave everything she had to me, and it made no difference.* And that made Linny shrink down in the wagon, hoping Mina could not, would not, see, so that her heart wouldn't break all over again.

Even if in the Plain they did not call it "breaking."

Because she was slumping and despairing, Linny missed the very beginning of what happened next.

They were at the intersection beyond the research hub when one of the gray men said, "Wait, who's that there?"

And as he pressed the button that stopped the wagon, a dart suddenly appeared in the side of his neck, and he dropped down to the left, as if he were a stone column kicked by the giant who had built the fairground bridge. And the Surveyor next to him had sprouted a dart of his own and was dangling over the side of the wagon.

"Down!" said Elias and Linny to each other, at almost exactly the same time, but it is hard to get really far down in the backseat of a wagon when your hands and feet are bound. She shut her eyes tight, though, willing herself invisible. And Elias, too. Let them both be invisible.

There were thumps and bumps for a minute or so, but no more shouting, and then a breathless, familiar voice said, "Well, hello, little guide of mine! Hello, hello!"

Elias must have opened his eyes before Linny, because he was already saying, "Who are you?" while Linny spluttered and tried to sit up again.

It was the Tinkerman, looking over at them from the front seat. He looked a little shaken, but pleased as punch.

"They were going to waste you! Waste you! So I had to stop them. They'll thank me in the end."

Linny peered over the edge of the wagon and saw the bodies of those Surveyors at the side of the road, where the Tinkerman must have dragged them. She shuddered at the suddenness with which a person could become an unmoving *thing*. She couldn't imagine those bodies ever thanking anyone again for anything.

"Oh, they'll wake up eventually," said the Tinkerman, who must have followed her gaze. "It's strong stuff, but not *that* strong. We should probably not waste too much time."

He had moved a bulky bag of his own into the front seat. Now he was looking at the wagon's buttons and levers, and he actually rubbed his hands together in glee, as ogres and bandits do in the worst stories.

The Half-Cat yowled forlornly from inside its sack.

"Oh, is that my own dear cat, as well?" said the Tinkerman. "Really, this is turning out to be a very good day."

"Thank you so much for the rescue, sir," said Elias, and Linny could tell from the stretched sound of his voice that his headache must be bad again. He would have to be remembering how much he hated being in the Plain. And being kidnapped by Surveyors had not helped. "But who are you, and where are you taking us?"

"He's Arthur Vix," said Linny. "The Tinkerman. Irika Pontis's sort-of father."

"Your gra—!"

Linny kicked his shins with her trussed-up legs. It was the best she could do, under the circumstances, to keep him quiet.

Elias's eyes were as wide as teacups. Linny could see that he was getting entirely the wrong idea about the Tinkerman.

"But let's hear what Mr. Vix has to say," she said to Elias, in her sweet-little-lamb voice. She hoped Elias would take the hint.

"Ha ha! What I have to say is, *research expedition*!" said the Tinkerman, starting the wagon machine. "Finally, finally under way. When you babbled about going home and ran off from the fair, well, I thought we might be losing our best chance, with you skedaddling back into the hills, so I came to see my dear Mina, just to check in on how her research was going. She's been working on that hillsickness remedy for a long time now. Sadly, still no cure, says Mina. But I'm heading into the wrinkled hills, antidote or not."

"You!" said Linny.

"Oh, yes. Who else better, to put my theory to the test? And imagine my surprise when I gathered, from various things her coworkers were saying, that my own recent guest, my impossible visitor, my future guide, was in the neighborhood! Well!"

He chuckled. The wind was blowing through his silver hair. He seemed very, very pleased with himself indeed.

"I heard enough to know they had captured someone, and then I set up my ambush. Criminality is so easy, it turns out, if you remember to bring enough darts. Here we are, happy as clams and on our way. Why did I slouch around so long, hoping they would give me official permission to test my theory? Who even gives permission for such things anymore? Who's in charge? The regent and that awful magician are glaring at each other over the Broken City like it's their own personal chessboard. They would have kept me waiting until the mountains wore down and the river ran dry!"

"What theory?" said Elias, that lummox.

"Don't encourage him," said Linny. "He said we're happy as clams, but we're *not*. We're tied up in *ropes*."

"Complexity, like water, flows downhill," said Vix modestly as he upped the speed of that wagon. "And can be tapped in to for power. This is the nutshell version I'm giving you now! Wrinkled places are complex, right? Even you can see that. The limit case of complexity is what you call Away. So, run a wire from there to the Plain, and your light bulbs will burn until the end of time. You can use that power to change the world. Like damming a river! Simple!"

"If the universe doesn't just go *pop*," said Linny. "Which I understand could potentially also happen. You shouldn't mess with Away. Your plan's the worst one I ever heard of. Don't pay attention to him, Elias."

Elias had been chewing over the Tinkerman's explanation, and his teacup eyes were narrowing now, like saucers being turned on their sides.

"So they'll use Away to power their grid," he said. "To make things go, I guess, but also to unwrinkle the world. Like what they did at the fair, only more so."

"Yes," said Linny and the Tinkerman at exactly the same time, only the Tinkerman added a happy exclamation point at the end.

"And my theory will be proved correct!"

That shut even Elias up for a while. He had probably never met anyone before who was willing to risk the end of the universe just to prove a stupid theory. He looked at Linny, and Linny looked at him. They were in very grave need of a backup plan.

"Excuse me, Mr. Vix," said Linny, trying sweetness again. "But my feet are falling asleep. Would you mind please untying us, now that we've been rescued?"

Almost to her surprise, the Tinkerman pulled the wagon to the side of the road and stopped it. "We'll need you in good shape when we get to the hills," he said. "Good shape and rested."

"Yes," said Linny, spreading the sweetness on thick. "But what if my feet have to be cut off because they haven't had any blood in them so long?"

She had gone a little overboard there; the Tinkerman was laughing.

"All right, all right," he said. "And we'll travel faster if you're resting. So, good night—"

And before Linny could say anything more, or even register what was happening, Vix had pulled out two more darts from that satchel of his, had turned around as casually as can be, and had stabbed one into Elias's shoulder and the other—ouch!—into Linny's own poor arm. Sharp as sharp, right through the sleeve of her dress. She wanted to shout, but before she got her mouth open, she had forgotten what shouting meant, forgotten what mouths were, and had slipped down into the utter dark.

30

TO THE EDGE

There was an infinite period of total nothingness that passed in no time at all. Space and time, both emptied out of everything that used to fill them. Nothing.

Until the nothingness was replaced by aching bones and a feeling of heaviness, and Linny realized she was lying flat on the ground, no longer in the wagon, and there was sunlight warming her eyelids.

She tried to open her eyes, but nothing happened.

How long had she been lost in nothingness?

It was coming back to her now. That treacherous Tinkerman!

She tried again with her eyes, and this time got one of them a tiny bit open. Just enough to catch a blurry glimpse of what looked like Elias, stretched out not far from her. The world started spinning, so she shut her eye and rested back in the comfortable darkness for another minute before trying again.

She opened her eyes more carefully, noticing this time that Elias's eyes were open, too, and he was looking at her.

"Where are we?" she whispered.

She could see the top of a hill to the right, and beyond that a forest that became wilder and denser as it marched up another, more complicated slope. Her heart jumped a little in hope. That didn't look like the Plain.

"Shh," said Elias. "You were really out there for a while. I mean, so was I, actually. Sheesh."

Then he smiled, a sweet ghost of a smile.

"You do realize *you* just asked *me* where we are," he said.

But by then Linny had moved her head just enough to let her eyes soak up the contours of the land all around, and she *did* know where they must be.

They were on a flat field, looking up toward the hills and the trees. A simple line of rocks ran past them and off as far in both directions as she could see. A butterfly of four different colors winkled through the air, but it was careful not to cross the line of those rocks and come over to them where they lay on the field.

"Wait," she said. "It's wrinkled over there."

There wasn't a river here, as there was in the Broken City, to mark the edge between wrinkled and Plain. The river came down from the hills and turned, and then turned again at the other end of the Broken City, beyond the fairgrounds. If they hadn't crossed the river, they must be far to one side of the world, where walking across a field might be enough to take you from Plain to wrinkled places. That was interesting to Linny. It was the sort of data that woke a person up.

"I know," said Elias. "He had to stop driving that wagon. He attached it to a power stump over there, see? And now he's fooling with his wires."

The Tinkerman appeared to be connecting an almost invisibly thin wire to some part of the metal charging station that the Surveyors had planted in the ground here, where the Plain bumped up against the wrinkled half of the world.

"Do you think you could run away, Linny?" said Elias, under his breath. "He did untie your feet."

She moved one foot and then another. They still felt oddly remote from the rest of her. Every part of her felt sort of remote, actually.

"Not quite yet," she said. "In a few minutes, maybe?"

It was already too late for that, though. The Tinkerman had noticed them watching him, and he came over now, an expectant bounce in his step.

"Awake from your naps?" he said. "Almost time for us to start walking."

"You knocked us out," said Linny. "We're not going anywhere with you."

"Oh, but you are," said the Tinkerman. "You'll come along like dutiful little children, I'm quite sure. Because I found some very interesting things, while you were sleeping."

He swept his hand to the right, and Linny saw her own lourka sack and the little bag from around her neck (only one card left in it) spread neatly out on the ground. There wasn't anything from Elias's pockets, because the river must have eaten everything when he was almost drowning.

"So? You knew I had a lourka," said Linny, but she saw immediately from the triumphant look on the Tinkerman's face that she was forgetting something else, something truly important.

The Tinkerman leaned a little closer, pulling a hand out of some hidden inside pocket in his jacket—and in that hand was a crystal vial, filled with a teaspoonful of leaf-green medicine, green as Sayra's eyes.

"What is this, you impossible girl?" he asked now. "Did you really think I wouldn't find it?"

"Hey!" said Linny, sitting all the way up now. "That's for Sayra!"

"Exactly," said the Tinkerman. "Exactly. So you'd better guide me up to Away, then, hadn't you? So we can see how powerful this antidote actually is. And maybe save your little friend. Who knows?"

"What about you?" said Elias. He no longer had any

illusions about the Tinkerman, Linny could tell. "You'll be hillsick all the way up."

"I'm tough," said the Tinkerman. "With a guide leading me along, I guess I'll manage."

And he tucked the vial back into his jacket, out of sight.

Linny and Elias couldn't think of anything to say. He had them. He really did. They wanted that medicine to get up to Away as much as he wanted to test his theory. And if the antidote was in the Tinkerman's hands, then they had to lead him into the hills.

"Oh, and here," said the Tinkerman, and he tossed Linny a handful of cloth—her birthday sash, with the silk rosebud still tucked into it. Linny felt her hand tremble as she hid it back in her pocket. "Just to show you how well-meaning I can be. Time for us to get going now, isn't it?"

But first he handed around some biscuits that tasted as rectangular as they looked.

Soon they were walking uphill, into the woods. Linny had her lourka slung over her back, but the Tinkerman had kept everything else. Elias had nothing, because the river had taken it all. And the Tinkerman was weighed down not just by the knapsack holding all his mechanisms and wires, but by the sack with the Half-Cat tied in it.

"Why don't you let the poor cat go, at least?" said

Elias, who had a soft spot for all creatures, no matter how wild or strange.

"That's my insurance policy, right there," said the Tinkerman. "Run away, and the cat gets one of those darts. You can imagine how lethal a human dose of that stuff would be for it, yes? A sad waste of a cat. But I think you'll see the logic of the business and not run away."

He held a spool of almost invisibly thin wire in his hands, and as he walked, he bent over every now and then to pound a metal stake as thin as a needle into the ground, so that the wire could run along almost, but not quite, touching the earth.

It would tire him out faster, that was the only positive side Linny could see. She didn't like his pounding needles into the poor, wrinkled ground. But when she scowled at him, he jogged the sack with the Half-Cat in it up and down and waved a dart in the air, and she turned away, seething.

Meanwhile, however, the trees were looking ever more like real trees, the rocks getting wilder and rockier, and Elias and Linny felt the wrinkledness of everything around them, and their hearts, despite the bind they were in at the moment, rejoiced.

Elias, who had been so bent and wobbly down in the Plain, was soon dancing up granite boulders just for the thrill of leaping off them again, as if he were one of the twins back in Lourka. Linny would have laughed at him if she hadn't been so glad to see him at home in the world again. And she was determined to stay close to the Tinkerman, to keep her eye on him, on the poor Half-Cat in that sack, and on the jacket where, in some hidden pocket, the vial with Sayra's antidote was traveling up the hills, ever closer to Away.

Linny was the guide. She couldn't help it, really. She followed the wrinkles of those hills as easily as breathing. She couldn't help knowing which way to go.

The Tinkerman huffed and puffed the first hour or so, but he kept unrolling his spool of wire and pounding in his needles. Then periods of frantic coughing joined his hard breathing, making him stop to gasp for air at regular intervals, while Linny and Elias watched him. Not with much compassion, it must be said. Linny had never felt more like a vulture circling. Or a wolf. She narrowed her eyes and felt the wolfish sharp-toothed thoughts take shape in her. If he would just weaken enough for her to grab that antidote and run!

But the Tinkerman, just as he had said, was stronger than he looked. Or maybe it was his single-minded dedication to his theory that kept him slogging on and on, unfurling wire and pounding in needle stakes, as the hill-sickness seeped into his legs and his belly and his lungs.

Eventually he was stopping every few paces to retch,

and then he went a new shade of green and staggered off into the bushes, looking so miserable that even Linny felt sorry for him, though the wolf in her kept calculating the time left before he could be toppled over with a Linny-sized shove.

He was in the bushes awhile, and when he came back, he looked sheepish and bedraggled, and Linny and Elias stayed silent, which was as close to compassion as they were willing to go. Soon enough he'd be on the ground for sure. They exchanged glances and nodded. Soon.

But after that near collapse, the Tinkerman seemed to get a second wind. He bent his face grimly toward the hillside ahead and marched on, perhaps even a little faster than before.

Sometimes nausea lifts for a while, after the worst has happened, so at first that was what Linny assumed was going on, but fifteen minutes passed, and he was still sticking to his pace, and whacking needles into the ground with verve. Maybe even slogging along a little bit faster. Some minutes later, Linny noticed it had been a very long time since he had had to stop to cough.

"Hunh," she said under her breath, for only Elias to hear, and she jerked her chin at the Tinkerman, striding on ahead of them now. It was a question and a comment, both at once.

"I know," said Elias. "Let me see something."

He trotted up to the Tinkerman and tapped him on the shoulder.

"Hey. You feeling better?" he said.

The Tinkerman turned around and blinked a few times.

"Why, yes," he said. "Now that you mention it. Must be getting used—"

But before he finished that sentence, Elias had done something entirely unlike himself: he had swung his fist right into the Tinkerman's cheek.

Linny, for her part, cried out and clenched her hands so tightly together that her fingernails dug into her own palm.

What they had both seen was the change in the Tinkerman's face. The green was entirely gone. His cheeks were slightly flushed, as you might expect from someone walking uphill for hour after hour, but he no longer looked ill.

"You lousy no-good thief," said Elias. "You've gone and swallowed it, haven't you?" And he reached quite roughly into the Tinkerman's jacket, only to find, as by then they both knew he would—the empty vial.

The Tinkerman had drunk the antidote. They had taken their eyes off him only while he had been off in the bushes, and then only out of politeness, but it had been long enough.

"So there's no point now," said Elias, looking at Linny. "Right?"

How had she let this happen? How had she let this happen? They had been so close! They had come so deep already into the wrinkled places, almost as if the hills had been helping them along (distances stretched and shrank like toffee in the wrinkled hills). And now they were standing there with a vigorous, red-faced Tinkerman, stronger and younger looking than he had any right to be, and Sayra's medicine, which they had suffered so much to find, was gone.

"Now, now, now," said the Tinkerman, flexing his strengthened arms a little. Elias's punch seemed to have left no trace of itself on his flushed cheek. "Don't go overreacting. In any case, I don't think you two are any match for me at the moment."

Linny ignored him. She put her hand on Elias's shoulder instead.

"I promised Sayra I'd come back," she said. "So I have to, anyway. Medicine or no medicine. I'll go there, and I'll be keeping my promise, and maybe I'll even think up something I can do for her, eventually. Can you keep him from following me?"

"Ha ha," said the Tinkerman.

Ignore him, she told herself. *Ignore him.*

"I can try," said Elias.

"I wanted to save her," said Linny. She was holding on to his arm now, almost as if Elias were something strong and true, like a house or a tree, that could keep her standing.

"I know," said Elias.

"If I get stuck there, tell my mother—"

"I won't go back to Lourka without you," said Elias grimly. "I'll find you."

They looked at each other.

Won't, he had said. Not *can't*. But *won't*.

"All right," said Linny. "Don't let him hurt you too much. He has darts."

And she turned and ran up the hill while Elias tackled the Tinkerman.

31

SAYRA

She ran and ran, while the world folded and refolded itself around her. A dragonfly changed its color from blue to red as it wobbled by. The water she scooped up from little streams sometimes had a hint of vanilla or cloves or something bright and indescribable. Home! It was beginning to feel like home.

As the sun slowly rolled toward the horizon, she found herself clambering over a wall of rocks, and a narrow valley opened before her, filled with golden trees. Not just yellow-orange-red, as trees sometimes are, even far from the wrinkled edges of the world; trees that actually glittered in the sun.

She ran a fingertip along one of those golden leaves, and it made a faint tinkling sound, like a bell. When the wind picked up, the whole grove chimed in for a moment, and as Linny hurried up the green grass of that valley, her head tipped a little back so she could see the sunlight playing on the golden leaves above her; for a moment it seemed impossible that there could be gray Surveyors anywhere eager to undo the wrinkledness of the world, or a Tinkerman with one greedy thought in his head and a bag full of darts.

At the top of the golden woods, she turned a kind of corner and found herself in a very wrinkled valley, not much bigger than she was. A pine tree with needles of many different colors stretched above her head, and there was a rock underneath it, suitable for sitting on, so she did.

Linny watched it for a while, still catching her own breath, and then she swung her bag around in front and got out her poor old lourka. It was a lot more battered-looking than it had been when she had first come up to the edge of Away, but it was still beautiful. And it was the way in. It was an instrument and a doorway, both at once.

"Sayra," she said aloud.

The word hovered there in that sliver's worth of valley. Where else could it go, after all?

Linny strummed the strings of her lourka, thinking of the songs that Sayra used to like most. The song about wind in summer trees, for instance—Sayra was fond of that one. She picked out the first notes, thumbing a kind of drone on the lowest string, underneath the music. Oh, it felt good to have the lourka out, even if her hands were so stiff and clumsy after her adventures that she dropped half the notes.

The leaves unfold
Their green and gold . . .

(Though to be singing that under a pine tree was funny!)

She thought of Elias, wrestling with the Tinkerman so she could run away, and she thought about the Half-Cat, trapped for way too long in the Tinkerman's sack, and for a moment worry almost hushed her.

But then, without even noticing what she was doing, she had started putting music to that worry, finding notes that sounded right for Elias—not as much a lummox as he used to be, after all—and then falling into riffs that seemed right for the Half-Cat, a tune that would be half one thing and half another, and in more than one way, just as the Half-Cat was both silver and gold, and both wrinkled and Plain.

The music hovered all around her, singing out her longing. And pulling some on the world, as a true song will do. For a time, Linny was as lost in her own song as another person would have been in the Upper Woods—

And then a rustling crash of a sound woke her up, and even though the noise was not "here," wherever here was, but quite some wrinkled distance away, Linny's head cleared.

How had she let herself get distracted like that? She had to keep her mind on Sayra. It was Sayra she wanted to play back into the world. She dug through her pockets and found the wrinkled sash Sayra had sewn for her, with its half-transparent flower that was also (as Linny's notes were transformed by Sayra's magic with stitches and silk) a song.

The lourka and the silk flower had come through the blackness of tunnels with her; they had been underground and locked up in fancy buildings and even to the edge of the Plain Sea. It was not surprising that they would look so bruised and scraped and battered—almost as battered as Linny herself! But here they all were, and all bent on remembering Sayra, who had always looked at Linny and seen a good person and a friend, when most of the rest of the world had seen only mischief and trouble.

She put the silk flower on the rock facing her and put her whole heart into the silly song that had inspired it.

> *Rose, rose, rose in the sun,*
> *Fly away fast before the long day's done!*
> *Look down at us from high in the sky*
> *And waggle your petals as you fly by. . . .*

The flower Sayra had made with such care blossomed,

reshaped itself, took wing, flew forward a couple of feet—
and disappeared.

Linny looked up from her lourka. Something had
changed in the air right before her. She could see through
the pine tree's branches, as if they had all of a sudden gone
transparent. Through them was another place, larger and
wilder than "here." Still a little blurry, but each note of
her song made the blue of that place beyond the branches
brighter and more vivid. There was a log there, under a
blue sky. And someone was sitting on the log.

Linny stood up and stepped into that picture, simple
as that.

The sounds around her changed, instantly.

In one way it was quiet (no birds), but far away, something very large roared and sighed and murmured.

But she was running already . . .

And crying out, "Sayra! Sayra!" as she ran . . .

Because it was surely Sayra, a somewhat blurry Sayra,
sitting on the log. Not looking in Linny's direction at all,
but gazing out over the edge of the bluff—they were on
a bluff—and at the churning waves of the ocean beyond.

(So much wilder, this ocean, than the Plain Sea at the
other end of the world.)

Even as Linny ran to that log on the bluff in Away,
however, a tiny thread of doubt curled into her joy.

For one thing, she could see the log and even the ocean

waves right through the girl's body, which was disconcerting.

For another thing, the almost-transparent girl on the
log hadn't jumped up to greet her or even spun around
with joy—as Sayra surely, surely, would have done. She
was only now beginning to turn her head, only now, as
Linny, struck by sudden shyness, stopped in her tracks a
step or two away.

"Sayra," said Linny. "I came back for you. Sayra!"

"Sayra," echoed the wispy girl on the log, and her
head had pivoted around enough that Linny could see
her strange, wild eyes.

Linny couldn't help it; she gasped. Sayra's eyes had
always been green, green, beautiful shining-leaf green, as
green as a story about emeralds or the sea. But this girl's
eyes were not just green *like* the sea, but filled with the
very sea itself.

In those eyes, the sea spilled back and forth, crashing
and rolling. It was as if this ghostly version of Sayra had
been staring so long at the ocean that the image of those
waves had just taken over her eyes, like ink rubbing off a
picture onto your hands.

The worst of it was, Sayra's ocean-filled eyes showed
no signs of knowing who Linny was.

"Sayra," she said again, in a wondering and wispy
voice.

"That's you," said Linny. "I'm not Sayra—I'm Linny."

The girl on the log stared at her, and the waves crashed and curled in her eyes.

They stood in silence for a while, staring at each other.

"Stop this. Come back," said Linny finally. "It's my fault you're here, and I can't stand it being my fault."

And because the girl on the log didn't move a muscle, just stared at Linny with the ocean washing through her eyes, Linny said, "Scoot over" and plopped herself down on the log beside Sayra, shoulder to shoulder, just like all those thousands of days in the woods, back when they were children tethered together in the village of Lourka. Only Sayra's shoulder was almost not there. It was the strangest thing. Linny had the impression that if she didn't focus like crazy, if she let her eyes close or her mind drift away, she might open her eyes and find no Sayra-like girl beside her at all.

At the edge of her vision she saw that there was the tiniest, most insubstantial of threads spinning out from Sayra to the sea. *That's why she's so faint,* thought Linny. *She must have been unraveling here already a very, very long time.*

Everything backward: the ocean like an enormous web, sucking all the little spiders dry. (Linny and Sayra had always liked spiders—Sayra for their spinning, and Linny for their plotting and planning.) And what was left, when you had unraveled into the endless sea?

The thought made Linny very tired. She had been running, it felt like, for practically ever. And now here was Sayra and yet no Sayra at all, somehow.

What were you supposed to do, when you got to Away, and the person you had come for was already gone?

But when Linny's eyes, defeated, fell away from the sky beyond the bluff, she saw, resting in the girl's ghostly hand, the ghostly silk butterfly-flower, still rippling through its wrinkled changes. The wings shivered and became petals. The petals changed color and suddenly were once again wings. It had found its way back to its maker.

There once had been a Sayra who had living, leaf-green eyes, and who cared enough about Linny to create something as wonderful as that flower, as a gift.

"You know, you made that," said Linny, and to her surprise the girl's hand trembled a little and closed around the silk.

Linny forced herself to look back into those ocean-filled eyes again. This time they seemed not just empty, but puzzled. Perhaps the girl was trying to figure something out. Perhaps she was simply staring for the sake of staring. It was hard to tell, so Linny turned back, with the lourka on her lap, to face the wild ocean of Away.

The Plain Sea, at the other end of the world, had

oozed forward and seeped back again, offering something astonishingly simple and simply wonderful: the Plainness of water. She remembered that, watching the Plain Sea, she had become something more abstract and more perfect than her messy, muddy self. Something numbers and equations could probably have described.

That Plainness had held her. What was holding Sayra here?

Here they were on a green bluff, and down below them the impossible ocean romped and played. It was the opposite of plain; it carried a frothy speckling of seaweed and shells on the backs of its waves. It came from somewhere and was going off to somewhere else, all of that complicated water. When Linny looked left and right, she saw the rocky green bluff continuing in the great distance, until the saltwater mist sent up by the waves blurred all the edges. It was a far and untamed place, and every now and then what seemed like the shadow of a melody or whisper went sailing by on its way out toward the sea, to join the wild song and dance there, and make it even wilder and more glorious.

Sayra's unraveling must also feed that sea. Linny twitched on the log. The little thread spinning off from the wispy edges of her friend—she couldn't stand it.

"You know you've got a loose thread there," said Linny. "You used to hate loose threads."

She nudged the almost-not-there shoulder next to hers, but it was like nudging a cloud.

And suddenly Linny just simply couldn't take it anymore. She jumped up, caught that unraveling thread in her hands, and snapped it free.

Linny hadn't thought anything through, of course; she didn't have a clue in her head what might happen next—just that Sayra, her Sayra, was unraveling before her eyes, and it was more than she could bear.

So she was caught by surprise when the half-transparent Sayra gave a high, thin wail of distress and flung herself after the vanishing thread—tripping toward the edge of that bluff like a balloon about to float away.

The bluff. The edge. The ocean beyond.

No!

Before she had time to think or reason or feel, Linny had already sprung so hard in Sayra's direction that both of them—one wispy pale, one battered, brown, and solid—tripped over each other's feet or over a lumpy bit of earth or who knows what, and they fell in a surprised heap of two to the ground.

32

COMPLICATIONS

"No! No! No!" Linny was shouting as she tried to pin the ghostly remnants of Sayra down, and Sayra—or the girl who had been Sayra, once long ago—wriggled inchwise toward the edge of the cliff, but already with just a little less conviction.

"What are you thinking, anyway?" said Linny, hanging on to her friend for dear life. "Don't you even care that there are people that can't stand losing you? Don't you even *care*?"

The girl with the ocean in her eyes looked up with doubt.

"Who are you?" she asked, and it was a little bit like the wind speaking.

"I'm Linny, Linny, Linny—don't you remember?" said Linny, almost as wild as that sea, and definitely grubbier. "I'm Linny, your friend, your mismatched twin. I told you to wait, and I know you tried. I *know* you tried. I went all the way down into the Plain to find a cure for you, because it was all my fault, and I, and I—"

Linny got a little stuck there, remembering the awfulness of that empty vial.

She had gone down into the Plain for medicines, and she had failed. She had brought nothing back. Nothing.

Absolutely nothing.

For a long time she lay there, hanging on to the almost-nothing-at-all that used to be her twin and friend, and she cried and cried and cried into Sayra's transparent and insubstantial shoulder. She had wanted so much to save her.

Then she lay there quietly with her eyes closed, sniffling a little, and dreamed of being a tiny child again, whose mother could make all the bad dreams go away, just by patting her on the back.

No, wait. Some faint hand really was patting her back, so gently it was almost nothing, almost just the breeze along the green bluff's edge.

Linny lay there frozen, as still as could be. Ghosts might be like wild rabbits, she figured: hard to tame and quick to startle. *I'll lie here forever,* she thought, *and then eventually I'll just open maybe the corner of one eye—*

But that was when a strange yowling hiss split the air in half, so near by that Linny forgot everything else and sat bolt upright and wide-eyed, breathing hard.

"Oh!" said someone's startled and familiar voice.

Just there to the left, the air had been torn, and through that impossible rip she could see the silver-golden face of the Half-Cat, hovering there in midair and midyowl.

"Help it! Oh!" pleaded that someone who sounded so much like Sayra.

And Linny, worn out, could not think of anything cleverer to do than to hold out the hand that was not holding on to Sayra and say, like any empty-headed fool, "Here, kitty kitty . . ."

Foolish as they were, the words worked like magic, just as if Linny had actually stepped forward and yanked the cat toward her by its mismatched ears. The Half-Cat suddenly tumbled forward, right into Away.

For the briefest of moments, there was half of a Half-Cat visible in the air—some tiny piece of Linny's brain was amused by that—and then the cat, all of it, was rolling on the ground, hissing and spitting and clearly very unhappy.

When it rose to its feet, the fur on both its golden and its silver sides was standing straight up. For a moment it looked more like an enormous, skinny, multicolored hedgehog than a cat.

Then Linny noticed, with a quick jolt of alarm, that a rope was tied to its frizzed-out tail, and the rope ran up and away and vanished in thin air.

The ghost of Sayra was pointing a half-transparent hand toward the place where the Half-Cat had popped into the world and where the rope now vanished. "*What?*" she asked.

"You're talking!" said Linny, but then she saw what Sayra had seen and fell silent, while her heart rattled and banged.

A hand had appeared out of nowhere, holding on to the rope. Around it, the air rippled and sparked.

For the smallest part of a second, she had thought *Elias*, but the hand was too long-fingered and pale to belong to him, so Elias's name turned to ice in her mouth.

Now another hand joined the first, feeling its way along the thread. Around the hands, the air whined in protest, and then gave way, and a body pulled itself into Away, while the Half-Cat yowled, and while Linny and Sayra huddled together, watching in horror.

"What is that? *Who* is that?" said Sayra, her arm trembling under Linny's hand.

"Shh," said Linny, but she had already recognized the man who had torn his way so rudely into this place. It was, of course, the Tinkerman.

The Tinkerman was pushing himself up, a little shakily, from the ground. His eyes were wide and triumphant, but his breath was ragged.

"Away!" he was saying to himself. "Did I do it? Is this Away? The cat is there—"

Only then did he turn his head far enough to see Linny and Sayra.

"That girl!" he said. "That girl who led us in. Thought it would work! Cat always follows the girl. And here I am." He seemed a little shell-shocked, but his cheeks were still unfairly ruddy, and his lungs unreasonably strong.

"He shouldn't be here," said the ghost of Sayra. She sounded uneasy.

"Quick, quick, quick, quick . . . ," the Tinkerman was saying as he turned to grab something out of his shoulder bag. "No time to waste. I'm here, here, really here!"

He was already digging more of those needles out of his pack, and unreeling a length of wire. Now Linny could see the wire vanishing into the air, as the rope leading back from the Half-Cat had done.

He still looked strong and hearty, which made the rage in Linny boil again. "What do you think you're doing? *And what did you do to Elias?*"

"Hush, girl," said the Tinkerman. "The boy attacked me—I had to defend myself. And you've done your part already. You called the cat. It heard you singing; it heard you calling; it came." He pounded one of his needles into the ground, and the earth trembled a little underfoot.

Next to Linny, Sayra gasped.

"Stop that!" said Linny to the Tinkerman. "I said, what are you doing? You can't do your experiments here—it's too dangerous."

"Complexity, like water, flows downhill," said Arthur

Vix in a whispered singsong of a voice, and he tapped another needle into the ground, slightly closer to the edge of the bluff where Away looked out over the wild, wild sea. "Doesn't it though? Doesn't it though? Can't you feel it?"

"He's hurting the ground," said the ghost of Sayra in a small voice at Linny's elbow. The transparent silk blossom, which had tucked itself into Sayra's equally transparent hair, fluttered a little, as if it had had a fright.

"*Stop that!*" said Linny again to that awful man, and something in her was getting so mad that she couldn't help it; she took a great risk. She let go of Sayra's half-transparent arm and ran across the springy turf of that bluff toward the Tinkerman and his needles and the machine made of copper wires and tubing that he was now fetching out of the depths of his backpack.

She hadn't decided whether to grab the machine or try to shove him onto the ground, and in the millisecond before she made up her mind, Mr. Vix jumped out of the way and bounded a few yards closer to the edge of the bluff, bending slightly again, to pound another of his little stakes into the ground.

Under his breath ran a singsong hum: "Runs downhill! Runs downhill! And even the hills will be made Plain!"

"It's burning," said a whisper from where Sayra was

still crouching, a few yards behind Linny's back.

The ground was indeed smoking slightly, from each of the places where he had planted a stake. And the smell of the smoke was sour and bitter, both at once, as if someone had sliced rancid almonds very thin and was letting them burn. He had pounded in his last stake. He stood there, fastening the last wires to the strange machine in his hand.

"Now we'll see!" he said. "Water conducts! Water conducts! When this hits the ocean, the circuit will close!"

"I won't let you," said Linny, slowly inching her way closer to the Tinkerman. She didn't like the smoke seeping out of the ground, all of those places where the man's needle stakes had pierced it. "Mina said . . . too dangerous . . . the universe . . . the soap bubble . . . it might all go *po*—"

But the Tinkerman didn't wait for Linny to finish her thought or her sentence. He just turned his back to her and, with a great heaving throw, lobbed the machine right over the cliff. It arced up into the sky—almost lazily, at first, as if it were considering sprouting wings and spending the rest of its life in the air—and then plunged out of sight beyond the bluff, down toward the roiling, complicated sea.

33

OUCH!

For a moment no one moved. The Tinkerman's thin wire hissed across the grass as the machine fell (the cliff must be taller than it looked), and the little puncture wounds where the stakes went into the turf of Away continued to send up their small tendrils of smoke, and everything and everyone was listening for the distant slap of a metal sphere, that might or might not bring the end of the world, hitting rocks or sand or the rolling surface of the sea.

Then the Half-Cat yowled and flung itself at the old man's back. He had been watching his spherical machine plummet toward the water, and to get a good look he had gotten very close—*very* close—to the true edge of the cliff.

"Hey!" said Arthur Vix, his hands going all windmillish as he struggled to keep his balance in the place where the bluff came to its abrupt green end.

And then, as if the air or the sea had simply reached up and grabbed him, Arthur Vix slipped right over the edge, with the Half-Cat still clinging to him, and he was gone.

Gone!

The ghost of Sayra made a scared little sound.

But that whimper was drowned out by a dreadful commotion rising up from the sea—that awful machine must have finally reached the water—and the needles stuck into the ground twitched in response.

That was when Linny got her mind back, or some percentage of it. She dove to the ground, close to the edge of the bluff, and yanked out the nearest of those strange smoking needle stakes, but just as she did so a brilliant, sparkling, burning, dreadful brightness came up over the edge of the cliff, running along the wire, right toward her hand.

"Linny!" said the half-transparent Sayra.

Linny hardly had enough time even to brace herself before the strange fire was engulfing her hand.

It hurt like the dickens.

It hurt a lot.

It *hurt*.

But it wasn't just pain. It also felt very odd. The hugeness of the ocean, the complexity of everything in Away, the wrinkledness of this part of the world—all of that was flooding into or over Linny.

It tickled at least as much as it hurt, and it made her gasp, and almost as soon as it broke over her, she felt she couldn't stand it, not one second more. But she hung on anyway.

The world had become very large, and Linny felt almost as large as the world.

Even though the wire was narrow, a whole ocean's worth of story and magic and complexity was coming along it, sucked up as if by a very thirsty straw, freed to—what was it the Tinkerman had kept saying? "Flow downhill."

And only Linny blocked it: Linny, standing there with the little spike burning in her hand. Linny, with tears of pain and amazement rolling down her cheeks, because the essence of Away was wrinkling through her, trying to get past her, and she could only stand there and hold on, like the flimsiest dam of leaves and twigs she and Sayra used to make together in the woods above Lourka. She held on and said no. If she did not hold on, all of Away's complicated magic would flow down this wire, flow right down into the Plain, and be used as power, to unmake the wrinkled places of the world.

Away fed itself through that wire and burned her hand trying to push itself through, and Linny stood her ground as well as she could. It was hopeless, of course. It was like trying to hold an ocean back with her arms.

But in that long, hopeless moment, she caught a glimpse of what a wrinkled world really meant: every drop of what passed for water in that ocean, every blade of grass growing on that bluff, every inch of Away, was itself a universe, and contained universes. If you squinted at those drops of water properly, you saw that all the stories of the world were here, all the stories and all the songs.

Even the Voices were part of that richness, stories within stories—Linny saw that now, in this moment when she could see all the wrinkled sides of everything.

But it was too much. The world was spinning and her ears were ringing and black fireworks were going off before her eyes—

And then there was a sudden zip of a sound, and the wire went slack, and Linny, all that pressure released, found herself rolling across the bumpy, cool, grass-scented ground. For a moment she couldn't see anything, and then the world began to form itself in front of her eyes.

Somewhere nearby, someone gasped.

"You're hurt!" said that voice, an echo of Sayra's real voice, quite close to Linny's ear. And kind fingers (like the echo of real fingers) brushed across Linny's arm.

"What happened?" said Linny. She felt like she had just fallen out of a tree.

"Oh, Linny, you're hurt," said the ghost, the echo, of Sayra. "Your poor hand."

Her hand? One hand was pressed at an awkward angle into the ground. The other one she couldn't feel at all.

"I think you closed the window," said that voice. An echo, an echo, but an echo that could talk! "How did you even do that?"

Linny forced her eyes open. The ghost of Sayra was looking down at her, a pale and worried face that shifted suddenly, when Linny blinked, into the echo of a grin. For the tiniest moment, Linny let herself think they were back in the hills above Lourka, back in the familiar woods, and falling out of familiar trees. Then she heard the sound of waves crashing not so far away, and saw the sky shining through Sayra's still-transparent shoulder, and she remembered where she was.

"What window?" she said, beginning to scramble back to her feet. And then: "Ow!"

Her right hand.

It had been numb until she tried to open it, and then it hurt so much she squeaked. She caught a glimpse of a dark slash across her palm, and then her hand was squeezing itself shut again against the pain.

"The wire burned you," said the ghost of Sayra. "You stopped the fire. But that window in the sky you all came through—it's gone."

She waved a transparent hand over Linny's shoulder, pointing away from the edge of the bluff.

Linny turned to look and saw . . . nothing.

There was no shimmering anymore of any invisible edge. The grass of the bluff went on back and back, under the strange trees.

She took a few steps toward where that edge, that window, had been, and the bizarre thing was, she felt no tugs in her, no whisper of direction anywhere. And for a moment, that made her feel dizzy and disoriented. They were truly stuck in Away, then.

And she had no idea at all which way might lead home.

She looked at the ghost of Sayra, which was watching her with those unreadable, ocean-filled eyes.

"Oh, Sayra," she said. "I'm so sorry. I wanted so much to save you. I went all the way to the Plain Sea, at the other end of the world, looking for the medicines that would cure you—"

She was so unbelievably sorry. It was her fault Sayra had been taken off to Away, and she had tried so hard to make it right, and it had all come to nothing anyway, and she was sorry to the bone about all of it.

"I waited and waited," said the ghost of Sayra. *"And you came back!"*

Linny looked at her again. It was the tone of voice that threw her for a moment. She was so miserable herself that she half expected Sayra, who was the one who had had to suffer all this lonely unraveling, to sound miserable, too. So it caught Linny by surprise, here at the end of hope and the end of the world, to hear that thrum of *joy* rising up under each one of Sayra's words.

"You did! You came back!" said half-transparent Sayra, and something more human than ocean smiled out of her green, green eyes.

It's not always what happens that is the most important thing. Sometimes it's how you tell the story.

"Sayra—" said Linny in wonder. Something enormous had just shifted a little in her. Something defeated and bitter and hard had cracked and was beginning to crumble away.

And at that very moment, there came a crushed, charming racket from the bluff nearest them, and the most bedraggled Half-Cat ever in the universe hauled itself over the edge of the cliff. Its fur managed to look both singed and dripping wet (smoking and steaming, both at once). All in all the Half-Cat looked very much as you would expect a cat to look, that had gone flying over the edge of a cliff. But it limped up to Linny with its tail held gracefully high, and at Linny's feet it paused to make some gagging, retching sounds until it spat up a mass of little shards of metal.

The Half-Cat must have bitten through the old man's awful wire. If Linny had had to hold on much longer, the whole of her would probably have been as burned and blackened as her poor hand.

Linny looked at it and felt that enormous shift continuing to happen in her. In her, and in all the world.

"You fell off the cliff!" she said to the Half-Cat. "I thought you must be squashed or drowned."

"Only eight lives left," said the ghost of Sayra, and she actually laughed.

"Not nearly that many," said Linny. "That Tinkerman did some terrible things to this cat."

"Six, then," said the ghost of Sayra, and she scratched it kindly with one of her transparent hands. The Half-Cat let her do it, too.

I'm stuck in Away with a Half-Cat and a half Sayra, thought Linny, looking up and down the bluff as she did so. It was so odd, not knowing which way to go. That part of her was muffled, or gone, or blind.

"Well," she said to the ghost of Sayra. "I guess we better get moving, if we're ever going to find our way home."

The ghost of Sayra smiled willingly and took the lightest of steps forward, but the wind came swooping in to catch her and float her right away. Linny grabbed that transparent arm in the nick of time.

"I'll have to carry you," said Linny. She could see she was going to have to be selfish about this. And stubborn. Because one thing was clear—sorry, ocean!—she was not letting Sayra go.

The ghost of your best friend in the world turns out to

weigh almost nothing. Linny cradled the half-transparent Sayra as easily in her arms as if she were made of air and light, which perhaps she sort of was, and the ghost of Sayra tucked her head cozily against Linny's shoulder, not minding too much, apparently, about the ocean.

"Tell me a story," said Sayra drowsily. "How you went all that way . . . down to the Plain—"

"Because it was my turn to save you. Don't you remember? That wolf you fought off! Then the snake bit you—my turn—and then I fell right out of the tree. And you carried me all the way home from the woods. How'd you even do that? So, my turn now."

"That's right, that's right," said Sayra, shifting her nonweight in Linny's arms. "I sewed you that wolf once."

"Look," said Linny, and she balanced the ghost of Sayra in the crook of her right arm for a moment, so she could fish around in her pocket with her unwounded hand. The birthday sash was there where it had been all along, a little battered, perhaps, but you could still read the pictures there: wolf, snake, tree.

"Oh, but that tree looks like a cabbage on a stick!" said Sayra. "I remember now. And I worked so hard on the wolf. The legs of the wolf. It's not right. It's not quite right."

"It's perfect," said Linny.

The ghost of Sayra turned the sash over and over in

her hands, and then she reached up and tied it with her nimble, fragile fingers around Linny's head, so she could see the embroidered pictures on it even while resting against Linny's shoulder there.

"Then what happened?" she said.

So Linny walked along the bluffs, holding Sayra in her arms, while she told the whole story, how she went down into the Plain and to the other end of the world to look for medicine for Sayra, and the Tinkerman had swallowed the antidote . . .

"But I waited and you came back to me," added Sayra, with a sleepy smile, "and then . . ."

And then the Half-Cat had gone over the cliff but somehow climbed back up to them again.

"And then . . ."

And then they walked and walked along the green bluffs at the end of the world.

"And then . . ."

And then they walked so far they finally, finally found their way home.

Stories can remake the world.

"Again!" said the ghost of Sayra, as greedy as one of the twins. "Tell it again!"

So Linny shifted her over to the other shoulder and told the whole story all over again, leaving nothing out, not the labyrinth, not the crown that she had found and then given away to the crowd to keep safe, not even the tomatoes on the way to the Plain Sea, and when she got back to them walking along the green bluffs of Away until finally, finally they found their way home, Sayra smiled and said the exact same thing, pummeling Linny a little, just to make the point, with one of her not-very-solid fists. "Again!"

And they went on that way for almost ever, telling and retelling the story, and eventually Sayra got too heavy for Linny's arms, and she had to put her down, but that was all right now, and they walked on along those endless bluffs, hand in hand, and under their feet a path formed in the world . . .

Until finally—

"Again!"

Finally—

"Again!"

They found their way—

Sayra and Linny saw it both at the same moment: the path brightening as if someone had thrown a door wide open. And they squeezed each other's hands and grinned mischief at each other and ran forward, singing out the end of the story as a glorious, mismatched chord:

"HOME

AGAIN!"

34

HOME AGAIN

Going through the door that led back into the world was like running into an enormous spiderweb in the air: it resisted, resisted, resisted. But Linny was stubborner than the air, and a moment later something had given way with a *pop*, and she had hit a different, rockier patch of ground with a splintering thud.

"Ouch!" said the ground. And the nearest tree hissed like a cat.

Because (Linny saw as she groggily pushed herself upright) the Half-Cat was clinging to that tree with its battered claws, and the ground that Linny had plummeted into was not ordinary leaf-and-turf ground at all, but rather Elias, who looked shocked as he scrabbled backward to get away from the person who had just clobbered him.

"What?" he said. "Linny! How'd you—"

But it wasn't Elias Linny was worried about.

The Half-Cat was through; Linny had come through; where was—

"Can you please scooch off my leg?" said Sayra, and indeed, there she was. Sayra, herself, and not a ghost, pushing Linny off her ankle and grinning at everything in the world.

"Well, how about that!" said Elias. "This time I seem to have gone and rescued you both!"

"*You* rescued us?" said Linny. She was feeling very bruised and sore; the splintering sound when she landed had come from the bag with the lourka in it, and her hand was now throbbing with the sort of pain that makes your ears ring. She opened her mouth to say something sarcastic, and then she remembered Elias tackling the Tinkerman, and she snapped her mouth right back shut again.

Which was just as well, because when she looked again, there was light dancing in Elias's eyes and actual tears on his eyelashes, and she saw, as any more reasonable person would have seen right away, that of course he had been kidding, about the rescuing thing.

She was so very glad he was alive, despite the Tinkerman's darts.

"Is that Elias?" said Sayra, and then she shook herself. "He looks strange."

She turned around and looked at Linny.

"So do you. You're both sort of stretched out and ragged. What did they do to you? You look older. You both look older."

She looked around at the tiny, very wrinkled valley, where red, feathery leaves were falling through the air like glowing ashes, and her eyes narrowed.

"What happened to me? How long was I gone?"

"Too long," said Elias. "I mean, actually I have no idea how long it's been. The Tinkerman jabbed me with one of his sleep needles, so I lost a bunch of time. And then I was looking for you up here—seemed like forever."

He paused, and then smiled, a very sweet smile, without even a dash of lummox in it.

"So I guess we're all a little older than we were."

"And *hungrier!*" said Linny. "Aren't you hungry, all of a sudden? Let's go home."

For a long moment Sayra and Elias just stood there staring at her.

"Don't you know what that means, *home*?" said Linny again. "What's wrong with you two?"

"You'll have to show us the way, you know," said Sayra gently.

So Linny took their hands and led them down the wrinkled valleys until they came to a bend in the hills that was already softer than the tight twists and strange turns near the edge of Away, and there below them were the familiar roofs of Lourka.

The sun was low in the sky, and they had to shade their eyes to look down at the village.

"Look!" whispered Sayra, tugging on Linny's arm.

A woman (very tiny indeed, from this distance) had just come around the corner of the house at the top of the village and was beckoning to someone—to two medium-little boys, running around like wild things, out there in the center of the lower meadow. Just the way that woman moved her hand through the air was as familiar to Linny as her own heartbeat.

And then she turned and looked up the slope, for all the world as if she had heard Sayra's whisper, which was impossible. She gazed right up the hill at them, and a gulp of a sob hiccuped its way out of Linny's throat.

The woman didn't even wave, exactly. She turned toward them, and straightened up in recognition, and held out her arms.

That's what joy looks like! If anyone ever asks you, now you know: it's your own mother standing at the end of the lower meadow, still quite far away, holding out her arms to welcome you home.

They were all running down the hill by this point, even the Half-Cat, though, being a cat, it was trying to make its run look leisurely, unhurried, engaged in by choice.

The wrinkled country must have wriggled itself a little to make the path down the hill shorter than usual. After all that long way, it was only a few seconds until Linny was in the fierce, strong arms of her mother, and the people of Lourka gathering all around.

35

GIRL WITH LOURKA

In the wrinkled parts of the world, people know how stories shape everything, so of course when the three children who had gone off to Away came dancing down out of the hills again, there was not only rejoicing. There was a pulling up of chairs and stools and a leaning in of the happy crowds and a posing of the old, powerful demand.

"Tell us what happened!"

They brought food, of course, as well as chairs, not to mention bandages for Linny's poor wounded hand (she impressed the twins with that black stripe across her palm), and they set everything up very comfortably on the village green, and the littlest children ran about in the grass, trying to catch blue and pink and brightest-gold fireflies with their pudgy hands.

Sayra sat on her mother's lap, her arms around her mother's neck. Her mother was still too much in the grip of shock and joy to say much in her own right, but the neighbors said what had been left of Sayra had finally faded completely away, just some hours before. That very day. And Sayra's poor mother had slipped to the floor, as if she, too, could think of nothing better to do than to fade away . . . only that was when the shouts had come from outside her cottage, and when she had opened her door—

But words alone have trouble with such things.

Each one of the three who had come down out of the wrinkled hills told the story as it had played out for her or for him, and the villagers hung on every word. They wanted to know more about Away, which was the strangeness that was nearest to them, and they were very curious, too, about the people, like Linny's aunt, who lived out their lives down on the Plain. And there was much headshaking and worry about the way the two halves of the Broken City kept trying to do harm to each other.

"*Madji* and Surveyors!" said Elias's mother in disgust. "Madmen and surlyfaces, more like!"

But they liked the description of the Bridge House (Linny's mother turned her head away, though, and Linny remembered that that was the house her own mother had grown up in, so long ago); they approved of the fair; they admired the wrinkled/machine-driven Half-Cat, frizzle-frazzled though it was by its encounter with the old man's dreadful wire. It wound through the legs of the crowd, showing off its gorgeous, bedraggled halfness, and pretending not to need or notice human beings of any kind.

Finally the baker dusted the flour off his hands and said, "She may be a wicked thing sometimes, our Linny, but seems like she's our door out and back, if you see what I mean. She could take a trader down to the Plain, y' know, and bring back all the various wonders—"

"Except that she's never leaving Lourka again!" said Linny's mother, with a sobbing gulp of a laugh. "How can you even suggest—no, I absolutely forbid it."

The silence that followed that was a very complicated silence. You could almost hear the thoughts of these people going in different directions all over the place.

Sayra raised her head off her mother's shoulder and said, "What about those people and their awful war? Linny said she'd come back to them, didn't she? They're holding her crown for her, and she's the Girl with the Lourka."

The older people in the village shifted their weight from foot to foot or scratched their arms inside their elbows. They were still (even after all of these marvels) made a little nervous by anything that linked girls and lourkas. Even though that had been the first thing Linny had said, and Sayra and Elias had said something like it, too: "The story has changed."

Weren't the three of them living proof of that?

The people of Lourka had been as trapped in the rut of the old story as they were lost in the wrinkle separating their village from the world.

Linny had had a long time to think over how it all must have happened, long, long ago. "The first Girl with the Lourka—the one they painted those pictures of—went down to the Plain, and the people here called that being taken off to Away, and they told the story that way for so long that it came true, of course, the way stories do up here, and that's eventually what happened to poor Sayra."

All right, makes sense. Even the eldest elders in the village could see how that might have happened, because anyone who lives in the wrinkled country knows how a story can sometimes surprise you by becoming real.

"Well, anyway," said Linny. "I can't go anywhere until I fix this." And she pulled the damaged lourka out of its grubby, tattered bag to show them all.

Some people still flinched for a moment, it's true, to see a lourka in a girl's hands, but the story had changed, the story had changed, and soon the lourka was being passed from hand to hand—even Sayra took it for a moment! Even Elias's mother!—and being not just pitied for its bangs and scrapes, but also (which swelled the heart of Linny, after all this time) *admired*.

"Child did this without a master's guiding!" said one of the oldest lourka makers. "Never seen such a thing."

"I'll help you mend it, Linny," said Linny's father. "Or I'll watch you mend it, maybe. Doesn't seem you need much help from me."

"But I learned everything by watching you," said Linny, her heart pounding and melting, both at once, under her thin ribs. No moment was ever as sweet as this: her own father, pleased to have her fixing her lourka. Welcoming her not just home, but into the workshops, where she had always been so unwanted!

Surely if *that* story could change, so could the story of the broader world, all that struggling between the wrinkled and Plain sides of the river.

"And what's this?" said Linny's father, running a finger over Sayra's sash, tied now like a headband, bright and bedraggled, about Linny's ears.

"Her wrinkled crown," said Sayra, with mischief back in her leaf-green eyes. The only thing still half-transparent about Sayra was that winged blossom of hers, and it fluttered now, up from her hair, and did a dance above their heads.

"It started the story that brought us all home," said Linny.

"And now let's get some sweaters on you tired young people," said Elias's mother. "Getting chilly out here!"

But none of them wanted to go home to their separate houses, on a day as extraordinary as this. So they made a fair of it, right there on the village green. The various households brought out food of different kinds, and someone built up a fire in the old stone ring, and the whole village sat around and laughed and ate together.

As the shadows lengthened across the green, even Sayra's mother finally began to believe that Sayra was truly back, and let her leave her arms (though not her sight) for a few minutes.

Sayra and Linny ate nutcake after nutcake, and smiled at each other like fools.

Then Elias leaned over them from behind and said, "Hey, what d'you think they're all talking about?"

And when Linny followed his pointing finger, she could see that some sort of conversation was winding its way through the grown-ups. They were gathering in little groups and getting into earnest discussions and then reshuffling themselves again.

"They don't seem mad or anything," said Sayra, licking sugar off her fingers. "I wouldn't worry about it. You know, I don't think I ever had one single thing to eat, when I was off in Away. What kind of strange place is that, where you would never have a nutcake and not even notice?"

"I'm not worried about what they're saying," said Elias. "I'm curious."

Then the smith banged some pieces of iron together,

and the crowd pulled itself together around Linny and Sayra and Elias.

"Linny," said Linny's mother. "Linny, dear. They've been telling me I am wrong."

"Wrong about what?" said Linny, feeling a little embarrassed.

"About keeping you here forever," said her mother, with a flash of a smile. "Though it seems reasonable enough to me."

"She did tell those people she would go back," said Sayra. "Didn't you, Linny?"

"My Girl with the Lourka," said her mother. "Who I came all the way up here to find!"

"Tell her our plan," said the baker. "Go ahead, spill!"

"You see," said Linny's father, stepping forward. "As the good baker said earlier, you're nothing less than our door, after a fashion. And we mean to make use of that, and to stand by you, too."

He took a deep breath.

"When your lourka's repaired and your body rested, child, it will be high time for you to go back down to Bend, don't you think?"

"And Angleside, too," said someone else from the crowd.

"Yes, to the wrinkled places *and* to the Plain," agreed her father. "Sounds like both have need of you, their Girl with a Lourka."

"But you won't be alone this time," said Linny's mother.

"Hey!" said Elias. "She wasn't always alone the first time."

He turned around so he could look right at Linny, and he smiled a quite nice, not very lummoxy smile.

"I know I wasn't much help the first time," he said. "But I'll come with you again, if you go back down."

"Me, too," said Sayra. "I'd like to see what the Plain looks like."

Linny gulped. "But your mother," she said. Actually, she could have been speaking to any of them. What mother would let go of her child twice in a single year? None of these mothers.

"Now you're not understanding what we mean," said Linny's father. "Linny, we mean *all* to go with you, since you can bring us back again, when the time comes."

"All of us, everybody," said her mother, and the crowd was full of nodding heads.

"Except maybe me and the sheep," said Elias's father. "But maybe even them!"

"And the horses and the kitties and the little flying birds!" said one of Linny's twin brothers.

"Don't be silly," said the other brother. "The birds won't come all that way."

"There will be drums and lourkas—think how lovely the noise will be!" said Linny's mother.

"And bright, bright banners," said Sayra's mother in a whisper. "No parade without banners!"

"Down from the wrinkled hills," said Linny's father. "To see the other places and explain how things are up here to those who don't know."

"A real wrinkled fair, we can show them—not their lourkas made of boxes!" said one of the oldest lourka makers.

"And to find my sister, Mina," said her mother. "She'll have people who'll join us, I'm sure."

Linny looked from face to face and couldn't even think of a single word to say. All those years spent chafing up here, and now, when the talk was of leaving again, she found herself feeling, for the first time in her life, truly at home.

"You'll be the Girl with Lourka then, for sure," said her father, and he laughed. "The Girl with *the whole village* of Lourka!"

Fireflies, laughter, the Half-Cat's purr, a thin thread of smoky tang from the fire, and someone picking out odd notes on a lourka, not so far away.

Linny breathed it all in, too happy for words. Then there was hope, after all! How lovely and how strange.

The stories will change, she thought to herself. *The stories will change, and the world will change—*

The wonderful world, both wrinkled and Plain!

ACKNOWLEDGMENTS

This story took shape during a hard and happy year. The people of HarperCollins have my awe and affection, both. Rosemary Brosnan, who blends kindness and wisdom in everything she does, was this book's first friend. Alexandra Cooper, an editor's editor, showed me a thousand ways it could be made better. Annie Berger kept everything on track. Alexei Esikoff and Laaren Brown went through the manuscript with sharp eyes and fine-toothed combs, and Heather Daugherty and Jen Bricking made a truly magical cover. Thank you all from the bottom of my heart. I'm grateful also to Andrea Brown and Taryn Fagerness.

I owe more than I can say to the friends who, through thick and thin, kept me walking, talking, and plotting. Dartmoor, Tilden Park, Mount Tamalpais, and Clouds Rest know our feet well. My love and gratitude go to Roo Hooke, Sharon Inkelas, Will Waters, Bill Roberts, and the stalwart members of the Berkeley Marina Dog-Walking Society.

Linda Williams introduced me to the glorious, cold water of Lake Tahoe. My colleagues at Berkeley were incredibly nice about the blue hair. Kristen Whissel and Mark Sandberg went many extra miles on my behalf: you guys are the best.

Jenn Reese, Christine Ashworth, Sally Felt, Yvonne Jocks, and Kristen Kittscher joined forces to make writing every day no matter what seem like a perfectly natural and possible thing to do.

Joan Balter taught me a great deal about the making of lourkas, although I think she thought I was asking about violins.

In France I benefited every single day from the positive spirit, intelligence, and general gutsiness of Hannah Konkel. Having Andrew Kahn and Nicholas Cronk as neighbors was a rare gift and a joy. Sisters, cousins, my father, siblings-in-law, nieces, godsons, and a nephew kept life lively everywhere.

My daughters—Ada Naiman, Eleanor Naiman, and Thera Naiman—are as musical as Linny and as stalwart. Bob Naiman makes the world a better place in every way. Eric Naiman is the best cook I know, and one of the world's most generous souls. Yes, Soushka *is* a good dog.

Sheila Engh, Kate Landis, and Michelle Oakes couldn't

stay to see this book appear, but I feel very lucky to have known them.

This book is dedicated, with love and affection, to Isa Helfgott and Jayne Williams.

Embark on a magical adventure through the streets of Paris with Maya.

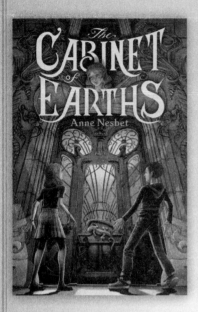

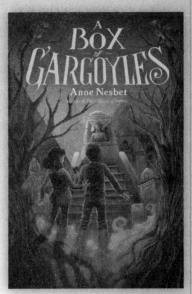

Praise for THE CABINET OF EARTHS:

"Reading this book is like discovering a treasure box
full of rare and wonderful things."

—Sarah Prineas, author of the Magic Thief series

"With imaginative alchemy, compelling action, and
sensitive characterizations, this novel will undoubtedly
win over fantasy fans."

—ALA *Booklist*

"A-shimmer with magic in plot, characters,
and literary style."

—*The Horn Book*